ALEX in WONDERLAND

ALEX in WONDERLAND

Simon James Green

SCHOLASTIC

Scholastic Children's Books
An imprint of Scholastic Ltd
Euston House, 24 Eversholt Street, London, NW1 1DB, UK
Registered office: Westfield Road, Southam, Warwickshire, CV47 0RA

First published in the UK by Scholastic Ltd, 2019

ISBN 978 1407 19424 0

A CIP catalogue record for this book
is available from the British Library.

Printed by CPI Group (UK) Ltd, Croydon, CR0 4YY

Papers used by Scholastic Children's Books are made
from wood grown in sustainable forests.

This is a v
dialogu
fictit

For Bella

CHAPTER ONE

They show me into the small, windowless room and the older guy must see the look of horror on my face because he says, "You do know you're not under arrest, right?" and I just smile and nod because *yes, I do know that*, but at the same time this room is *somewhat scary*. I'd assumed how they show it on TV was all over the top, for dramatic effect, but it turns out it's not. The room is bare, with grubby white walls and four plastic chairs around a small table with metal legs and a wooden top, into which someone has scraped the words "EAT YOUR GREENS".

Eat your greens? Sure, it's all very community-spirited to graffiti a public health message in a police interview room, but—

It hits me. It's code. It's got to be. Some sort of warning, an anagram maybe, about how I shouldn't trust them, they'll stitch me up, don't drink the water they poison it, get out while you can, that type of thing.

But then I think, never mind that, this is actually all very *serious* and perhaps there are even worse things to worry about. Example: what if they do a . . . you know, *a cavity search*?

But then, why would they even do that anyway? It can't be a routine thing.

It's not a routine thing, is it?

I swallow hard, palms sweating, as I sit down, Dad pulling up the chair next to me, the two police officers on the other side of the table – an older white guy with a craggy face, and a slightly younger black guy, forties maybe, who's the one in charge. I wish they could have put me with a kindly, cardigan-wearing officer with a gentle voice, in a room with sofas and a few pot plants, or something. Why haven't they done that?

BECAUSE THEY ARE GOING TO STRIP YOU AND CAVITY SEARCH YOU, THAT'S WHY! THEY'RE GOING TO BEND YOU OVER AND RAM THEIR LATEX-GLOVED HANDS UP YOUR—

"Sure you don't want a drink?" Craggy Face asks.

I lamely hold up my plastic bottle of Lucozade and hope they don't notice how much my hand is shaking. A sure sign of guilt.

Dad chuckles. "He has way too much sugar!"

Oh yes, very funny. Aren't kids just *the worst*?!

The policemen both laugh too, as Craggy Face tips four sachets of demerara into his plastic cup of vending machine coffee, with absolutely no hint of irony. He stirs his drink, then looks up at me and smiles. Maybe he's playing "nice cop". Maybe it'll be the other guy who ROUGHLY SHOVES HIS HAND UP MY— "So, I'm DS Hunter, and this is DI Griffin," he says.

DI Griffin smiles too, then he leans forward and says, "Nice T-shirt, Alex." It's a distorted chequered design, in black and lime green, and it is quite nice. I like it. I love it, actually. "Don't think I could get away with it, but it looks good on you," DI Griffin continues.

I give Dad a glance and a little raise of my eyebrows, which I know is smug, but I've been proven right, *so*. Dad wanted me to wear a proper shirt. I refused. Too hot for that, plus I felt it made me look like I was trying too hard. And that might look . . . well, guilty. By way of compromise, I'd agreed to wear my tan chinos, rather than some shorts. You know it's serious when Dad insists on the chinos. Or at least, you know *Dad* thinks it's serious. He responds to me being right by rolling his eyes a little and sitting back in his chair, like he thinks my victory is meaningless. He would have been here in a full-on dinner suit if he could have been.

DI Griffin is still acting all mesmerized by my T-shirt. "Where's it from?" he says.

My eyes widen. Something in his voice makes me feel he thinks I *stole* it. "I bought it," I say, immediately worrying that makes it sound like I didn't. And in actual fact, *I didn't.* So, here we are, first question in, and I'm already LYING TO THE POLICE. There are good reasons for this. And it's not just about my ineptitude in any situation where I have to be in close proximity to another human being. The T-shirt was actually a present, it's just I don't want to say who from, not in front of Dad. *Not yet.* If I say, it'll raise questions, and now isn't the time to tell him all about that. Especially when I don't even know if . . . well, anyway. This is a new low, even for me. But in for a penny: "Online," I mutter, looking down at the "EAT YOUR GREENS" on the table and wondering if it's actually a clever reminder that you shouldn't try to challenge the system. Do as you're told, eat your greens, brush your teeth, be a good boy, and don't tell lies. But the lies are mounting up. They'll impound my computer, forensically examine it, and when they do, aside from the sites *you know I visit but we all know I shouldn't,* they'll also find no evidence I've ever bought a T-shirt online.

DI Griffin nods. He's not an idiot. No way is he buying this platter of crap I'm serving him.

I clear my throat, give my messy blond hair a scratch, look at him, look away, look at my fingernails and look back again. It's an assortment of nervous tics that must read: GUILTY AS SIN. Why are we talking about my T-shirt, anyway? This is some clever psychological tactic, isn't it? He's buttering me up, being all nicey-nicey, so that I relax and incriminate myself. "I haven't done anything wrong," I add.

"Alex, we're not suggesting you have," DI Griffin says. "You're here voluntarily and you're free to go at any time."

I think about going. It would be pretty nice to go, right now. But going would look weird. It would look *guilty*. If I was innocent, I would just be all "La, la, la! Of course I'll help with your enquiries!" and everything would be fine and we'd probably have a laugh and stuff.

DI Griffin runs his tongue over his lips. "Why don't you just tell us everything? The whole thing."

"Everything?"

DI Griffin nods. "From start to finish, Alex. Don't leave anything out. You might not think something important, but any tiny detail, some insignificant thing, it might just help us."

"OK." I guess that sounds fine. It's not like I have to hide anything. I mean, there are some bits to this that I'd *like* to hide. Especially with Dad sitting next to me and two blokes that I don't even know opposite. But the trouble with hiding stuff is that then other bits don't make sense and you end up lying, like I've already lied. *Frigging twice.* Little connections and motivations are lost, and expert interviewers, like DI Griffin surely is, would spot that a mile off. Then he'd be all, "If you're hiding that, WHAT ELSE ARE YOU HIDING MISTER MAN?!

SPREAD YOUR GODDAMN LEGS AND BEND OVER RIGHT NOW," as he snaps those gloves on and—I swallow again. "Everything, then?" My voice sounds squeaky.

DI Griffin nods, smiles at me and flips open a notepad. "Everything, Alex."

CHAPTER TWO

She told me via text because she's a coward.

> Hey Alex! How you doing?
>
> OK thanks. You?
>
> Cool. So don't know if Will told you, but we're off on holiday tomorrow! Yay!

She doesn't know if Will told me? Jesus, why didn't she just *ask* Will, since she was dating him and he was probably sitting next to her as she typed this serious-made-to-sound-casual rubbish. Will had *not* told me. At least, not officially. Nor had she. And they were both supposed to be my mates. Although I did know something was going on, because I saw them both shopping in the chemist's the week before. Actually, I *heard* them first – discussing the merits of different brands of suntan lotion, just the other side of the shelving from where I was looking for any sort of shower gel that wasn't aggressively masculine and full of weird ingredients like silver or charcoal.

"Forecast says it'll be over thirty-five *every day*, babe – you'll need at least factor thirty."

I froze, then slowly squatted down behind the shelves, not that they could see me over the top anyway, but being lower down made me *feel* more hidden.

"So, I'm not gonna get a tan, then?"

"You're so pale though, babe... No, get the spray stuff, it's easier."

I didn't want them to see me because it would have been awkward, right? Awkward because last year we all went on holiday together – Annie's parents rented a villa in Spain, and they let me and Will stay in the spare room for free. That was before Annie and Will got together and everything was normal. It was when I stupidly hoped I might be in with a chance with Will, even though he was a straight boy (*slaps forehead repeatedly*), and that maybe at some point over the ten nights we would be sharing a bedroom, he would finally open up to me about his confused feelings towards other boys, and ideally me specifically.

Well, that didn't happen.

All that did happen over those ten nights is that Will talked *a lot* about how much he fancied Annie, and I spent *a lot* of time locked in the bathroom, relieving myself of all the stress.

I'm sorry, that's probably too much information.

But anyway, they became a couple and they had clearly decided they wanted to do couple things and there was no space for me any more. And there in the chemist's, that was the exact moment I realized that my long-anticipated glorious summer after finishing GCSEs, just hanging with my mates, with no worries and nothing to do except mess about in whatever sun the fickle English summer deigned to throw our way, was totally wrecked.

But before I had a chance to contemplate the car crash of my summer any further, it got worse:

"We really need to tell Alex," Annie said.

"Yeah, but what do we say, though?" I could imagine Will flapping about awkwardly, avoiding her eyes, not wanting this conversation, because that's what Will does. That was one of the main reasons we became friends – he hates talking as much as I do. We could literally sit for hours, in total silence, playing video games, and we'd both be happy as pigs in shit.

"Well, we gotta say *something*," she said. "He thinks we're all gonna be hanging the whole summer, so it's not fair on him." She paused and sighed. "Poor Alex."

Poor Alex?! I was actually frozen to the spot at this point, because now I was some sort of charity case. I was a person to feel sorry for. Don't get me wrong, I am *well aware* of my own terrible plight – I've lived my constantly disappointing life for a full sixteen years now, so I'm well acquainted with the damp squib that is my existence, but for OTHER PEOPLE to also know this?! It was mortifying.

I had to get out of there before they discovered me behind the shelf, and before I heard any more devastating revelations. If I worked my way back towards the far left corner of the store, I was probably safe. I could hover there, pretend to look at stuff, and wait until they'd gone. I stood up, and my eyes met those of the security guard, who was watching me from the end of the aisle. I grabbed a bottle of "Hydro Force Power Wash – With Active Carbon" (why do they think guys require this level of industrial cleaning?), to try to show I wasn't a shoplifter, and I scurried off along the aisle, something hot and unpleasant pumping through my veins. *Poor Alex. Poor Alex.* Were they just hanging out with me because they felt bad for me? Like the kid picked last for a sports team, was I just a burden they were reluctantly letting join in? I couldn't believe that's what they thought of me. I couldn't believe Will hadn't told me about the secret holiday. I couldn't believe how . . . *empty* this whole thing had made me feel. Yes, I get that people find love. It's not that I begrudge them that. I just don't see why that suddenly means friends have to be excluded, like you can't be part of their little gang any more. It would have been nice to go on holiday with them again. I wouldn't have been any trouble. I never am. I've even got that in writing on one of my reports, from Mrs Harper, history: "He's not any trouble."

I must have been on autopilot, because I unexpectedly arrived, breathless, at the checkouts, with a basket stacked high with random products I must have picked off the shelves as I stormed past. I didn't know what the hell I'd been doing, or even how long I'd been doing it, but the security guard was watching again, so I must have been acting pretty weird.

Also, I was very confident there was no way I'd have enough money in my account to pay for all this. But, nevertheless, there I was. Trying anyway.

A blonde girl, face thick with foundation – "I'm Dolly – here to help!" – gave me a half-hearted smile. "Do you want a carrier?"

Whilst the obvious answer would have been yes due to the volume of goods I'd acquired, the five-pence charge she would have added for the carrier could have been the straw that broke the camel's back, financially. "No," I said, with as much confidence as I could manage, like I could deal with this. Like the carrying situation was in hand. "No carrier."

She looked at me doubtfully and started scanning the items through the till.

"Alex?"

I froze. It was Will's voice. Right behind me.

"Will?!" I said, with too much surprise, because it was clearly him, holding a basket of goods in a shop in the town where we both live, so his being there shouldn't have been *that* shocking.

Will nodded at me. "Cool, man," he said, pushing his free hand through his dark brown hair. He was looking less skinny than usual. Like he'd been going to the gym. I tried not to look too much.

"I'm just in the chemist," Will said. "Getting some . . . stuff."

I glanced at his basket – several bottles of suntan lotion, after sun, eye masks, inflatable travel pillows and those little miniature toiletries you can take through airport security. I flicked my eyes up to him, because if he was going to tell me about how he was going on holiday *without me*, this would probably have been the time – what with all the evidence and all.

But he bottled it. "Annie's here, actually. . . I think she's . . . looking at shampoo."

"Yeah, shampoo's . . . good," I said. "*Hair.*"

"Hair. Right! Ha! So . . . *Alex* . . . you got plans for the summer?"

OK, so here it was. This was the lead-up. I couldn't tell him the truth, which was "nothing", because it sounded utterly pathetic. And I couldn't say "doing stuff with you guys" because it sounded too needy, and anyway, I knew I wouldn't be doing that now.

And as annoyed as I was, Will and Annie were also friends, and I didn't want to make them feel bad.

I blew out a breath. "*Loads,*" I said.

"Cool..." Will nodded, clearly expecting more. Expecting *details.*

"What about you?" I said. *Deflection – my favourite tactic.*

Will nodded. "Hey, maybe later in the summer we should all go to a festival or something."

I noted his use of the word "later". This was Will's way of telling me he wouldn't be around during the first part. I should probably have considered myself told at this point.

"Sure," I said, because being rammed into a muddy field with thousands of pissed-up happy people is about as far away from my comfort zone as you can get. "Or a barbecue?" A barbecue sounded safer to me. I could probably get on board with that.

"Totally!" Will said, with way too much enthusiasm. "Everyone loves meat!"

"Not vegetarians," I reminded him.

He nodded, sadly. "Not vegetarians." There was a time he would have laughed at that.

Dolly coughed to get my attention. "Thirty-five pounds, fifty," she said.

I looked in horror, first at the numbers on the little screen and then at what I'd actually bought, which, in the absence of a carrier bag, was all laid out on the countertop: my Stallion Man Beefcake Wash With Active Red-Blooded Testosterone (or whatever the hell it was), a bath bomb (actually, I really like them, so fine), sanitary towels, two pots of baby food, a pregnancy test kit, some "Glam Crystals" glitter eyeliner, and two large boxes, each containing twenty-four own-brand condoms.

I felt Will's eyes scanning the items too, as a shocked silence fell across us all.

Dolly's eyes flicked from the condoms to me. I am sixteen, but I'm a young sixteen, you know? I don't necessarily look like I should be having sex. I certainly don't come across as *confident* enough to be having that much sex. Not forty-eight condoms' worth. Even one condom would be pushing it, believability-wise. And with these goods, I was aware I was also giving the impression I had one baby at home, and another potentially on the way. Maybe she would think that's why I needed all the condoms. Maybe she would think I had finally seen sense, and understood the importance of safe sex.

My cheeks were glowing. I could see Will out of the corner of my eye, and he was just sort of *staring*, open-mouthed. Also, there was no way I would have enough money in my account to cover this; I had about fifteen quid, tops.

But I optimistically let Dolly try my debit card anyway, because you never knew; sometimes banks accidentally deposited tens of thousands in people's accounts due to some processing error.

That hadn't happened in this instance.

"It's not going through," Dolly said, giving me a sympathetic look.

"Oh," I muttered.

"On me, mate," Will croaked as he pushed his basket on to the counter. "Just put it on mine," he told Dolly.

"Oh, er, really?" I said, staring down at my trainers.

He was staring down at his trainers too. "What are mates for?" he said, finally.

"Huh, thanks," I said. I looked up at the cashier. "And a bag, please?"

"Alex?" The softness in his voice caught me off guard. I swallowed and finally met his eyes. "We'll have a nice summer. We'll definitely plan stuff. Like, I know me and Annie are together now, and I guess there's some stuff I'll be doing with her, but you're still my mate, so we'll do stuff too."

I got why he couldn't tell me. He genuinely felt bad. He knew everything was changing, and he was clinging on. I didn't blame him. I cried when I got home after the year eleven leavers prom. Everyone was moving off in different directions, growing up, chasing dreams, excited for whatever came next. But I didn't want to let go of the known and comfortable. It was horrible. It felt like everyone was jumping into the river of our futures and being swept away by the rapids of life, and I wasn't even in the water. I couldn't be. I can't swim.

Like, not metaphorically. I literally can't swim.

"Yeah, yeah, totally," I said. "It'll be great."

"It's gonna be a *sweeeeeeeeet* summer, man!" Will said, although something in his voice made me think he didn't quite believe that.

I sighed as Will put his PIN into the machine and it all effortlessly went through. At that point, I was pretty much resigned to it being The Vile Summer of Total Arse. All signs pointed in that direction. Turned out I was wrong. It *was* going to be *sweeeeeeet.* Just not in any way I was expecting.

I was also going to use all the condoms.

Just not in any way *you* might be expecting.

CHAPTER THREE

I sent Annie a text back:

Have a good time.

I was pretty confident she would pick up on the fact I didn't say "great" time, didn't use an exclamation mark, and didn't put any kisses. I wanted her to know I was hurt. But I didn't have chance to wallow in any further self-pity (something I do really well, by the way – I have numerous playlists for it and everything), because Kendra was coming up the stairs, calling my name.

Kendra and Dad met on Tinder, not that either of them knew I knew that. She had a peroxide-blonde bob and, like most people with too much money and no class, drove a white Mercedes with personalized plates: K3 NDRA – the three forming a backwards "E" that made it look like her name had been written by a toddler.

The severe hair, combined with her penchant for wearing turtleneck sweaters, meant she looked a bit like an android in a movie. Like, she didn't want to reveal her neck, because that was where the little compartment that accessed her circuit board was. Ultimately, androids always turn rogue and wipe out the humans with a cold, ruthless efficiency, so I was constantly on my guard with her.

"There you are," she said, pushing my bedroom door open. One of these days, she'll regret not knocking and end up seeing me doing something awful that she wouldn't want to see . . . like smiling, or enjoying my life, for example. I did my best to not have resting "I'm totally indifferent towards you" face. That was one of my first faults that Kendra pointed out to me, by the way, when she moved in, six months ago. The truth is, she's not my kind of person. She's flashy and pushy, and she's rude to waiters. But I was doing my best for Dad, toning my real feelings towards her down, because he seemed to like her and I guess I just want him to be happy. Indifference was the best I could manage. Anything more positive would have been too tall an order.

She wrinkled her nose. "Do you need to open a window?"

OK, here is a fact: my room does *not* smell. It doesn't. I'm really clean and tidy – there's no clothes dumped all over the place, no old food under my bed, and I Febreze the living daylights out of everything several times a week. But that was never good enough for Kendra. Kendra was always *convinced* she could smell something. It drives me mad when people say teenage boys smell, because we don't. Well, not all of us anyway. And no more than anyone else smells. And she could talk. You should smell her when she comes back from hot yoga.

She also loves eating beef jerky, by the way, and that stuff reeks.

But I opened the window.

Kendra perched on the edge of the bed. I stayed by the window. She rubbed her fingers along a tiny bit of my duvet. "When did you last wash this?"

"Last week." That was more or less true.

She narrowed her eyes at me. "In the washing machine?"

"Yeah?" What did she think I'd done? Carried it down to the river and rubbed it over some rocks?

Kendra took a breath and nodded. "So that's why there was fabric softener in the pre-wash compartment."

"Huh?"

"What compartment did you put the fabric softener in, Alex?"

I just stared at her. I'm not even sure I used fabric softener. What compartment? I squeezed some liquid into one of those plastic balls you put straight in.

She shook her head. "OK! We'll have a little lesson about how to use the washing machine then!"

Couldn't wait for that.

"It's a *Neff* appliance," she added.

I didn't know what to do with that information.

"*Expensive*," she explained. "So it's a good idea to use them correctly, in accordance with the instructions." She looked me in the eye. "Right?"

"Right," I said.

"Are you going to stand there or come and sit down?" she asked. "I thought we should have a little chat."

My stomach lurched at the anticipated horror. "Little chats" are never fun. I perched on the edge of the bed by my pillows, as far away from Kendra as possible, looking down at my white socks.

"It's OK, Alex, we're not going to talk about *private teenage boy stuff*."

Well, thank god for that.

"What are your plans for the summer?"

Actually, let's just talk about private teenage boy stuff.

"*What are you going to do with all that time?*" she said, in a way that made it very clear I should definitely be doing something really constructive. Sitting in my room playing Fortnite probably wasn't going to cut it.

I swallowed and shrugged. "Well, Mum and Dad always said that if I knuckled down for the exams, the summer was mine, so—"

"Well, your mum's on that commune with her female friend, *so...*" Kendra countered.

I flicked my eyes away from her. It's not a commune. She's joined a voluntary group for a year, committed to various environmental causes. It's a sustainable eco-village in South America. And this whole "female friend" business annoyed me too. There was an insult hidden in it, but I couldn't quite work out how.

"Also," Kendra said, "you should know, because you're old enough to know, despite what your dad thinks, that money is pretty tight. The divorce costs money, and your mum is being pretty inflexible. It's fine, no one wants to see her out on the streets, but we're all having to work extra hard to give her what she wants."

I didn't think that was true about Mum for one minute; I'd ask Dad later. But OK, I got it. She wanted me to get a job. And I had no objection to doing some work and earning a bit of cash. The independence would be a good thing, to be honest, then I wouldn't have to endure Kendra saying "Don't spend it all on sugary drinks!" every time Dad gave me my allowance. Trouble was, my ideal job would be getting paid to be in a science experiment to study the effects on humans of solitary confinement. I'd gone as far as to look if there were any opportunities in that field, but apparently humans need contact with one another, and solitary confinement for extended periods is cruel. I couldn't understand it. It sounded pretty much *perfect* to me.

But there should be loads of other options. Although

Newsands had been in permanent recession for as long as I can remember, it had recently turned a corner. Thanks to the rock-bottom housing market, lots of middle-aged Londoners had started buying places and doing them up, apparently loving the "faded seaside glamour" of the town. They were opening galleries in empty shop units, and pop-up street-food stalls on the rotting pier. They were spending money. And when people spend money, more stuff opens, creating *job opportunities.* Surely one of them would be right for me? I could work in a gallery. They're notorious for having no one visit them.

"OK," I said.

"Is that an 'OK, I'll get a part-time job'?"

"I'll try."

"Well, that's great!" Kendra said. "Pulling your weight a bit – your dad and I would really appreciate it!"

I nodded and looked down at my socks again.

"What do you think your selling points are?"

I looked up. "Huh?"

"Tough job market out there, Alex. What do you think is going to make you stand out from the crowd? If I was taking someone on, how would you convince me it should be you?"

She was staring right at me, expecting an answer, and I couldn't think of a single thing that made me "stand out from the crowd" unless my insane levels of misfortune qualify me for some sort of world record.

"Come on!" she demanded. "You've got ten seconds – sell yourself!"

"No, I—"

"What's so special about *you*?"

"Yeah, but—"

"What's going to seal the deal?!"

"I—"

"Are you confident?"

"No."

"Good at maths?"

"Not really."

"Team player?"

"I dunno, I guess some people say I'm pretty good at oral."

She stopped dead and stared at me for five silent seconds. "You're. Good. At. *Oral*."

It was only when she spelled out what I'd just said that I realized what I'd just said.

She cleared her throat. "You know, Alex, you really shouldn't be sharing that sort of—"

"Oral communication. It's part of the English syllabus," I muttered quickly. I stared harder than ever at my socks, the heat billowing from my cheeks.

She laughed. "Talking?"

I sighed, unsteadily. "Uh-huh."

She laughed again. "OK, so you're telling me you're predicted a good grade for *talking* to *people* in *public*? Well, you do like to hide your light under a bushel, don't you?! *Wow.*"

I didn't like that "wow". Also, at no point did I use the term "good grade". I just said other people thought I was pretty good at it. Which they do. Relative to my other predicted grades – which, just so you know, are pretty ropey.

"OK, well," she said, "being able to *talk* to people is a good skill. A *valuable* skill. That could put you in the running for all sorts of customer service positions."

Oh, *brilliant.*

"Just do me a favour and don't refer to it as... Don't use the word 'oral', OK? That's something quite different."

Did she imagine I didn't know that?

"Could lead to all sorts of misunderstandings and trouble," she said.

I should be so lucky.

"But it's good to hear you're on board. Glad you're engaged in this. Committed. I admire that in a young person."

"OK," I said.

"Especially one like you."

I looked at her with wide eyes.

"Well," she said, "I just mean you can be a bit..."

"Withdrawn?" I offered after a long pause, because it's basically true.

"Sure." She shrugged. "I was going to say 'antisocial'

but let's go with 'withdrawn'. Sounds a bit better, doesn't it? Like when people say 'passed away' instead of 'died'."

I looked straight down at my socks again. This was unbelievable.

There was a silence. I could feel her robotic eyes scanning my room. There was nothing for her to latch on to in here. The boxes of condoms were well hidden and there was no evidence of anything else she wouldn't approve of.

"Why have you got so many cushions in here?" she said.

"I like them."

She stood up and surveyed the cushions with this massive air of suspicion. I know it's probably stereotypical, but I saw these pictures in a travel magazine of luxury hotel rooms, and I liked all the cushions they would put on the beds. I like making things look nice. I wanted *sophistication.* I wanted my room to look like I had style and maturity. I don't think there's anything wrong with that, so I didn't understand why she was looking at me in such a weird way. I couldn't quite place it. Mild disgust?

"Loop me in with the job progress," she said, turning and walking out.

I sat on my bed in despair, the entire summer now looking nothing remotely like what I'd expected.

"He's got a lot of cushions in his room, Tom!" I heard her say to my dad as she got to the bottom of the stairs.

"I know, what's that about?" Dad replied.

Great. So everyone was thinking stuff about me and was busy contemplating how I had some sort of dysfunctional cushion thing going on.

"Well, you know what teenage boys are like. They'll try to hump anything," she said, laughing.

I stared into the middle distance, so shocked I couldn't move.

For the record, I'd never tried to hump a cushion.

At least, I hadn't until that point.

Sorry, that's probably too much information again.

CHAPTER FOUR

I decided to change my clothes. Board shorts and a baggy T-shirt weren't really going to cut it. I reluctantly pulled my chinos on, along with a white shirt and the only tie I had that wasn't my school tie. It was actually one of Dad's old ties, which he lent me when he and Mum took me to a posh restaurant to announce their divorce, and after telling me it was "all amicable" and we'd "still be doing fun things as a family", we spent the whole meal in agonizing silence, until Mum stormed out, saying to Dad, "You couldn't even make an effort for this!" A tie of happy memories. It had a horrible pattern, and was very wide, but it would have to do. I ran some wax through my hair and tried to make it do something that wasn't random sticking up in all directions. I couldn't say I was particularly successful.

"Do I look OK?" I said, walking into the kitchen.

"You're wearing *that* tie?" Kendra said, perched on a

stool at the end of the breakfast bar, looking up from her laptop.

"Yes?"

"OK then."

"Why? Do you think it's—"

She held her hand up, distracted by her ringing mobile, which she answered with her other hand. "Georgie? Do we have news?"

I waited while Kendra jabbered on about whatever the hell it is she actually does. Property or something. I looked down at my tie. Maybe it *was* wrong, I didn't know. My chinos also had a little stain on them, just by the flies, and that was definitely not a good look. I glanced back up when I realized it had gone silent.

Kendra was looking at me, her cupped hand over the mobile. "Alex?"

"Yeah?"

"Just be *confident*? OK? Walk into wherever has a vacancy, and say what you want. Don't 'um' and 'ah', just say it. What do you want?"

"What do I want?" I repeated.

A flash of annoyance crossed her face. "Yes! What do you want?"

"A job?"

"With confidence!"

"I want a job."

She nodded. "Thank you."

I licked my finger and tried rubbing the little stain by my flies.

"Alex?!"

I looked up.

"*Stop playing with it.*" She lifted the phone back to her ear. "Sorry, Georgie. Just trying to coach the boy in a few job-hunting skills." She looked at me, mouthed "*Go!*" and got back to the call. "Yeah, no, *he is a bit*," I heard her say as I walked towards the front door.

I didn't even want to know what I was *a bit*.

One result from the influx of Londoners to Newsands was the increase in the number of shops aimed at pretentious types. There was a café now, for example, that did stuff on toast that really had no place being on toast. And the place I was standing outside of now had also recently opened.

RAW

That was its name. The interior had a stripped industrial feel: air-conditioning ducts on the ceiling, bare brick walls, polished concrete floor, and those old-fashioned light bulbs, where you can see the filaments, hanging down from the ceiling.

RAW sold clothes – although not many, by the looks of it. A few rails were sparsely scattered around the store, each of which had only one or two garments hanging from them, and there were some tables, also with just a couple of tops or trousers folded on them.

It was quite dark inside. And the music was quite loud. Occasionally, you would get a fleeting glance of an aloof, cool figure, casting their eyes lazily over a T-shirt, like they were the judge on a TV talent show and the T-shirt really needed to work to impress them. I felt like I was being watched. And I felt like whoever was watching me was also laughing and bitching about how someone with my (lack of) fashion sense had no place being in a place like RAW. But they had a small sign by the door advertising "Sales assistants required – apply within" so I guessed that, depending on their level of desperation, they might give me a chance.

I repeated Kendra's words, like some sort of affirming mantra. *Walk in. Say what you want. Don't "um" and "ah".*

Well, I'd already walked in, so now I really needed to tell someone what I wanted.

I looked around. There was absolutely no one who appeared to be actually in charge. There wasn't even an obvious place to pay for stuff, which I could just hover near. I mean, *stride confidently up to.*

Then over in the corner, I saw two women – early twenties, maybe. They were putting some clothes back on a rack and had that disinterested, superior and disdainful thing going on which I think is a prerequisite for anyone working in a high-end clothes shop.

My chest was tight.

Say what you want.

Heart hammering.

I gritted my teeth and strode over to them, although my legs felt like jelly. "Hi, I'm here about the job?" I said. I'm pretty sure my voice was wobbling all over the place, but the whole thing is a bit of a blur.

The women glanced at one another. It was a sort of . . . mildly disgusted glance. Like someone had just farted.

I put my hands in my pockets to help add an air of *cool* to the proceedings. I shouldn't have said anything else, but there was this terrible, awkward silence, so I did. "I'm good at. . ." *Don't say oral! "Selling."* Yes, Alex, good! This is a shop, they'll like it if you can sell stuff. "I, er . . . I can *sell* really good. I mean, *well.* I could sell . . . a glass of water to a drowning man, that's me. So. *Boom.*"

I wasn't sure what the "boom" was about.

Nor were the women, by the looks of things.

One of them nodded and called over to this guy who was riffling through some shirts in the corner. "Spence! This guy's here about the job?"

Spence came over, all skinny jeans, hipster moustache and shirtsleeves rolled up to display his tats. "Cool, man! OK, quick-fire questions—"

"Here?" I blurted out.

Spence winked. "I like to keep it spontaneous."

The women nodded.

Spence put his finger in the air, and everyone held

their breath, waiting for his divine inspiration. "*Fashion.* Art, or basic human need?"

I had no idea what type of fuckery I'd just walked into, but I wanted to get the hell out as fast as possible. The women made appreciative murmurs as they considered the question. Spence looked smug. You just knew he probably came to work on a penny-farthing and liked his coffee made as complicated as possible.

I wanted to tell everyone, "Sorry, only joking about wanting a job, please get back to your smashed avocados and obscure folk music!" but I had to answer. "Um—*clothes* are a basic human need. *Fashion* is art." Not bad, I thought. Kind of makes sense.

"Is art not a basic human need then?" Spence frowned. "Does art not contribute to our understanding of life, of the world . . . *of ourselves*?"

"But . . . you presented it as either-or," I protested. *This guy!* I bet he was really fun at parties.

"Challenge the question, my man!" Spence declared. "Think for yourself! The status quo enslaves us all!"

I swallowed and nodded.

Then he laughed. "Mate, we're playin' with ya. We don't even work here!"

I froze while they all had a good giggle, picked up the bags they suddenly had from the floor, and started making their way out of the store.

"Good luck finding a job!" one of the girls called back to me.

"Make sure you tell them how you can sell to people good!" the other said.

I stared down at my suede high-tops.

I was such a total disaster zone it was a miracle charities didn't regularly airlift supplies to me.

My stomach was tight and cramped. So was my throat. I started biting one of my fingernails, only remembering that Kendra had made me start putting that anti-bite liquid on them when my mouth filled with a foul bitter taste. I turned and walked out. Maybe I could sort myself out, regroup, try again later.

Or maybe I could try "Splash Down!"? That was the water park that occupied a huge patch of land down the far end of the front. Splash Down! didn't have employees – they had "dream makers", and being a Splash Down! dream maker was considered the best summer job any kid in town could get. As long as you didn't mind entertaining annoying brats and their incredibly rude parents, it paid well, and it was supposed to be legendary amounts of fun – not least because of the end-of-season pool party they hosted every year, which employees got free entry to, and free drinks all night.

I tried to boost my confidence after the humiliation in RAW by striding along the front, thinking about times when things had gone well. It turned out that was quite challenging, so I thought about Caramel Crème Frappuccinos instead, which at least was a happy thing. I took a breath, removed my tie (Splash Down! was definitely not a "tie" sort of place. It was really a Speedos sort of place, but, huh, no way was that happening), and walked up to the information kiosk just inside the entrance, the screams and cackles of people having a good time *in water* drifting over from the main pools. "Hi," I said to the girl behind the counter. She was about my age, pink hair, and a stud in her nose. "I was wondering about the dream maker jobs?"

"Fantastic!" she squealed. I had no idea how anyone who was sixteen could be so happy. "You're in luck!"

I blinked at her. That would truly be a first.

She was bubbling over with excitement. "We're holding the last of our audition days for this season's new dream makers tomorrow!"

I let the words "audition day" sink in. "Uh-huh?" I muttered.

"So, it's gonna be *so good*?" she said. "Starts with team-building activities in the morning, where you'll be making rafts, doing assault courses and an orienteering exercise around the park; then there's a talent show?"

"Talent show?" I said.

"So, like, everyone who works here has a talent?" She was one of those people for whom most sentences were a question. "So, you'll need to show us yours?

Maybe it's singing? Or magic? Maybe you've got a dancing dog?"

I could put my toe in my mouth, that was literally it. (Don't ask about the sequence of events that led to me finding that out.)

"All through these sessions, people get cut if we don't feel you've got what it takes. . ."

This was sounding better by the minute.

"And if you make it through the talent section, then it's instant death."

I nodded. "What. . . How does that work, then?"

Her eyes lit up. "Everyone gets two minutes to speak, without hesitation or repetition, about themselves. If we get bored, we buzz, and that's it, you're dead. Or at least you won't have a job here, so you may as well be dead!" She laughed like that was funny. Although, in terms of how things worked socially in Newsands, certainly amongst the teen population, it was basically true. All the cool, popular kids got to work and party at the water park in the summer. The rest of us just skulked on the sidelines, pretending like we didn't care. "Make us laugh, make us cry, just *entertain* us. That's a true dream maker, right there." And she gave me this stupid *wink,* like she really thought she was *it,* you know?

I wondered if that was true. I wondered if I really made them cry, if I told them some sad, tragic story about my gran's stroke or something, that they would be so "entertained" they'd give me a job on the spot.

"Registration is nine a.m. tomorrow!" she beamed.

"I'll be there," I said, smiling.

I would not be there. Every kid in a ten-mile vicinity would be turning up for that tomorrow. There was no way I'd survive building a raft with a group of other teenagers. They would all confidently get on with it and then sail away, probably forgetting about me, and leaving me on the side. That was literally what happened on the year nine trip to Paris, when I got left in a service station in Calais, and they only realized when they got to Dover. And that was my fault for "being so quiet". Quiet kids have it rough in a world that loves noise.

I walked out of the park and trudged along the front, jobless and friendless. A pathetic little loner with forty-eight own-brand condoms and an unfortunate reputation for humping cushions. This was not how the summer after GCSEs was meant to be. This was not how *sixteen* was meant to be. I was supposed to be engaged in *revelries*.

I was reaching for my phone so I could put on my Pity Party playlist when I heard the shouting:

"Hey! Oi! Mate?!"

I did what I always did in situations where someone random appears to want my attention: I kept my head down and carried on walking.

"Mate! Mate! Hey, MATE!"

But, OK, this guy wasn't giving up, and my pulse was increasing in line with his volume.

"MAAATE!"

I looked up.

"Fancy a lemonade, mate?"

I stared at him. It was the lad in the giant fibreglass lemon by the entrance to the pier. Every year, some sucker would take the job standing in the stupid thing, serving fresh lemonade to the tourists, and also lemon sorbet and lollies. It's all lemon-themed . . . obviously. It's a lemon. Be weird if it sold hot dogs. It's always been considered a bit of a duff job. It doesn't pay well, mainly because the stand is not that popular. I don't think fresh lemonade appeals to a lot of people round here; I think they'd rather down an energy drink. Or super-strength lager.

He was grinning at me. I hadn't seen him before, so I guessed he must go to a different school. He was black, my age, athletic-looking, with a cheeky sort of face that certainly *seemed* to be friendly, although appearances can be deceptive.

"I'm OK, thanks," I muttered, bowing my head and heading off again.

Lemon Boy (unlikely to be his name, but would have to do for now) whistled. "Man! What does a guy have to do to sell some lemonade around here?"

I vaguely shrugged, and flashed him the briefest of apologetic smiles. The fact is I don't actually like fresh lemonade. I've got a seriously sweet tooth and it's usually too sour for me.

"I am *so* gonna get fired," he sighed.

OK, great, so now I felt sorry for him. You should know there's only so much I can take, in terms of guilt trips. I made the mistake of glancing at Lemon Boy again, and his eyes lit up with *so much hope* I just couldn't disappoint him. I swallowed and approached the lemon.

Lemon Boy watched me, shook his head and smiled. "Bad day?"

Huh. I guessed he'd noticed the little cloud of rain that perpetually follows me around.

"Know what'd help?" he said.

A guardian angel? A genie in a bottle? Frankly, I'd settle for a fairy godmother right now, even the hilariously useless type who accidentally turn pumpkins into pigs in tutus, or whatever.

"*Lemonade,*" he said.

Well, I should have guessed. "OK, then."

Lemon Boy worked his magic and placed a plastic cup of lemonade on the counter. "Straw?" he asked.

"Straw," I said, demonstrating the extent of my charisma and repartee by just repeating his words back to him. I watched as Lemon Boy tried to insert the straw into the tight little hole in the top of the lid. A couple of failed attempts, and the hole finally yielded. In it went, but he must have been squeezing the cup too hard, because a shot of lemonade squirted out of the top.

"Easy, tiger!" he laughed.

The one thing in life I am grateful for is that mind reading is not an actual thing. If you could see what went through my head sometimes, I think you'd be pretty disappointed in me.

"Give it a try," he said, pushing the lemonade towards me. "You're my first customer, I wanna check it tastes OK."

I gave the straw a tentative suck. The bitter sourness hit the sides of my tongue, and I had to seriously fight the urge to wince. I swallowed it down, my mouth stinging. "Mmmmm."

Lemon Boy raised his eyebrows. "Nice?"

"So nice."

He looked pleased. "It's my first batch."

I took another painful acidic sip, my left eye starting to water as I swallowed. "Nice," I croaked as my throat constricted. I hadn't the heart to tell him the truth, although maybe that was just cruel. Maybe he *needed* to know this stuff seriously needed more sugar. If he got the sack, maybe that would be my fault now.

I put my hand in my pocket to get some coins, but he said, "On the house, mate!"

"Oh, really, but—"

"LADIES!" Lemon Boy shouted as he saw two girls over my shoulder. "Fancy a nice refreshing glass of *the best* home-made lemonade you'll ever taste?"

The girls giggled to each other and came over. I wasn't

sure what to do. It felt rude, just slinking off, but I didn't have any reason to stay. Worse, every moment of indecision and hesitation was making this whole situation a million times more difficult to remove myself from.

"Two glasses, yeah?" Lemon Boy smiled at the girls. He turned back to me and caught me just staring at him. "Anything else, mate?"

"Oh, er, no," I said, looking quickly away.

Lemon Boy suddenly grinned. "Oh! I know what you want!"

"Huh? No, I—"

He produced a lemon ice lolly from his freezer and handed it to me. "He's having a bad day," he explained to the girls, who gave me sympathetic smiles.

I nodded a thank-you because I didn't want to interrupt him with any of my stupid words, and backed away from the lemon.

"Make sure you tell your mates!" Lemon Boy shouted after me. "There's a hot new lemonade maker in town!"

The girls giggled again. I held up my ice lolly like I was toasting him (should have used the actual drink, it would have made more sense), and nodded.

I didn't mention I hadn't got any mates *to* tell. I think it would have overly complicated the situation, and if he felt any more sorry for me, I think he'd just have given me the whole stand.

What little confidence I'd mustered for this job

hunt had ebbed away. I needed half an hour to do something else, build it up again. I very nearly turned left and walked down the pier, but I didn't fancy any of the fairground rides at the far end, and all the sideshows required either throwing something or aiming something, neither of which are skills I really possess. Also, there were already quite a lot of people milling about down there, and you know, *crowds.* I sighed and turned the other way, and despite myself, a smile crept across my face.

Wonderland: it occupied the biggest retail unit on Newsands' seafront – a monstrosity of austere architecture that I think was built in the sixties, but was done up like some sort of fantasia. A huge pink-and-yellow plastic frontage was studded with lights that glittered and twinkled, with golden ones making the name "Wonderland" in the middle. Right outside the entrances were the kiddie games – the mini cars and fire engines you could ride for fifty pence, a row of claw grabbers, stuffed with cuddly toys and an assortment of shiny trinkets (some of which may *or may not* have been iPhones), giving passers-by a little taste of the delights within. Neon signs above the doors advertised "Air-Conditioning Throughout" and "Play to Win" – and there was a handy ATM in the wall at the side, just in case you needed some cash, and you *would* need some.

Yeah, it was tacky. And, yes, it was gaudy. But

Wonderland was an escape – like junk food when you're feeling low. There was something magical about those flashing little bulbs outside, the electronic music from the machines, and the occasional sound of an avalanche of coins from a jackpot win. The rows upon rows of games always made me giddy: Pirate Treasure, Pharaoh's Fortune, Jungle Fever, Titan Cash Vaults, the old-school arcade machines and the brand new 4D and VR experiences. Hell, even the change machines twinkled at you like they wanted you to come over and play with them. Put a quid in the slot, and Zoltan will tell you your fortune, delivered on a small printed card at the base of the machine. Another quid gets you the worst hot dog you'll ever experience, or a bag of candyfloss, or a pink-and-white striped paper bag of popcorn. Or there's the Mirror Maze, or the bingo, or pinball or Dance Dance Revolution or Mario Kart or just good old retro Pac-Man. Once you were in, you had no idea if it was light or dark outside, you were just suspended in time, the lights glittering like crystals, like this place was a million dollars. Like *you* were a million dollars.

Maybe it was some sort of sorcery, but it calls you in. It called *me* in, anyway.

CHAPTER FIVE

Listen, I'm not an idiot. I knew this place was as crooked as they come. It's not that the games are gaffed as such, it's just they work in such a way that you never really win. Everyone knows if you win a bit on the coin pushers, you're gonna put it straight back in again because it always looks like a whole heap of coins are about to fall off that moving ledge. They never do, but it *looks* like it. And then a lot of the games churn out streams of golden tickets that you can collect and put towards something from the prize booth. Even if you're crap at a game, you'll usually get a few tickets, and a mediocre performance can easily net you fifty. Never mind that a tiny toy rabbit is five hundred tickets, you quickly have fistfuls of the things, and you feel like you'll surely be able to buy a Porsche.

I mooched about, the few coins I had already burning a hole in my pocket. It was pretty empty in there that day. I nodded at Kemal, who was hovering by the fruit machines with his notepad, as usual. Kemal reckoned he was working on a method – a way of telling when one of the machines was going to give up its jackpot. We weren't exactly mates – more two loners who occasionally exchanged pointless small talk. I spent a bit of time with him last Easter break, when Will was mysteriously often "busy" (which I know now was because he was permanently suckered to Annie) and I didn't have anything else to do except sometimes hang out in Wonderland. After I'd apparently gained his trust by offering him one of my treat-sized Mars Bars, Kem showed me his lists, with columns of all the machines and the frequency with which they were paying out. He had scribblings of equations and probability calculations and everything. Reckoned he was going to be a millionaire one day. Reckoned it was foolproof.

I reckoned he lost about a hundred quid that break.

"See that one there," Kem said, coming over to me whilst keeping his eyes fixed on one machine that an elderly lady was sitting at. "*Hot AF*."

Point of reference: when Kem says something is "hot" he's not talking about the old lady – he means the machine. He means he thinks it's about to pay out a massive win. At least, I hope that's what he means.

I raised an eyebrow. "Yeah?"

He nodded sagely, like it was a dead cert. I'd seen that look before. It hardly ever *was* a dead cert. I don't think those machines work on a basis where mathematical probability would ever help you. Kem never seemed to mind that he always lost his money, though. "Investment in R & D, innit?" he always used to tell me. "Gotta speculate to accumulate."

"How come you're in here, anyway?" Kem asked. "Not seen you in ages."

"Just bored." I shrugged.

"Are you wishing away your summer break?!"

"No. . ."

"You're *unbelievable*!"

I chuckled. Kem was good fun and I thought I should probably make more of an effort to get to know him better. I knew his family was Turkish (he'd told me), and I knew his hair was way better than mine (that much was obvious, he had a proper quiff going on and everything), and even though he sometimes wore wrap-around Oakley sunglasses, he was actually an OK guy. There was a girl he was trying to impress. He wouldn't tell me who she was, but he described her with words like "enchanting" and "mysterious", which I took to mean she wouldn't speak to him. Anyway, all this attempting to win the jackpot malarkey was apparently just so he could impress *her*. I don't know, he went on a lot about how he wanted some souped-up car when he was seventeen, and how he wanted to take her to Cyprus, like fast cars and flashy holidays were all girls needed to be wooed.

"Showtime!" Kem suddenly shouted, as the old lady

slid off her stool and hobbled away from the fruit machine. He was over there in a flash, kissing the first of his coins and putting it in the slot. "Let's bring it home, boys!"

I couldn't help but smile. "I'm gonna get some candyfloss."

"Bad for you, all that sugar," Kem said, not taking his eyes away from the machine, and smacking the "spin" button with the palm of his hand.

"Bad for you, all that gambling," I replied.

But he wasn't listening. He jabbed at the "hold" button and slapped "spin" again. I've never been able to get my head around all the complicated lights and noises those machines have. My tastes are far simpler. I paid a quid for a bag of candyfloss, and changed another quid into two-pence pieces for the Penny Falls – alternately stuffing candyfloss into my mouth and coins into the slot as the moving shelves gradually shuffled the coins forward towards the pay-out hole. There were a couple of five- and ten-pound notes in there too, plus a shiny-looking watch, although, like always, they never actually got beyond the edge.

I was down to my last five coins in no time, and I'd only won about another ten that were sitting in the tray at the bottom of the machine. I considered changing another quid, but then I happened to glance at a couple of kids I recognized from two years below me at school – some boy leaning against the side of a Pac-Man machine, whilst the girl pressed into him, grinding her pelvis into his, mouths all over each other. I got a familiar heavy ache in my stomach, like, *would I ever get to do that with anyone?* And I kind of didn't feel like playing any more.

I started to realize that I'd wasted too much time on the unobtainable. I'd wasted nearly *two years* on Will, ever hopeful that he was definitely in the grip of some sexual confusion that would result in him gently placing his lips against mine. *Unobtainable.*

Lusting after unobtainable people was how I'd come out to my whole family. I was thirteen and a half, sitting in my pyjamas in the lounge, with Mum, Dad and Gran, watching a TV talent show. And there he was. *Alfie McDonald.* This beautiful sixteen-year-old, the best sort of boy, *soft,* not afraid to cry, loved his mum and nan, took his dog for walks and liked cooking. I also bet he would spoon me whilst I slept, whilst listening to mellow indie music. He sang a ballad-y cover of "Born This Way" and all the judges stood up at the end.

And it was then I realized it wasn't just the judges that were standing up.

I casually and slowly manoeuvred a cushion from the sofa over my lap, but when Mum asked me to get another Martini and lemonade for Gran from the kitchen, and I said I would "in a minute" there ensued a terrible and lengthy argument about why I couldn't get her the drink "right now" that resulted in the full horror of everything being revealed. Later that night, Mum came into my bedroom, sat on the edge of my bed, and asked me if I liked boys, which, under the circumstances, I felt like replying "No shit, Sherlock" to, but I just said "Maybe", because I wasn't sure how she would take it, and I thought it might soften the blow if I introduced a small element of doubt into my answer.

She kissed me on the cheek and told me she loved me, before adding, "We won't mention it to Auntie Pat because she's a homophobic old bitch and we want her to leave you something in her will."

So every year, for the last three years, we've seen Auntie Pat at Christmas, and every year she asks me if I'm "courting a lovely young lady" and every year I just shake my head, look down at my trainers, then ask if I can have a biscuit, as a way of taking everyone's attention off my love life. It's pathetic.

Stupid Alfie McDonald – I had to stop wanting what I had no chance of getting.

But then maybe there was Lemon Boy. The free lemonade, the free lemon lolly . . . those two facts didn't completely stack up to a declaration of romantic interest, but they weren't a bad start. I didn't think I fancied him, but maybe feelings could grow . . . maybe that's how it's meant to happen, you know, rather than crazy instant lust, something more grounded and rooted in actual feelings. . .

"AAAAAAAAH! AAAAAAAAAARGH!"

I looked over towards the "Museum of Curiosities" where a teenage girl had just slammed out of the exit, breathless with apparent terror. "Oh, man!" she gasped, taking a couple of deep breaths. "*Shit*."

She was making enough of a drama for Kem to have noticed too. I looked at him and rolled my eyes – she must be a tourist, because everyone round here knows the trick that place pulls. You pay your quid to get in, and the first part of the "museum" is all these exhibits of supposedly weird things – big bell jars containing mermaids in formaldehyde, fake taxidermy, including a pushmi-pullyu from *Doctor Dolittle* – I mean, *please*. It's all dark in there, and they play creepy music, so it sort of gets you in the mood a bit. And then there's this door with a sign on which reads: *Behold the fearsome gorilla-men – half human, half gorilla. Enter only if you dare!*

Well, first of all, I was always pretty sure that gorillas shared most of our DNA anyway, so they essentially probably *are* half human, but that aside, what you get beyond that door is what looks like two stuffed life-sized gorillas with human masks taped to their faces. Proper crap, right? Except when you walk past, one of them stands up and grabs you, and asks for a banana. You're not expecting it, and props to the guy in the costume for staying so still, but it's full-on naff, and most people just walk out smiling.

Anyway, I'd just put another couple of coins into the

machine when I heard another scream. I looked up and there was this eight-year-old boy who'd just run out of the museum, and he looked like he was crying. And then his mum walked over and hissed, "Oscar, have you wet yourself?"

And Oscar shook his head, denying everything, even though he'd blatantly got this massive wet patch all over the front of his shorts, and now, *now* I was intrigued. Whenever I'd come here in the past, people would come out of that place laughing. I'd never seen anyone leave screaming, or having pissed themselves.

I stuffed another handful of candyfloss in my mouth and strolled over to the entrance of the museum. "One ticket, please," I said to the girl manning it. She was pale as a vampire, and looked just as friendly. Tragic, black and heavy eye make-up. Dark purple lips.

"There's no tickets, you just cross my palm with gold and you may enter," she said.

I figured by "gold" she just meant a regular pound coin, so I gave her my last and she lazily gestured to the door like I'd totally ruined her day. I pushed my way through into the darkened room, with everything just as I remembered. I nosed around, reminding myself about all the crap exhibits: some old photos that purported to show the Loch Ness Monster (but could just as easily have been an old tyre floating in a reservoir); the skeleton of a unicorn (pretty hard to verify, but sure); some creatures that are apparently imps, stuffed and mounted (although to me they looked suspiciously like spray-painted gerbils with horns stuck on their heads); and the crappiest thing of all, this creature in a cage, also dead and stuffed, that is supposedly the *Kludde* – a malicious spirit from a desolate part of the Flemish countryside, which takes the form of a winged black dog. Now, I'm not pointing fingers, but the owner of this place used to have a big, black Labrador called Sally, which sadly died two years ago, just a few weeks before the *Kludde* appeared, so you form your own judgement on that.

I could have bought another bag of candyfloss with my last pound, instead of wasting it on this massive disappointment. I shook my head, beating myself up about how Wonderland gets you *every single time*, like everyone who walks in has "sucker" written on their foreheads.

I pushed through the door to the gorilla-men and walked directly up to the one sitting down, who promptly stood up. "Got a banana?" he said. I did my best attempt at a scowl, shook my head and turned towards the—

"AAAAAAAAAAAAARGHHH!" There in my face, *that face*! Haunted! Gaunt! It's the SCREAM face from SCREAM, the movie SCREAM, I was SCREAMING, it was SCREAMING, who the

Adrenaline splintered and surged
Jerking away
Running towards

Slipping

The floor . . . wet. . .

Piss! I'm slipping in kiddie piss!

And then

I'm falling, flying, forward, backwards? Towards . . . and—

CHAPTER SIX

"Lemons. . . Lemonade. . ."

The focus started to come back, the haze became shapes. . .

"*Lemon Boy. . .*"

And the shapes became more solid. . .

A face. Looming over me.

A girl. A short girl. A short black girl, Afro pushed back with a hairband.

And *ping!* I was back in the room. Only on my back, on the floor, with a killer headache, but I was back.

"I literally thought you might be dead," she said.

"I'm not," I replied.

I tried to shift myself up, but she pushed me back down. "*Chill.* You banged your head. Ben's coming with a wet flannel and some paracetamol."

I closed my eyes, partly because of the throbbing, and partly because I seriously wondered if this day, and life in general, could get much worse. I was pretty sure I was lying in the piss too. Something felt *damp*.

"Stay with me," the girl insisted. "Keep your eyes open."

"I'm just resting," I told her.

"Open!" she demanded. "I saw it on Netflix. I gotta keep talking to you, stop you slipping away, until the ambulance gets here. Well . . . not that we've called an ambulance, but until you're recovered, anyway."

I snapped my eyes open. "You haven't called an ambulance?"

"We were going to. If you didn't wake up within a minute. Do you want an ambulance?"

"I dunno. Does it seem serious?"

"You just kinda . . . ran at the door, kinda slipped, and kinda banged your head on it." She chuckled, like this was actually amusing. "Never seen a reaction like that! That was pretty special! Ha!"

I narrowed my eyes at her. "Was it you in the Scream mask?"

She reached behind her and put the damn thing in front of her face. "Boo!" she said. "You proper pissed yourself."

A grim thought crossed my mind. "I didn't though, did I?"

"I don't think so. Did you?"

I sighed and closed my eyes again. "That's why I slipped. Kid before me did."

I heard the door push open and glanced over as a boy my age walked in, dressed in a furry gorilla outfit, except for the head part, which he had under his arm, along with a mound of soggy toilet roll in one hand. "No flannel – got loo roll instead," he said. "Oh, is he awake?" The boy peered down at me, like I was an exhibit in the stupid Curiosity Museum. "Hey." He smiled.

"Hey," I said. He looked a bit hot and sweaty, with flushed red cheeks, but he had kind eyes and dark hair, short around the back and sides and slightly longer on top, that if it wasn't for the fact he'd been wearing a gorilla head for god knows how long, would probably not be sticking up at random angles.

"I'm Ben," he said.

"Alex."

He smiled again. He had *dimples.* Bloody hell.

"Do you want some wet toilet roll on your head?" He extended the dripping mound towards me.

"Not massively," I said.

"Do as you're told," the girl said, grabbing the toilet roll from Ben and pressing it against my forehead. "Take the swelling down."

"Is there swelling?"

"Yeah, a bit. You proper whacked it," she said. She turned to Ben. "Did you tell Maggie?"

"Yeah, she's on her way," Ben replied.

"She's gonna kill us and I can't get fired right now,"

the girl said, turning back to me and then narrowing her eyes. "Are you staring at my breasts?"

"You're looming right over me," I told her. I mean, they were literally taking up my entire field of vision. "Also, I'm gay."

"Being gay doesn't stop you looking at my breasts though."

"No, but. . ." I wasn't sure, maybe she was right. In any case, I was too concussed for this chat.

"I *thought* you were gay," the girl continued. "My gaydar is always spot on, isn't it, Ben? A1 accurate, right, Ben?"

Ben sort of shrugged. "Apparently."

"And when you were coming round you were muttering stuff," she continued.

I swallowed. "*What stuff?*"

"About some boy."

"*What boy?*"

"*Lemon* Boy. Who's he?"

"No one."

"Sounds sexy."

"It's no one," I said. "I was delirious. People say stuff they don't mean when they're delirious."

The girl blew out her cheeks and shook her head. "Not necessarily true, Alex, because this girl, yeah? She's one of my best friends, and she had to have this tooth out before she could have braces fitted, but she's dead scared of dentists, yeah? So she had to be sedated, and she wanted me to come with her, 'cause her mum had legs, bums and tums that afternoon, and she's gotta have someone with her, to get her home OK after the sedation, yeah?"

I could feel myself drifting off again. "Yeah?" I muttered.

"Right," the girl continued, "so the procedure goes fine, but after, as she's coming round from the sedation, she starts muttering all this stuff – like, *'I love you, Efia'*, and *'I've got feelings for you, Efia'*."

"Is your name Efia?" I asked.

"Yes, I told you that."

I knew she hadn't, but I also knew it was pointless disagreeing with her. "Maybe she was just delirious," I said.

Efia shook her head. "No, because when I asked her about it later, she goes dead serious, and says all this stuff about how she didn't want me to find out like that, but it was basically true and how she's a lesbian. I mean, I'm bi, but I wasn't into her, you know?"

I sighed. "Right."

"All I'm saying is, whoever this *Lemon Boy* is, you are *smitten*. You are *luuuuurving him*. You are. . ."

"I get the picture."

"WHAT THE BLOODY HELL HAVE YOU LITTLE *SPUNKERS* DONE NOW?"

I twisted my head round to where the somewhat

fearsome figure of the woman I knew to be Maggie Clapp stood in the doorway. You know how, in small towns, some residents become local celebrities? So, maybe they're the mayor, or they once worked on local radio, or, like my dad, you're the guy who came up with the winning entry to Brownfield's Foods' "name our new margarine" competition, which was, I kid you not, "Butter Me Up". Well, Maggie Clapp was very much a local celebrity, mainly because she was known for ruling Wonderland with an iron fist, taking crap from no one, and, legend had it, once hospitalizing three troublesome blokes on a stag weekend with nothing but her bare hands and some tricks she learned from an ex-lover who used to be a KGB spy. She was a big woman – tall and broad, and it was entirely believable she could hospitalize three rowdy blokes, with or without the KGB tricks.

She took a long drag from an electric cigarette then blew a plume of steam into the room.

A sweet caramel scent hit me.

"Frig me sideways," she muttered, walking towards me. "This is exactly why I dread hiring you kids over the summer!"

Efia opened her mouth to speak, but Maggie held her hand up at her. "But you're cheap, so it's swings and roundabouts." She sighed and shook her head at them both. "Is he gonna sue?" She bent down to look at me. "Are you gonna sue?"

I shrugged. How should I know? It hadn't occurred to me I could claim money for my accident, but there was a chance this could make me way more than any job could. That is, if there was any actual damage. I wiggled my toes about – not paralysed. I guessed we'd only be looking at five figures then.

"He slipped and whacked his head on the door," Ben said.

"Very unfortunate," Maggie said. "But accidents happen. No one's fault."

"He slipped on some wet on the floor," Ben added.

Maggie screwed her face up a bit. "Some *wet*?"

"Some . . . *pee*," Ben said.

Maggie had another long suck on her electric cigarette and looked at Ben. "Some *pee*? Who the frig's been pissing in here?"

"I guess we should have mopped it up, but—" Ben looked down to where I was still lying. "I think he's sat in it."

Maggie gave me a look that I'm quite familiar with, which was somewhere between sympathy and disgust. "All right, kid—"

"*Alex*," Ben interrupted.

A flicker of annoyance passed over Maggie's face. "*Alex*. Does anything hurt?"

"My head, mainly," I said, leaving the door open for other possibilities, if they were potentially lucrative.

Maggie nodded, looking up and down my stricken form. "Bit of mild concussion, huh? Bit of a knock – be better by morning. No harm done, right?"

I shrugged.

"Your parents here?" she asked.

"I'm sixteen," I told her. I hated it when people thought I was younger than I was, but my blond hair, baby face and complete lack of even a hint of facial hair tend to suggest I am.

Her eyes lit up a bit. "Sixteen, are ya? I see." She nodded, then looked at Ben and Efia. "Know him, do you?"

"What school do you go to?" Ben asked.

"Castlegrove."

"Ah. I go to Sherwood Academy and Efia's at St Mary's High. Isn't Castlegrove in special measures?"

"Yes," I said, increasingly feeling like I should be too. That's what I needed. I just needed someone to identify that I was a calamity, and have a team of people sent in to rectify me, until I was "outstanding" or at least "good". But there I was, no friends, no job, sitting in a little puddle of piss, a loser in the heart of *Loserville.* And I didn't want to go home, because I knew how small and pathetic Kendra was going to make me feel, I knew how—

It was then it occurred to me that I didn't know where my candyfloss was. I came in with it, I knew that much, but now. . .

"Um, where's my candyfloss?" I muttered.

"Oh," Efia said. "There wasn't much left."

My eyes widened.

"I ate it," she added.

So, I don't know if it was the bump to the head, or just this realization of how bad stuff was, or maybe this candyfloss business finally tipped me over the edge, but I started to cry at this point. Just sniffles to begin with, but pretty soon I was gulping down buckets of air and bawling my eyes out.

"Frigging hell," Maggie said.

"I'll . . . buy you some more?" Efia offered.

"Come on, mate," Ben said. "It's not so bad."

"It *is* so bad!" I managed to say.

"Give him a tissue!" Maggie told Ben.

"I haven't got a tissue!" Ben replied.

Maggie threw her hands in the air. "Well, that's a lesson, right there! Always have a tissue on you! You'll always find a need for a tissue."

"Have *you* got a tissue?" Ben asked her.

(I'm still bawling at this point, by the way, it being pretty obvious no one cared about me, it was all about the tissues.)

"Thank you, *Benjamin*," Maggie sniffed. "I just used mine in the lav, *someone* used the last of the bog roll."

"He's still crying," Efia said.

They all looked down at me, like a small rodent

they'd just accidentally run over in their car, and they were debating whether to put me out of my misery or just let nature take its course. "I have such bad luck," I sobbed.

Maggie sucked in a breath. "No such thing really, son," she said. "People make their own luck, by and large."

OK, so that didn't account for all those innocent people killed by, I don't know, shark attacks, or deadly pandemics, or even the poor woman at number twenty-five who got killed by a toasted sandwich maker, because none of those people deserved their bad luck through anything they did, but that aside, she was blaming me. Maggie was saying my horrible life was all my own fault.

I wiped my eyes with the palms of my hands. "All I . . . wanted was . . . to get a . . . huh . . . summer job, so everyone would . . . huh . . . leave me a-lone."

Maggie rolled her eyes. "Listen, if it's a summer job you're after. . ." she sighed, "I *suppose* we could use another pair of hands, since it's high season."

I stopped crying like a kid offered candy, propped myself up on my elbows, and looked at her. "Really?"

Maggie glanced down at me. "Part-time, summer only, four pounds an hour, or four fifty if you'll take cash-in-hand and keep it casual."

"I could keep it casual," I said, sitting up further.

"And you agree to drop any . . . claims against me or this place for your little . . . misfortune."

So! Here was the trade-off. Was she only offering me a job to put a stop to me suing her? Did that mean she thought I had a good chance of *sizeable compensation*? But then there would have to be a big old court case, me in the witness box, doubtless being made to say things I don't mean by some hotshot lawyer, branded an opportunist, a liar. The alternative was at least a guaranteed income and, um . . . working here with some nice people. And no, I didn't mean specifically *Ben*, because I didn't even know if he was (a) single or (b) interested in boys, so that would definitely have been stupid.

I nodded my agreement. "OK then."

Maggie sucked on her electric cigarette again and blew another cloud of caramel steam in my face. "Start tomorrow then. Ben and Efia will walk you home – to make sure you're OK after that little trifling bump, better safe than sorry." She looked at Ben and Efia. "It's quiet today, so you two can have the rest of the day off."

Efia's eyes lit up. "Paid?"

"Of course not," Maggie said. "This is a zero-hours contract."

"Oh, come on!" Ben said.

Maggie shook her head. "Works both ways, Benjamin. Flexible for me, when I don't have the hours going; flexible for you when you want to get drunk and have sex with each other, or whatever teenagers normally do."

I can't be sure because I had my eyes closed in

mortification, but I was pretty sure we all had our eyes closed in mortification.

"See if you can get up," Maggie suggested. "Nice and slow. . ."

I opened my eyes, then put my left hand on the floor to steady myself for the heave up. Ben held a hand out for me to take, but like a muppet, I just looked at it, like he was offering me a random fish or something.

"Grab my hand," he suggested.

So I did. And he pulled me upright.

"All right?" he said.

I nodded.

He smiled. *Dimples*. Bloody hell.

CHAPTER SEVEN

"This is me," I said, stopping on the pavement outside my house. I would have invited them in – we'd had a nice enough chat on the walk over here – but I didn't want them to meet Kendra. She would put them off me in a micro-second. "Probably just need to lie down for a bit and I'll be fine," I added, just to make it clear I needed to be alone and wouldn't be offering them refreshments. I flicked my eyes across to Ben and gave him a small smile and a nod. *Yeah.* That's about the extent of my flirting ability. Also, as you would probably expect, he looked even better out of the gorilla outfit. He was the same height as me, but a little broader, with a very slight smattering of freckles across his nose that I could quickly become obsessed with. Well, those and his dimples. And his brown eyes, they were nice too, and—

"Wanna do something later?" Ben asked.

"OK?" I said.

Ben shrugged. "Just hang out at mine for a bit?"

"Sure."

"Bring a bottle," Ben said.

"Really?" *No, Alex, play it cool, can't you?!* "I mean, yep. Like . . . *wine,* or—"

"If you like," he said. "Or whatever."

"OK then."

I had no idea. Did he just mean Sprite?

"My place isn't as nice as yours," he said.

Efia rolled her eyes. "Your place is *fine.*"

"Not as nice as this though." He gave me a little smile. "*Nice.*"

I flicked my eyes away. I guess it is quite a nice house. It's a Victorian semi, quite big, and Mum and Dad spent a lot of time and money when they first bought it doing it up, modernizing, so there's a loft conversion, and an extended kitchen at the back. And since Kendra's moved in, she's continued in the same vein, paying to have the sash windows replaced, and putting two matching box tree shrubs either side of the front door. "Thanks," I said, kicking my high-tops on the pavement.

"Seven, OK? Give you time to sleep off your headache," Ben said. "I'll message you my address."

I nodded.

"Don't bring wine," Efia added.

"OK then."

"Bring *vodka,*" she said.

At least I had firm instructions now. That was good.

Less chance I'd mess up with firm instructions. I nodded my goodbyes to both of them and walked up to my front door, pretty pleased that I'd just been invited to some sort of party, which meant they must have liked me on some level.

"I know you don't like curry, but we're having curry," Kendra said, busy unpacking two carriers of takeaway food as I mooched through to the kitchen, after lying down for a few hours.

I looked in horror at the silver containers on the counter, which had things like "jalfrezi" written on them. "I don't like—"

"Curry, I know," Kendra interrupted, "but we all have to do things we don't like sometimes – it's called 'being an adult'. Plus, if you eat something you don't like five times, you actually train your brain into liking it, did you know that?"

I shook my head as she lifted the lid off a biryani. "Like a lot of kids," she continued, "you've just got immature taste buds. Not your fault, as such, considering what your mother fed you your whole life, but it's time to start educating yourself a bit, Alex. Time to embrace the rich variety of world cuisine. You can't just eat chicken dippers for all eternity."

I didn't see why not.

She broke off a bit of poppadom, dipped it in some mango chutney and looked at me. "Let's have the bad news then," she said, putting it in her mouth.

"I got a job."

She actually stopped chewing for a brief moment, then raised her eyebrows and swallowed. "Where?"

"Wonderland."

She made a sort of slightly disgusted face. "That place on the front? That *amusement arcade*?"

"It's more than just a—"

"What are you going to be doing? It's all automated, isn't it? Just a bunch of losers wasting their benefits money playing games they can't ever win." She laughed hard at this "joke".

I looked down at the floor.

"I suppose they need people to clean, do they?"

"Maybe," I muttered.

"Huh," she said, getting some plates from the cupboard. "Just make sure your vaccinations are up to date, that's all I'm saying."

Dad came through. "Ah, Alex, I know you don't like curry, but—"

"We're having curry," I said.

He looked mildly apologetic. "Kendra's treat."

Some treat. "Thanks, Kendra," I said.

"You're welcome," she chirped, taking the plates and takeaway containers over to the table. "Come and sit down then. Alex has some news, Tom!"

Dad smiled. "Yeah?"

"He's got a job!" Kendra said.

Dad's smile grew wider. "Yeah? That's great—"

"At Wonderland," Kendra added. "Tell your dad all about it, Alex."

I shrugged. "I mean, that's basically it."

Kendra started spooning rice on to all our plates. "I told him I hoped his vaccinations are up to date!" And she laughed again.

Dad laughed too. "It's not that bad. All seaside towns have places like Wonderland."

"It's the sort of place," Kendra said, "that towns like Newsands *don't* need." She looked at me. "Balti, jalfrezi or bhuna?"

"What's most mild?" I asked.

"They're all *medium.* Which isn't, before you moan, *hot.* It's about the delicate spice mix, that's what you need to understand. There's a bit of heat, but not too much. Trust me."

"Can I have a bit of balti then?" I said.

"You may," Kendra replied, spooning some on my plate and handing it to me.

She busied herself fixing the food on to her and Dad's plates, while I took a tentative mouthful of rice and a tiny bit of curry. Holy Christ! It was hot as hell. And there was nothing for me to drink on the table. I shot up and filled a mug with water from the tap, drinking it down.

"Spare us the theatrics," Kendra muttered.

I finished the mug off and gasped air, then refilled it again and returned to the table.

"Do you want some water, Tom?" Kendra said, just as I sat down.

"Sure," Dad said, "I'll—"

"Alex?" she smiled. "Since you were up anyway, water for the table might have been nice?"

"Oh. Sorry," I said. I got up again and filled a water jug, bringing two tumblers over with it.

"Thanks," Kendra said. "Next time, some ice and lemon could also work well."

I shifted my chair back again.

"Whoa!" Dad frowned, stopping me. "What did you do to your head?"

I flinched away from him. "Nothing. Just hit it."

"How?"

"Walked into a door."

Kendra shook her head and shovelled a forkful of curry into her mouth. "Mm! It's so good, that new place – this is absolutely delicious."

"Yeah, it's good," Dad agreed, still looking at me.

"So fresh too!" Kendra tore off a piece of naan and mopped up some sauce.

"Did someone hit you?" Dad asked me.

"No, Dad, it's fine. I literally walked into a door."

Dad opened his mouth, about to call me out on what

he thought was my bullshit (but was actually my life) when his mobile started ringing. "Hold that thought," he said, getting up from the table and answering his phone.

I watched as Dad headed out through the back door, which meant it was probably Mum on the other end, talking about the divorce. I flicked my eyes back to Kendra, who was now helping herself to a spoonful of jalfrezi. "I'm not feeling very hungry, to be honest," I told her.

"Well, there's nothing else if you don't eat this, Alex," Kendra said. "I've thrown out the chicken dippers."

I stared at her. *She had thrown out the chicken dippers?!*

"Processed food is basically poison," she explained. "I know your mum was just trying to keep you happy by giving you what you wanted, but sometimes being a parent means you have to play the bad guy. I'm not your mate, I'm your stepmum."

My description of what she was would have been somewhat ruder and had more expletives in it. "I've kind of got somewhere I need to be," I told her.

"'Kind of' or *you have*?" Kendra said.

"I'm meant to be seeing some. . ."

Kendra raised an eyebrow.

"Friends?"

Her eyes widened. *"Friends?"*

I swallowed. "So, um, yes, I'll probably just go and do that then."

I nodded my goodbyes.

Kendra just shrugged and spooned some more curry on to her plate.

"Tell him about the letters."

Efia was lying back in the hammock that was stretched between the two larger trees at the bottom of Ben's garden. His house may have been quite small, but the garden was big, with a vegetable patch, pond, and a lot of lawn. I only know that because when I arrived, it had still been light. I hadn't even noticed it get dark, but our little encampment was now lit up by some tea lights inside empty pasta sauce jars, which was actually a lot more magical and beautiful than I've maybe made it sound. Ben was squatting on an orange spacehopper that belonged to his little brother, and I was on a white plastic patio chair. Ben's dog, a cute West Highland Terrier called Artoo Dogtoo, lay asleep by my feet, completely unaffected by our laughter and general chatter, which, since we were on our third vodka and Cokes (which on an empty stomach wasn't ideal), was pretty loud. Anyway, in between all the general hooting and guffawing, they were giving me the lowdown on everything I needed to know about Wonderland.

"If he doesn't know about the letters," Efia repeated, "Maggie's gonna snap at him, and. . ." She glanced over towards me. "I'm not sure he'll be able to handle it."

I sat up in the chair a bit, trying to look like I could "handle" it.

Ben blew his cheeks out. "OK, so, when the post comes each morning, one of us needs to sort through it. Now, what you'll find is a lot of very angry letters, printed in red ink, with words like 'Final Demand' and 'Urgent Action Required' written on them."

I nodded. "Take those to Maggie."

"No," Ben said. "Do *not* take those to Maggie. Those ones aren't important . . . apparently. Take those, she'll bite your head off and tell you you're playing right into the hands of the capitalist elite." He took a sip of his drink. "The ones you take to Maggie are the ones that say they're gonna send actual bailiffs or repossess us. They're the ones she'll sort out, as and when they appear. The rest – you just file them."

"In the bin," Efia added.

Ben shrugged. "Yeah, wherever really, she's not interested in them."

"Is Wonderland in trouble?" I asked.

Efia snorted. "I think the term might be 'screwed'," she said, staring up at the stars.

Ben tutted. "We don't know that for sure."

"Town's becoming too cool now," Efia said. "Mum got made redundant from her bar job 'cause they turned it into a trendy gastropub and then didn't rehire any of the old staff."

"That sucks," I said.

Efia sighed. "*Gentrification*, isn't it? And I'm not sure the hipsters want amusement arcades, either. I'm sure it'll last the summer though," Efia said. "If it's the job you're worried about."

I took another gulp of vodka. It wasn't the job I was worried about. It was the increasing sense we were all being edged out. There was too much change happening in Newsands. It was *our* town. It didn't belong to people from London. Surely some things we should be able to keep?

Efia was looking at me, grinning. "So, *Alex*, have you got a boyfriend?"

"Um, no," I said. "What about. . ." I mean, he would almost certainly be with someone because fate is never *that* kind to me, so why was I even asking? "You guys?"

"I'm single," Efia said, brightly. "My last relationship was last summer, with this girl who was staying on some kind of summer camp. Oh my god. She was a nightmare. Turned out she was a kleptomaniac. Literally, anywhere we went, she would nick stuff. It was really stressful." She looked expectantly at Ben, who just smiled and nodded. "Ben's got a *girlfriend*. . ."

Of course. Fate was being as predictable as ever.

Ben crossed his arms. "Why did you say it like that?"

"Like what?" Efia said.

"Like with that little edge in your voice when you said 'girlfriend'?"

Efia chuckled. "OK, well, maybe it's because you never speak about her and she's a total mystery. Maybe that's the reason."

Ben's eyes widened. "I've spoken about her!"

Efia shifted in the hammock and turned to me. "On the day we first met, he told me 'Bella' was travelling over the summer, and when I asked 'Who's Bella?' Ben said, 'My girlfriend' and then deflected my attention by asking if I fancied going for YO! Sushi one day after work, because then all I could think about was panko prawns and not the enigma that is 'Bella'." She leaned slightly further forward towards me and lowered her voice a bit, like it was secret. "He's cunning like that."

Ben blew a breath out. "I mean, OK, I guess I'm just not one of those people who talks about themselves a lot—"

"No, no, no, no!" Efia chirped. "I know plenty about *you*. It's Bella who remains cloaked in secrecy . . . but that's fine, maybe it's private, and I respect that. And I believe you."

Ben stared at her. "What do you mean, you *believe* me?"

"That's she real."

"Of course she's real! Oh my god, Efia, she's real!"

Efia held her hands up. "OK! Sorry! You're *very* defensive, it's weird."

"She's *real*! I have . . . a photo!" Ben started pulling his phone out of his pocket.

"Does it have a Getty Images watermark?" Efia smirked.

I couldn't help but snort. "Oooh! She . . . that is . . . ha! That's . . . yeah," I said.

"Why would I go to the effort of finding and paying for stock photographs of my imaginary girlfriend when I could just pull something off Google?" Ben shook his head. "Makes no sense. And why would I lie anyway?"

"Because boys are full of crap," Efia announced. "Thank you for coming to my TED Talk."

"You're such a wind-up merchant!" Ben shook his head and smiled at her. *Dimples.* I really needed to get over those dimples. Especially now. Now he had a girlfriend. However vague she was. I took a good mouthful of my drink, telling myself, firmly, that I must not, under any circumstances, repeat my previous mistakes. I must not fall for this boy. This couldn't be Will all over again.

I became aware of something warm, moist and slightly rough tickling me, and glanced down to see Artoo Dogtoo enthusiastically licking my ankle. He looked up, as if to check if this was OK, so I gave him a small nod, and he happily carried on. At least someone thought I was tasty.

Efia was still smiling back at Ben. "How did you and Bella meet anyway?"

"School. We're in the same year."

"Ohh!" Efia said. "So she lives round here?"

A flicker of annoyance flashed across Ben's face. "Yes!

Did you think she was just an internet girlfriend who's really a fifty-year-old man who's trying to get me to send him dick pics?" He looked between us both. "I mean, not that I would send dick pics to anyone, but you get what I mean?"

"Uh-huh," Efia said. "Parents?"

"*Yes,* massive surprise, but she does have parents – she wasn't genetically engineered and raised in a laboratory." He took a breath, and looked like he was making a real effort to dial back the sarcasm about ten notches. "Mum's a GP, dad runs a software company."

"Oooo!" Efia cooed. "Minted."

Ben shrugged. "I guess. Don't know what she's doing with a pauper like me."

I held my finger in the air and they both looked at me. "It's not . . . money . . . shouldn't always . . . a thing, see?" It appeared my lips weren't working properly. Either it was the concussion or the vodka.

"Heartfelt and important words, buddy," Ben said, patting my leg.

I downed the remainder of my drink.

"Artoo Dogtoo! *No!*" Ben said, clocking what was still happening around my ankles. "No licking!"

"He's fine," I said.

Ben cocked his head, and Artoo Dogtoo cocked his head back, both staring at one another in this battle-of-wills, until Artoo made a little whimper of defeat, and lay down on the grass, paws out in front, resting his chin on top of them.

"Good boy," Ben said.

Efia leaned back in the hammock. "I think we need to fix Alex up with someone this summer. Maybe with this mysterious Lemon Boy character, whoever he is!"

I shook my head.

"Yeah, who is he?" Ben asked.

"He's no one."

"Ah, so he is *someone*!" Efia said, triumphantly. "Do you like him?"

I shrugged, when I should have said just said no.

"Awwwww!" Efia said.

"Awwwww!" Ben said.

I chewed my lip a bit. "Can I ... go on ... spacehopper?"

Ben slid off it and rolled it over to me. "Knock yourself out. Not literally. You've had enough of that for one day."

I squatted down on top of it, grasping the rubber horns in my hands. Had a little bounce. Yep, it was still fun.

"Take her out for a spin if you like," Ben said.

I did like. To be clear, I wouldn't normally bounce around someone's garden on an inflatable toy designed for five-year-olds, but it was maybe the concussion. Or the vodka. To this day, we can't really be sure, and that's the story I'm sticking with.

I zoomed off, straight down the lawn. It was kind of like . . . flying . . . big leaps . . . through the night air. . . Please don't think me lame, but it was weirdly exhilarating. I think it was maybe because it was quite dark, so I couldn't see that well. I can't cope with roller coasters, or pretty much any ride that spins you about at fairgrounds, so I think I have a low excitement threshold. And this *was* exciting. I think I was squealing. Artoo Dogtoo was running alongside me, jumping up in the air with every one of my bounces and barking in delight. I could hear Ben and Efia laughing. I felt like every teenager in every Hollywood movie who had ever had the best time of their lives.

"I'm the KING OF THE WORLD!" I shouted as I glided through the air, hitting the ground then ricocheting back up again. "I FEEL INFINITE!"

And I did! I felt infinite!

And then I suddenly felt very wet.

And I was in the fish pond.

Just sort of *stunned* and *in the pond*.

How did I even. . .

I started giggling.

And I don't really remember what happened after that, but I'm pretty sure there was a big fish floating next to me, and I think I'd killed it.

CHAPTER EIGHT

I woke up in my own bed – fully naked – and I didn't want to think about how that happened. I stared up at the ceiling, wondering quite how I managed to suddenly get so drunk. One moment, I seemed fine, the next I remember feeling a bit less miserable than usual . . . and the next thing, I'm sitting in a pond next to a dead fish.

I wondered if Ben would forgive me about the fish.

I wondered if I'd said a load of stupid stuff and my new friends now thought I was awful.

I wondered if I should just email Wonderland and say I was very sorry, but I knew I'd ruined everything and for everyone's benefit I would never darken their doors again.

I had a shower and a think.

The house was thankfully empty.

Had some Coco Pops.

Found my clothes from last night draped over

a clothes horse in the garden, drying in the already blisteringly hot sun.

Found a note from Kendra: *Your father and I will be having a chat with you later.*

Decided to brave Wonderland after all.

I made an excellent first impression by arriving over an hour late, and despite being determined to find Ben and Efia, was immediately collared by the vampire-esque girl who had been manning the entrance to the Museum of Curiosities the day before. She introduced herself as "Eve" and I'm pretty sure she said she was a Wiccan, unless, in my slightly hungover state, I hadn't realized that was actually her last name. Eve had been charged with running my "orientation session", which involved us drifting around the deserted interior of Wonderland, whilst she languidly gestured towards the odd fire exit and complained about how there was never any nut milk in the staffroom fridge, only "bovine mammary secretions" which made me come *this close* to puking. She handed me a duster, can of lemon Pledge, and my uniform of a bright yellow polo shirt with the Wonderland mascot embroidered on the left breast – a pink flamingo with a top hat and cane – and I was all ready for my first day of gainful employment. My first task was wiping down all the machines, which quickly became smeared with fingerprints and general grease. Before she floated away, Eve offered to do the tarot for me later, flagging up the possibility of a "sacrificial offering" if it turned out the cards weren't in my favour. Let's just say I was pretty confident I would be killing goats and hanging chickens upside down by closing time.

Left to my own devices, I was torn between trying to find Ben and Efia, and actually doing the job I was being paid for. "Be mature," I told myself as I lifted the can of lemon Pledge towards the steering wheel of one of the driving simulators, "this is work time now." But then I caught sight of Efia coming out of the staffroom, so dashed over to her instead.

"I'm really sorry and I totally understand if you don't want to speak to me again." I sighed and gave Efia a nod. "If it's best, I'll go."

"Mate, it's fine."

I stared at her.

"It's all good," she added.

I swallowed. "Can you . . . is there anything specific that I did that was awful? Besides the fish. I remember the fish."

"Aaah, *yeeeah*," she said, with a slight grimace.

"Does Ben hate me? Where is Ben? Was the fish his? Did I get him in trouble?"

"Talk to Ben," she told me. "He's cleaning the Mirror Maze. I gotta go."

"But—"

"But, mate, seriously, you were just enjoying yourself."

Enjoying myself? Now I really *was* worried. That sounded distinctly out of character.

Efia hurried off towards the Museum of Curiosities. I wanted to talk to Ben, but I also couldn't face it. Why had Efia been so vague? "Talk to Ben." What was so bad that she couldn't tell me herself?

So, I just put it all off instead and buried myself in my work, like that would somehow make the whole thing not real. I'd just finished wiping the Perspex windows on one of the Penny Falls machines (this was one for high rollers – it had ten-pence pieces in it – way out of my reach), when this kid, probably around thirteen or fourteen, came right up and put his entire, greasy hand right on to the glass. His skin was a sickly pale white, like he'd never been out in daylight, and the combination of trackie bottoms, a stud in his ear, and tired, red and swollen eyes, made me super-wary of him. He moved around the machine, casing which slot he was going to use, and then put his other hand on another bit of glass. So now there were two greasy handprints smeared on the machine. And then he *looked at me.*

And then he *licked the machine with his tongue.*

And then he looked at me again, a look that said, *What you gonna do about it?*

I pretended I hadn't seen, even though I was looking right at him in utter disgust, and just sniffed, turned and walked over to Drake, who was this lanky guy in his mid-twenties, who was permanent staff, and in charge of the prize booth where you could exchange your golden tickets. The booth was an Aladdin's cave of treasures: stuffed toys of all sizes, bags of sweets and chocolate, and at the higher end of the scale, even mobile phones and PlayStations – not that I'd ever seen anyone walk out with one of them. Drake's gaunt appearance, greasy shoulder-length hair and general air of despair was somewhat, in my humble opinion, at odds with the magic of the prize booth, but I was a newbie, and I knew to keep my mouth shut.

"That kid just licked the machine," I said to Drake, hoping that maybe he would sort it out. If *I* told the kid off, he'd probably just see it as a challenge, and relish licking everything in the entire place, and that would be me, wiping lick off the machines for the rest of eternity.

Drake stared at me for about ten seconds, expressionless. "Do you want any weed?" he finally said.

I blinked at him.

He raised his eyebrows. "No?"

"Um . . . no. Thanks," I said.

He nodded, took a slurp of his tea, and emptied a bag of coins into his palm. I watched as he placed each one individually into the slot in his coin tray. "Post's here," he said, when he finally glanced up.

I turned to see the postman hovering over by the row of mechanical grabber machines and headed over to take the little pile of envelopes from him, ignoring the kid by the Penny Falls, who had swung his leg up on to the machine when he saw me, and had started to hump it. I started tearing open the letters, just like Ben and Efia had told me. The first was just some marketing material about discounted office supplies, and the second was an overdue electricity bill, which I knew I was to "file". But it was the third one that concerned me. It was a blank sheet of A4, one line of typing:

TIMES UP WONDERLAND

I mean, it was all in caps, the sure sign of a lunatic, but still, this type of letter had not been mentioned to me – did I take it to Maggie, or not?

I would have asked Efia, but she was busy in the Museum of Curiosities, so I'd have to brace myself and ask Ben. But I'd have to *find* Ben first, since he was inconveniently still somewhere in the Mirror Maze. Meanwhile, the kid was now slamming his hands against the window of the coin pusher machine, trying to dislodge the cash, so I pointed to the little sign that was taped on to one of the panels. "What does that say?" I asked.

The kid looked at me, blankly. "Dunno. Can't read."

I locked eyes with him. He seemed genuine. "OK," I said. I mean, if he can't read, he can't read. "This machine is alarmed. Please don't rock it," I told him.

The kid nodded.

I nodded back. We had an understanding. I turned to walk away.

The kid started slamming the machine again.

I took a deep breath, but I wasn't sure what else to do about it, so I just pretended like I hadn't noticed, walked around the "Cleaning in Progress" sign outside the Mirror Maze, and pushed my way in. The maze is essentially a series of boxed sections, some of which have mirrors as sides, some that have clear Perspex, and some that are actually doors that swing open into the next part. At the centre, there's a totally crazy "free-form" section where you literally have five of you staring back at yourself. It's probably the best-value attraction at Wonderland, because it's a quid to get in, but can often be half an hour to get out again.

"Um – Ben?" I called out.

"Yeah?"

"It's me . . . Alex?"

"Yeah?"

Oh god, he'd gone monosyllabic, he hated me.

"Um . . . sorry about the fish."

Silence. Then: "No worries."

Oh god, maybe it was precious. Some of those things are worth a lot of money, I think.

"Um – Ben?"

"Yeah?"

"Where are you?"

There was a pause, and then: "Over towards the left."

"My left?"

"If you're facing forward having just walked in, yeah."

I'd done the maze twice, but I couldn't remember it well enough to know the route. The panel in front of me pushed open, so I walked into the next section, where I smacked straight into a clear Perspex wall. "Ow!"

"Careful!" Ben shouted.

"Do I. . . Which way is it?" I asked.

"Which bit are you in?"

I mean, *the bit with mirrors* – how should I know?! Left was a fixed mirror, so I was more than happy to ignore my sorry, grim-looking hungover reflection and head right, which was a mirror door. Into the next section, and I soon hit my stride, keeping my hands out in front of me to feel for the see-through panels, pushing through mirrors, and generally working my way over to the left-hand side of the maze.

"I'm waving at you!" he called out.

I did a one-eighty turn, and there he was, a few sections away, reflected in one of the angled mirrors, giving me a dopey wave and a dimpled grin. *Bloody hell.*

"How do I—"

"Should be a door to your right, I think!" he said. "No, not that right, the other right!"

"You mean the left?"

"Argh, I don't know, I don't know what's real any more in here!" He collapsed in laughter. "This place messes with your head!"

I tried my left, which opened into a new section, with an angled mirror I could walk around. Ben was seemingly in front of me, but I knew better than to dart forward . . . and I was right. He pressed his nose up against the clear panel and made a mournful little puppy dog face, while he gently pawed at the glass. I one hundred per cent put all the cuteness of that out of my mind and pressed on, opening the mirror door on my left, then forward, then a right turn and—

"Yay!" Ben said, putting his hand up for a high five.

I half-heartedly slapped his hand. "Hi."

"Hello."

We were practically nose-to-nose in the small, metre-cubed section. He was looking right at me, but I couldn't look back. Plus, if I'd known I was going to be standing this close to him, I would have popped a mint. I bowed my head, so I didn't have to look or breathe at him. "About the fish—" I began.

"Alex—"

"I'm really . . . spectacularly sorry though."

He put his hand on my shoulder. "It's fine."

I glanced up at him and he smiled, as if to confirm he wasn't lying about that. "What happened after?" I asked.

"Well . . . you were dripping in pond water and covered in algae, so we tried to suggest you take a shower at my place, but . . . you wouldn't."

"Why not?"

"Apparently you don't take your clothes off on a first date."

I closed my eyes.

Ben chuckled. "We all say stupid stuff if we've had a drink, Alex."

"Uh-huh."

"So we walked you home instead—"

"What am I saying at this point?" I asked. "Am I talking?"

"You *are*."

I waited for the details. "Just tell me," I said, after a long pause.

"You told a policeman you liked his 'big manly helmet'. You let two women from a hen party lick your cheek and when they had, you shouted, 'Yay! I'm not a virgin any more!' You stood on the wall by the fountains and shouted, 'I love chicken dippers! I love Lemon Boy!' and when we got you back home you needed to pee so badly you just did it in one of those nice box tree shrubs by your front door. That's when your mum came out and you were like, 'Look out everyone! It's the *Borg Queen*!'"

I stared straight ahead, through the Perspex wall behind him, to the next section and a mirror that reflected back the biggest knob currently residing on the planet.

"From Star Trek, right?" Ben added.

I nodded. "Yeeeeah."

"Then you started giggling and running through a list of other female villains, kind of aimed at her."

"Great. That's . . . what did *she* do?"

"Um . . . she turned and went inside, just after you'd called her 'Bride of Chucky', I think, although it might have been after 'Cruella de Vil'."

I felt a bit sick.

"No harm done," Ben said. "I mean, OK, maybe calling your mum 'The Borg Queen' isn't the biggest compliment in the world, but she seems cool enough, I'm sure she'll laugh about it."

I took an unsteady breath. *If only he knew.* "She's not my mum, she's my dad's girlfriend. This came," I said, handing him the all-in-caps note: TIMES UP WONDERLAND.

Ben looked down at it, then slowly back up at me. "Kids being stupid?"

"Maybe it's kids being stupid."

"They missed the apostrophe in the 'time's' of 'time's up' – that suggests to me it's kids."

"Or ninety per cent of the population who can't correctly use an apostrophe – including me."

Ben laughed.

"What?"

"I like your sense of humour," he said.

I smiled and looked down at my trainers.

He folded the note and put it in the pocket of his chino shorts. "Let's go and show Maggie."

"OK," I said. "Um ... you know the way out, right?"

Ben tapped his head. "Got the route memorized." And then he produced another piece of paper from his back pocket. "But, we've also got a map!" He unfolded it and showed me a plan of the maze with a red line indicating the route towards the exit. "For if there's a fire or medical emergency or something," he explained, handing it to me, then confidently pushing his way out through the indicated doors.

We were back out on the main floor in next to no time, which was still pretty much deserted, all the games and machines flashing away, glittering, but to no avail. Maybe it was still too early for many people to be out.

Maggie glanced very briefly up from behind her desk as Ben knocked, and we walked into her small office towards the rear. The entire room was a chaotic mess: random boxes piled on top of each other, a huge (dead) pot plant on the floor in the corner, an old arcade game with a smashed screen, and a battered filing cabinet with papers and files bulging out of it. On the wall behind Maggie's desk was a long piece of wood with hooks screwed into it, from which hung the keys to the various machines, so you could get in to them to take money out, or refill them with prizes. "I could have sworn you two were working separately," she muttered.

"Alex came to find me because a thing came," Ben explained.

Maggie gave him a withering look and Ben held out the note, which she took, scanned her eyes over, and handed back to him. "Right?" she sniffed.

"Didn't know if it was important," Ben said.

"How should I know?" she said. "What is it you kids say? 'Haters gonna hate'?"

My eyes widened. "Do we have haters?"

She turned her attention to me. "Why were you late?"

"Oh, I . . . um, it won't happen again, I'm really sorry."

She nodded. "Strike one, Alex."

"How many strikes do I have?"

"Two," she said.

I chewed my lip. "Isn't it normally three?"

Maggie gave me a sarcastic smile. "There's nothing normal about Wonderland, Alex."

Ben waved the note again. "So who hates us then?"

"No idea. The world is full of people with a chip on their shoulder about something. Maybe someone got annoyed because they didn't win a teddy bear. Oh!" She looked like she'd just thought of something, or realized who the culprit was. "*Maybe* the owner of Wonderland wanted to send a message to the staff that TIME WAS UP for finishing their cleaning duties and could they please, for the love of sweet Jesus, get on with it!"

"Shouldn't we tell the police though?" Ben asked.

"Christ!" Maggie said, slamming her palms down on her desk.

"Maybe it's a hate crime," I added.

Maggie guffawed, then went deadly serious. "OK. Get out."

"What shall I do with the note?" Ben asked, as Maggie came round the desk and started pushing us towards the door.

"You can shove it up your pert little arse for all I care, sweetheart."

Ben opened his mouth to speak again, but Maggie stopped him. "I'm doing the lunch rota – you're both taking the early slot together, OK?"

We both looked at each other. Well, to be accurate, I looked at his lips, which were incredibly kissable, and then up to his eyes, which were incredibly beautiful. I released an unsteady breath.

"I'll take that as a yes," Maggie said. She gave us both a long stare then rolled her eyes. "Now, if you could possibly bear to spend the rest of the morning apart, it would be *great* if you could finish your jobs. OK, boys?"

We both nodded and Maggie gently closed the door in our faces.

"What did she mean by that?" Ben said. "*Bear to spend the rest of the morning apart.*"

I shrugged because whatever Maggie was implying, she was quite wrong. I was, at this point, fairly confident I had the Ben situation under control. He was nice, *yes*, but he was straight, he had a girlfriend, I'd accepted those basic facts, and I knew nothing could happen between us. I was fine with that. It didn't matter how cute he was, I wasn't going to fall for another one. I had this. I *so* had this.

I so *hadn't*.

CHAPTER NINE

You know what else I *hadn't*? Any lunch. In all the panic of running out of the house late, it hadn't even occurred to me. Nor had I brought any lunch money, as such, although I did have a quid on me, so I was saved to an extent – or at least, I *thought* I was – until the woman at the chicken and kebab shop was less than helpful:

"How much just for fries?" I asked.

"Two pounds."

"What about a half portion?"

"We don't do them."

"What about a child's portion?"

"A quid."

"Ah, OK—"

"But you gotta be under twelve."

"Oh."

"Can't make exceptions, else everyone will be wanting favours."

I nodded. "I understand."

I did consider trying to find an "under twelve" and asking him/her to buy some fries on my behalf, but I'm aware it's not a good look, hanging around, approaching little kids and offering them money. So I plodded back, empty-handed, to where Ben was waiting on a bench on the promenade, legs stretched out in front of him, texting.

"No fries?" he said, slipping his phone back in the pocket of his shorts.

"They wouldn't let me have any."

Ben frowned. "They're a *shop*!"

"Yeah, well, I wanted a child's portion but I don't count as a child, even though, if it comes to anything fun that children aren't allowed to have or do, *then* I'm a child."

Ben gave a knowing laugh. "I hear you." He prised the lid off his Tupperware lunchbox and held it out towards me. "Help yourself."

I smiled and shook my head. "That's yours. I'm not having your lunch."

"I've got plenty."

"Thank you and everything, but I can't."

Ben cocked his head. "Why not? These are bacon and avocado on crusty farmhouse white," he said, nodding towards the sandwiches. "Trust me, they're good."

"I'm not even really hungry," I told him, which was a lie because my hangover had worn off and I was starving.

Ben snorted, grabbed one the sandwiches, and

waggled it in front of my face. "Eat me! Eat me!" he said in a squeaky little voice.

"Is that meant to be the sandwich talking?"

"Uh-huh." He waggled it about again and did the voice. "I'm a sandwich!" He bundled it into my hands. "Eat up, else there's no dessert."

"Ahhh—"

"Eat!" he insisted.

OK, so I ate, and he was right, those sandwiches *were* good. More than good actually; they were particularly awesome. Even the bread, which is normally the most depressing part of any sandwich, was as sensational as bread is capable of getting. "Who made these?" I asked.

"Me."

I swallowed a mouthful down. "No way. It was your mum."

He shook his head. "It was me." He split open a bag of salt and vinegar crisps and laid them flat between us on the bench. "And I hope you agree, they're the best you ever had?"

"They're *excellent*," I said.

"Right? The freshness of the bread is paramount, but beyond that, the genius lies in the textures and flavour combinations: crisp, salty bacon against the soft mellowness of the avocado, with just a hint of tart ketchup running across it. I can't vouch for the health credentials, but it sure tastes good."

"Which means they're probably really bad for you," I said.

"My favourite type of food is definitely the lethal type," Ben said. "If I never have to eat a lentil, I reckon I will die a happy man."

"To pies!" I said. "And cake and doughnuts and all the bad foods!"

And as if on cue, Ben produced a tub of homemade rocky roads, chock full of all the really good stuff, like marshmallows and cherries, and my first lunch break as an economically active member of society became as perfect as it could possibly get.

Maggie called us all into the staffroom for a meeting that afternoon. I was sitting next to Ben on the small circle of chairs that had been set up; Efia was opposite, next to Drake, with Eve in between, plus a spare chair for Maggie, who was riffling through some papers by the sink.

"Did Ben forgive you about the fish?" Efia said, looking across at me, smirking.

I glanced at Ben, then back at her. "I hope so. I mean, he gave me some of his rocky roads, so I *think* so." I glanced at Ben briefly again, and smiled.

"Aww," Efia said. The way she was looking at us both, it made my stomach flutter.

"Anyway, I don't think he wants to talk about any of *that*," Ben said. "Let's just leave it."

Efia shrugged and popped some gum in her mouth.

I looked at Ben again, who just nodded at me, and then back to Efia, who was looking down but smiling.

Great. There was something else about last night, wasn't there? Something they weren't telling me. I looked down at my trainers before the awkward got dialled up any further.

"Minus eight hundred quid."

I looked up again as Maggie walked to the edge of our little circle, waving a sheet of paper with figures on it about.

She didn't sit. "That's what we lost last week."

Drake sniffed, pulled out a tobacco pouch and started making a roll-up. "Like, went missing, you mean?"

Maggie smacked him on the back of his head with the paper. "No, you great lummox. Do you understand profit and loss? Accounts? That was the difference between what we made and what our outgoings were."

"We spent more than we made?" Drake said.

"Just like the week before, and the week before that," Maggie said. She took a long drag on her e-cigarette. It was minty today. "I'm going to carry out an audit of all the machines and games – see which ones aren't paying their way – and in the meantime, we need to get more punters in. Ours is a numbers game – get 'em through the door, and they'll spend. But we gotta get 'em through the door in the first place."

"I'm not doing it," Drake said.

Maggie blew a plume of steam out at him.

"I know where this is going, and I'm not doing it," he continued. "Get one of the newbies to do it."

Maggie looked between me, Ben and Efia. "Who wants to volunteer?" she said.

Only a fool volunteers for something before they know exactly what it is. Ben clearly felt the same. "What is it exactly?"

"Thank you, Ben," Maggie said. "I like it when people don't hesitate to step up."

Ben's eyes widened a little. "Yeah, but—"

Before he could finish, Maggie had spun round, grabbed a big black bin liner from the table and emptied the contents on the floor in the middle of the circle: a large oval-shaped section, covered in bright pink fluff and feathers, a long pink neck section, attached to a head, some pink diving flippers and a pair of pink tights. It looked like cartoon flamingo roadkill. "Ta-da." Maggie said, with very little enthusiasm.

"What's . . . this?" Ben said, weakly. I think he knew what was probably coming.

"It's the costume that will enable you to become the living embodiment of our famous mascot," Maggie smiled.

Drake sniggered.

"Walk around town in it this afternoon, handing out flyers for ten free games tokens and a free drink," she continued. "Pose for some pictures, talk to the kids – everyone loves a flamingo."

I thought that was quite a bold statement and I didn't see why it would be true particularly.

Ben gingerly picked up the tights. "I have to wear these?"

"Flamingos have pink legs, dude," Drake grinned.

Ben sighed. He sort of looked . . . crushed. I didn't blame him.

"I can wear my boxers underneath, right?" he asked, eyes pleading.

Maggie rolled her eyes. I wasn't sure if that was a yes or a no. I felt so sorry for him. And Ben was . . . such a nice guy. He'd been so sweet to me. *He'd shared his lunch with me. He got me home safe. He didn't mind that I killed his fish.*

I swallowed. I didn't want to, but I owed him. That's what friends did. It couldn't all be a one-way street. "I don't mind," I muttered.

I felt all the eyes in the room flick to me. "You want to do it, Alex?" Maggie said.

"Sure," I said. I looked up at her, tried to smile but physically couldn't. "I'd love to." I think a little bit of sick came up.

"Alex, it's fine, I don't mind—" Ben said.

"No, it's OK. Anyway, I owe you, so." I looked at him and nodded. He nodded back and smiled. It was worth it, just to see that smile and the, er . . . accompanying dimples, of course.

"Oh, my heart!" Efia said, clasping her hands to her chest. "This is *too cute.*"

Ben narrowed his eyes. "*Efia.*"

"No, but seriously," she said, "Alex is making the ultimate sacrifice for you. Everything he holds dear – his self-esteem, dignity, and any vestige of cool he possibly had, he's prepared to give it all up – *for you.*"

I wasn't keen on her use of "vestige of cool" – I mean, I wasn't massively cool, I knew that, but I think she made me sound a lot worse than I actually was.

Ben folded his arms. "He's not my boyfriend," he told the group.

Everyone just stared at him, because that kinda came out of nowhere.

"What?" Ben said, going red. "I'm just saying."

Efia put her head in her hands. "Oh my god."

I didn't know what to do. He sounded quite adamant too. A dull ache in my stomach told me I was sad and disappointed, which meant I wasn't doing a very good job of convincing myself not to fancy him and not to construct wild fantasies in my head about me and him doing stuff like taking bubble baths together, which. . . I blew my cheeks out. *Oh boy.*

Maggie was staring at me. "Alex?"

"Huh? What? It's true, he's not my boyfriend," I told her. I looked at Ben and nodded. He was just staring back, open-mouthed. "We only just met, really," I added.

Maggie rolled her eyes. "I meant, are you OK to be the flamingo?"

"Oh, I really don't mind." I shrugged. "How bad can it be anyway?" It couldn't possibly be more horrific than this staff meeting.

I looked around the group. Everyone was looking down at the floor.

The fluffy pink middle section sat around my hips and had a pair of fake human legs attached to the front, so as to give the impression I was actually riding the flamingo – which, as far as I know, is not really a thing, but anyway. I wore my uniform polo shirt on my top half, and I had some "reins" attached to the neck section, which I held in my hands, juggling also the flyers I had to hand out. The tights were predictably horrific, leaving not much to the imagination towards the, er ... upper portion, and the pink diving flippers ensured that *this* flamingo, far from being a graceful, nimble sort of creature, slapped along the pavement in fits and starts, like some sort of demented, injured yeti.

"You look really good," Ben said as I flip-flopped out of the staffroom.

"It's OK," I said. "You don't have to lie."

"Aww, look at your little legs!" he said, adjusting the fake ones attached to the front of the pink middle.

"Look at his *real* ones." Efia grinned, joining us. "You have *great* legs, Alex."

"Thanks."

"Message from Maggie," Efia said. "Steer as much trade away from the pier as you can – tell people you heard someone got E. coli from one of their hot dogs."

I nodded. "Do we hate the pier then?"

"Oh, Alex, *yes*," Efia said. "Yes, we do! *Rivals*, mate!"

"And don't mention to Maggie that you've even ever been there," Ben added. "I came in with a bag of pier doughnuts the other week, and she went proper crazy at me. Made me put them out for the seagulls."

"Noted," I said. "I should go. The sooner I've got rid of the flyers, the sooner this'll be over."

"Hey, Alex?"

I looked straight into Ben's eyes and a million butterflies fluttered in my stomach. He awkwardly gave me what felt like a slightly reluctant hug. "Thanks for volunteering," he muttered.

"Huh." I swallowed as he gave my shoulder a little squeeze. "It's nothing." And I flip-flopped quickly away before anything in my tights started to suggest it might indeed be *something*.

Once on the promenade, it was pretty much as I expected – completely hideous, and I'm not sure my pulse dropped below 120 bpm the entire time. I attracted quite a few wolf whistles from men and women alike (I just bowed my head and pretended I didn't hear them), a few people took photos with me (including one man who stood behind me and posed like he was anally violating the flamingo – I just smiled inanely, like I didn't know what was going on), and I made two toddlers cry, which was crazy because they were the ones pointing at me and saying, "Look, Mummy! A pink elephant!" and the mum said, "It's not an elephant – it's an *ostrich*," and I only went over to kindly explain I was a *flamingo*, but the kids started screaming, and the mum got sniffy and said, "I'm not sure scaring children is in your remit," like her stupid children's hysterical reaction was my fault and like she knew what my "remit" was anyway.

However, I did manage to hand out a few flyers and after a while it wasn't going as badly. Then the universe must have remembered that I hadn't had any bad luck for half an hour, and I was well overdue. And so, right on cue, there's this huge roar of fierce barking, and I turned to see approximately thirty kilograms of angry, savage muscle and teeth on four legs hurtling towards me with terminal velocity. An old-ish man with a kind face (presumably the dog's owner) shouted from some distance away, "It's OK, he hates flightless birds."

Leaving aside the fact that a flamingo is *not* a flightless bird (unless he *also* mistook me for an ostrich, of course), there was no part of this situation that was remotely "OK". In what world is a massive feral beast with dripping fangs, running towards a living creature that it openly "hates", ever going to be "OK"?

"Mate, I would run," a worried-looking bloke said to me.

"DON'T RUN!" the owner shouted, now puffing and tottering towards me as well, because of course this dog's owner wouldn't be fit enough to actually sprint up to his dog and call him off. "YOU'LL BE FINE IF YOU STAY STILL!"

The violent barking suggested otherwise, and I know it sounds unlikely when I say this dog had red eyes, but I think it seriously did have – and that is not normal.

"Mate – RUN!" another random passer-by implored me.

All I could see bolting towards me was TEETH.

"Dear Christ!" some woman said.

"That kid's gonna get *maimed*!" (Another voice.)

"RUN!" a man screamed.

I ran.

Or, rather, I rapidly flip-flopped along the promenade. I didn't dare look back, but the barking was getting louder, as was the rapid thud of heavy paws galloping on tarmac. I ran straight past the fibreglass lemon, hoping, *maybe*, that Lemon Boy wouldn't recognize me, although that was the least of my worries right then, as I had visions of this thing taking a huge chunk out of one of the legs Efia had so recently admired.

It was then I had an idea – dogs can't do stairs. So I struggled down the steps that led to the beach.

Except, of course, dogs *can* do stairs, and the brutish thug of a dog was hurtling down them right after me.

"SHIIIIIT!" I squealed, now left with no option but to head directly for the sea, because in my panicked brain, dogs can't swim, although of course, they totally can.

I ploughed through a huge sandcastle town that some father and daughter were building, looking over my shoulder seconds later, to see the dog also charge through, leaving a plume of sand and debris in its wake, like Godzilla tearing through New York.

I ran forward, splashing through the waves, hoping to hell the owner would arrive any second to call his stupid animal off and then—

Then there's nothing underneath my feet but water.

And I'm plunging down.

I forgot the water gets deep quickly on this beach – one minute it's fine, and the next there's this ledge you basically fall off.

And I don't know why it didn't occur to me, like, twenty seconds ago, but I can't swim.

So now I'm—

A very different panic floods my body as I flail my arms about

And there's water in my mouth and I'm swallowing it and

"HELP!" I gasped.

And it's stinging my eyes and there's thick mucus

dripping out of my nose and down the back of my throat and I can't actually see, and I can't breathe, and I'm just gulping in salt water and I bob up with the swell of the current, and then this huge wave, towering over me, crashes down on my head and

CHAPTER TEN

Arms.

I was vaguely aware of strong arms around my waist.

"You're OK, mate, I got you."

And being pulled back to shore.

No barking now.

It was pretty hazy, but the next thing I knew, I was lying on the beach, between two legs, black *muscular* legs, sort of propped up against some very hard abs, head lolling against a chest, and I didn't know if this was maybe heaven, but I felt very safe and very calm.

And then I spewed up what felt like ten litres of seawater and all of my lunch, and it took every ounce of willpower not to curl up into the foetal position and bawl my stinging eyes out.

"All right, mate, you're all right," the boy said, soothingly rubbing my back.

I recognized the voice. The slight London twang.

A quick glance over my shoulder, and seeing that cheeky face and those sparkling eyes confirmed it. It was Lemon Boy. But I suddenly felt so bad I didn't even want to think about that right now.

I heard feet pounding down the beach behind me. "Alex?! Alex?!"

"I think your friends are coming," Lemon Boy said.

Efia arrived first and took in the scene. "Wow," she said. "Are you alive?"

I nodded.

Ben arrived, breathless. "Alex?"

"Yeah, I'm OK," I croaked. "You can call off the ambulance."

Efia looked sheepish. "Um, we didn't— We heard the commotion and just saw you darting down to the beach and then. . ." Efia looked at Lemon Boy and I saw the little smile play on her lips. It was then I realized that Lemon Boy was nearly naked, if not for his boxers. "Are you a lifeguard?" Efia asked him.

"Nah. I work in the lemon," Lemon Boy said. "I saw he was in trouble and just ran in after him."

"You work in the lemon," Efia repeated. I didn't even need to be looking to know she and Ben were locking eyes at that exact moment, making all the connections. *"A boy who works in the lemon."*

"Yeah," Lemon Boy said. "Don't know why Carl had that dog off its leash – he knows what it's like!"

"Wh . . . who's . . . Carl?" I muttered.

"Carl Hudson – bloke who owns the pier," Lemon Boy said.

Efia shook her head. "This is war."

"Probably best to leave it, Efia," Ben said.

"But he's hurt one of our own!"

I started shivering and Lemon Boy wrapped his arms around me tighter, hugging me to his chest. "We need to get him somewhere warm," he said.

"I'm fine," I said, because honestly, apart from dripping in mucus, the stinging eyes, the nausea and exhaustion, this was actually starting to feel pretty nice. I would warm up soon enough right here.

"C'mon, let's get you back to the staffroom and sort you out," Ben said.

I glanced down at my sorrowful, wet body. Some seaweed was tangled around my foot, and my sodden hair was stuck down to my forehead. Pink tights . . . but where was the rest of the flamingo outfit? "But . . . the flamingo. . ." I muttered.

"Think that's long gone, mate," Lemon Boy said, nodding towards the vast ocean in front of us.

"Gone. . ." I repeated. I was surely going to get fired now. This was strike two, no doubt about it.

"It doesn't matter," Ben said. "We'll just explain to Maggie that it wasn't your fault and that Carl Hudson basically set his dog on you – she'll understand."

Something told me that was somewhat optimistic. I took a deep breath, which set me off hacking and heaving my guts up again, before spluttering out another lungful of seawater and mucus. "I'm sorry this is so unattractive," I gasped.

"No one cares about that, mate," Lemon Boy said.

I couldn't work out if that was a good or bad thing.

"Let's look at the evidence," Efia said, handing me a mug of sweet tea as I sat huddled under a blanket on one of the plastic staffroom chairs. "A really hot *boy* who works in the *lemon* stand saw you were in mortal danger, so didn't just call for help, he full-on *stripped off his clothes* and ran into the water like this whole thing was *Baywatch* or something. He ran into the water, Alex – *in just his boxers* – to save your life."

I shrugged.

"That boy, that *handsome* boy, who by the way has *great abs* and seems really sweet and genuine, is *the* Lemon Boy you often speak of."

"I don't often speak of him," I said.

"You do," Efia told me. She held up her hand to prevent my further protests. "And I do not blame you. He is a fine, *fine* boy. He is deeply fine. He *is* Lemon Boy, right?"

I looked at Ben, who was all ears, then at Efia, who was grinning at me. "Yeah, I guess."

"Bingo!" Efia high-fived Ben.

I sighed. It barely mattered now anyway – even if

Lemon Boy turned out to be into boys, I'd blown my chances, for sure. Puking your guts up in front of someone is hardly appealing, and nor was the needy "oh help me please I'm drowning" situation I'd found myself in. I was like an actual child, and whilst I was, admittedly, an actual child, it didn't mean I had to act like one all the time.

"You look cold," Ben said, throwing me his hoodie. "Put this on."

"I'm fine with just my T-shirt."

Ben gave me *oh really now?* eyes. "Put. It. On." He crossed his arms. "Seriously, you'll get pneumonia or something."

I pulled it over my head. It was soft and smelled of him.

Maggie walked in, and I immediately stood up. "I'm so sorry, I'll pay you back for the flamingo – take it out of my wages."

"Sit down," she said. Then she looked at Efia and Ben. "I need a minute with him."

Efia and Ben both gave each other a look, distinctly along the lines of *oh man you are so screwed*, and backed out of the door, closing it behind them.

"It was a really big dog," I told Maggie, hoping this fact would count as a mitigating circumstance.

"Sit down, Alex."

I shuffled back into my seat and she pulled a chair up opposite me. "You're not cut out for this, are you?"

My eyes widened in panic. "No, I . . . am! I'm sorry, I promise, I'll do better tomorrow, I'll—"

"I'm not talking about the job," she said. "I'm talking about *life*."

I stared at her and I think my mouth fell open a bit.

"You knock yourself unconscious yesterday, today you nearly drown. . . If I believed in witchcraft, I'd say you were cursed."

I nodded. The idea had crossed my mind.

Maggie gave me this terrible, sad smile, then opened her mouth to say the words I'd been dreading. "You're—"

"I understand!" I said, immediately standing up again. "It's OK, you're right, I'm sorry, I'll go."

". . .a full-on, balls-out muppet," Maggie continued. "But I'm not going to fire you."

"Oh. Right." I sat back down. "Really?" Because, in all honesty, I would fire me.

Maggie gave me a smile. An actual smile. Not a sarcastic one, not a grimace, but, I don't know, almost approaching *affectionate*, I think. "Stop beating yourself up. Shit happens, *get over it*." She leaned towards me. "If you fight against something, it tends to just fight you back. So don't fight. Let it be. *Own the awkward*, Alex."

"But won't my life just be complete shi— Excuse me, *completely terrible* then?"

"No," she sniffed. "It'll be better because you'll stop worrying about things that don't matter. Everyone makes mistakes. Everyone gets themselves in a pickle sometimes. Everyone makes a fool of themselves in front of a boy they like."

I puffed my cheeks out. "Wha— Well, I wouldn't know about that, no boys being liked over here right now, I can tell you, and that is the truth." I was pretty sure that didn't sound convincing, so I added, "No, siree!" making it even less so.

She looked at me with unimpressed eyes. "That was just a hypothetical."

"Oh." I nodded. "Yes."

"Although the lady doth protest too much, methinks," she added. "Do you think I didn't notice how you were with Ben in my office earlier?"

My eyes nearly popped out. "Ben? I was normal!"

"Your cheeks were pink," she told me, very matter-of-factly.

"I have pink cheeks! I can't help it, they're just my cheeks!" I mean, how can I help what my cheeks are doing? I mean, I am *sorry* for having blood going round my body, *seriously*?

"And you were doing an excellent job of not looking at him."

"Proving I don't fancy him!"

"Proving, without a doubt, that you do."

I sighed. This was no good at all. Everyone was on to me. Was Ben on to me too? Was I making him feel awkward and uncomfortable with my apparently obvious lust for him? The way Maggie was talking, I was about as subtle as a panting and drooling dog whenever Ben walked into the room.

"Just try and enjoy it, Alex," Maggie said.

I looked at her, blankly.

"*Life,*" she clarified. Her face was stone, devoid of emotion. I wondered if she took her own advice.

"OK, well, thank you, and I *am* truly sorry," I said.

"Stop apologizing."

"OK. But I'm an idiot."

She raised her eyebrows at me.

I shook my head. "Not an idiot?"

Maggie nodded.

"But it won't happen again, I'll be better, I'll improve, I—" Maggie was glaring at me. ". . .I am OK as I am?"

Maggie sighed and stood up. "I knew a lad like you once."

She stared at me for a moment, a fond smile on her lips. It was disarming, so I just stared back. And just as I was about to ask who, she turned and left, pausing at the door. "Also," she said, "I'm going to whip Carl Hudson's sorry arse." She gave me a quick smile, then walked out.

Ben and Efia were standing immediately outside the door and came straight in.

"Are you sacked?" Efia asked. "Maybe you can claim for unlawful dismissal. I'm pretty sure she can't fire you just because you're unlucky."

"No, I'm still here," I said. "But I've got to *enjoy* being unlucky. Got to enjoy being me." I smiled at them both. "If you're awkward and you know it, clap your hands!" I sang, clapping my hands.

Ben joined in on the claps – bless.

"Who's the lad she knew like me?" I asked.

Efia looked blank. "What?"

"Apparently she knew a lad like me once?"

"Ohhh," Efia said, after a pause. "Maybe she means . . . she had a son. I mean, that's what I heard."

Ben nodded. "I heard that too. Wonderland was created in his memory, 'cause Maggie and her ex took him to Coney Island as a kid, and he got obsessed with the fun fair there."

"What happened to him?" I asked.

Ben shrugged. "Went missing, I heard. I'm not sure. Kinda awkward to ask her. Guess it's none of our business." He checked the time on his phone. "I've gotta go. I'm FaceTiming Bella and I need to be near some good Wi-Fi."

"Oh!" Efia smiled. "And where is Bella calling from today? Atlantis? Camelot? *Wakanda?*"

"Lithuania." Ben rolled his eyes and nodded at me. "I'm glad you didn't drown."

"Me too."

Efia smiled at us both.

"I'm just saying I'm glad he didn't drown," Ben said.

Efia blew out a breath and held up her hands.

"Lunch on me tomorrow," I told him. "I'll do the sandwiches – although I'm not sure they'll be as nice as yours, or your mum's, or whatever."

Ben shook his head. "I told you, I made them." He smiled at me. "Later, then."

When he'd gone, Efia turned to me. "Why you mentioning his mum for?"

I shrugged. "They just seemed like very accomplished sandwiches for a teenage boy to make. I know our limitations."

She nodded. "She died though, Alex."

I suddenly felt cold again. "When?" I managed to say.

"Last year, like practically *this time* last year." She looked down at the floor, then back up at me. "I mean, you weren't to know that."

"But he . . . he seems. . ."

"Fine? Yeah, I know he does. He has to. He's holding it together for his little brother, and his dad's a total mess."

I stared at her, the fingers of my right hand gently squeezing hold of the left sleeve of the hoodie he'd lent me. "Poor Ben."

CHAPTER ELEVEN

Dad shoved the bunch of petrol-station flowers he'd bought me into my hands as he put his key in the lock.

"Aren't lilies flowers of death?" I said.

"She likes them."

Of course she did.

"I'm not saying she has to be your best mate, Alex, but it'd be nice if you two could just get along? Yeah? Be civil to one another."

"You know I was drunk? You know I don't really think of her as the Borg Queen, right?"

"Well, that's what you *said*."

I sighed.

"And we'll talk about the drunk part after you've apologized to her."

"I'm sixteen though."

"*Precisely*."

Dad led me through the hall and pushed me into the

lounge while he carried on towards the kitchen. Kendra was sitting on the sofa, laptop on her knees, typing away. She put a finger up, instructing me to wait, finished whatever she was doing, clicked the mousepad, shut the laptop up and looked at me.

I waited to see if she was going to speak.

She didn't.

"I'm sorry, these are for you," I said, quickly offering the flowers after a pause that lasted way too long.

She stared at me, unblinking.

"They're lilies."

Kendra glanced at the flowers, sniffed, then looked back at me again.

"I'm really sorry, I didn't mean it, I . . . I'd had a drink and I . . . it won't happen again."

Kendra sighed. "The thing is, you *did* mean it, didn't you? You don't like me. Why don't you just admit that fact first, get it all out in the open, and then we can go from there."

I ran my tongue over my lips. This felt like a trap. It felt like standing here and openly admitting how much I hated Kendra would definitely be the wrong thing to do, even though she'd just told me to say it. "No," I squeaked. "I like you."

She stared at me.

"I *really* like you," I added.

A look of disgust and mild alarm flickered across her face.

"Oh, god, not like that," I said.

"Good, Alex, I should hope not." She scowled at me. "Are you going to give me the flowers?"

I handed them to her. "Lilies," I said.

"Yes, you said." She dropped them on the sofa next to her. "I hope they didn't cost too much."

"They didn't." I gave her a reassuring smile and then clocked her frown. "I mean, they were competitively priced. I wouldn't waste money, that's something you've taught me and . . . but I wanted to spend *some* money to show how sorry I was."

This was all too much. I seriously considered just telling her exactly what I thought of her and letting thermonuclear war commence. But just as my hand was hovering over the big red button (is that really how they launch nuclear missiles – seems a bit obvious and naff?), Dad walked in.

"All OK?" he said, giving this hopeful little smile, which was kind of pathetic.

I nodded.

"Good," Dad said. "Sit down then, please."

Oh, *brilliant,* things were about to get even better.

"Now, obviously," Dad continued, "you're sixteen, and I'm sure you feel like you want a bit more freedom – seeing friends, staying out, parties and so on. And that's fine. That's *normal.* But with freedom comes *responsibility.*"

Which is odd, because responsibility sounds like the antithesis of freedom, but OK. I wondered whether he had memorized this verbatim from some useless teen parenting site.

"And, Alex, drinking to excess is not being responsible, is it?" Dad said.

"I think it was because I didn't eat any dinner though," I told him.

"No," Kendra said. "It was because you consumed excessive quantities of alcohol."

I looked down at my shoes.

"Alex? Don't do that looking at your shoes thing – you need to look at us, please," Dad said.

I swallowed and looked back up.

"Now, Kendra and I have spoken, and despite your poor behaviour towards both her and the box tree shrubs she kindly bought for the front of the house, we've decided not to ground you."

"Sorry about the shrubs," I said. "Oh, and thank you."

"OK," Dad said. "But I do want us to be adult about this. And you need to promise us both that there won't be a repeat."

"Sure," I said. "No drinking."

"Alex, I'm not naive enough to imagine you're not going to drink again – of course you will. I'm just saying, act responsibly. Don't do it to excess. Don't get so off your face your mates have to bring you home and you end up urinating all over the front of the house."

"Huh. No."

"OK," Dad said.

I nodded.

Kendra was notably silent. What was the betting she was originally pushing for the death penalty for my punishment? Anyway, maybe that was it now, and I could just go and lock myself away in my room for a bit. Like, six months or so.

"So!" Dad said. "*Ben.*"

My eyes widened. "Er . . . yeah?"

"He seems like a nice lad."

I nodded slowly. "He . . . is."

Dad smiled. "Well, *good.* I'm glad. *Pleased for you.*"

"Wait . . . *what*? What do you mean?"

"Pleased you've found a nice boyfriend," Dad said.

"*What?! No!*"

Dad's face dropped. Poor guy, he's well aware of his son's inability to attract romantic interest and I think he's always felt sorry for me. And in this case, maybe he just saw Ben and *assumed,* for some reason. I don't know, wishful thinking or whatever.

"Right," Dad said. "But last night, you said—"

I was bolt upright. "No! *What did I say?!*"

"Kendra opened the door, you were weeing in the shrub, Kendra went to get me, I arrived and said, 'Come on, mate, put it away', you refused and I'm not going to stop you mid-flow—"

"Can you *please* stop talking about me peeing in the shrub and get to the important bit!"

"I offered my hand to the girl, Efia, to introduce myself, and then to the lad you're with, and you . . . you said, 'Hands off – *he's mine*.'"

I closed my eyes.

"So, I mean, I naturally assumed. . ." Dad continued. "And especially when you then added . . . well. . ."

I kept my eyes closed. "What?" I muttered.

"'*He's a hottie, don't you think? He's. . .*'"

"Ohhh. . ."

"'*He is. . .*'"

"Please stop."

"'*He's finger lickin' good!*' So, forgive me if I got it wrong, Alex, but from what I was hearing, it sounded like you'd got yourself a boyfriend at last."

I emitted some sort of deep, guttural groan. I'd suspected there was more to the story, because of the way Efia and Ben had been acting, I just didn't think it would be this bad. I'd made an absolute idiot of myself. Worse (or possibly better, depending on how you look at it), I couldn't even remember any of this. I dreaded to think what Ben must think of me.

"Did *he* say anything?" I said.

"Ben? Um . . . no, he just . . . he looked a bit sheepish

now you mention it, but at the time I thought he was just bashful about meeting his boyfriend's dad while you were in that condition."

"And Efia?"

Dad nodded. "Yeah, well, that's the other thing—"

Oh god, there was more...

"She said, 'I hope they have a chocolate fountain at the wedding reception,' and I laughed, and said, 'Yes, definitely, they're my favourite thing, especially with fresh strawberries', and she said, 'No, mate – *marshmallows*, and—'"

"Dad!" I said. "No one is getting married. Least of all me. And even more least of all to Ben. He's got a girlfriend."

"He could be bi!" Dad said triumphantly, as though he deserved points for knowing about different sexualities.

"Could be," I agreed, "but he still has a girlfriend, and I'm not going to be that person who splits other people up."

Kendra grabbed the flowers. "I hope that wasn't a dig," she said, walking out.

I stared after her.

"You may not say much," Dad said, "but when you do..."

"Huh, yeah," I muttered.

And then Dad laughed, which was something, at least.

And I had a little chuckle too, but only a small one, because at this point I was mainly thinking two things:

1) I must never be allowed near alcohol again.
2) I needed to apologize to Ben and really make it up to him, not just for this new piece of hideousness, but for going on about his dead mum so much. And then I needed to seriously back off from doing anything that suggested I fancied him.

I also needed to prove my worth to Maggie. In twenty-four hours I had managed to screw up *so much stuff* it was almost beyond belief.

"What you gonna do, then?" Dad said.

I took a deep breath. "I'm going to get some bacon and avocado, and make the best goddam sandwiches that boy has ever tasted."

Dad nodded. "There's both in the fridge. We've got some bread too."

"No," I said. "None of your shop-bought bread. I need some flour and I need some yeast. This has got to be perfect."

CHAPTER TWELVE

Kem sidled up to me as I skulked out of the staffroom the next day. "So, *Alex*, my man," Kem said, eyes twinkling. "Got any insider tips, now you're working here?"

I blinked at him. "Like what?"

"Well, like *anything*? This girl, yeah? She's proper special. I'm gonna need some serious dollar to impress her!" His face was animated with excitement, like I held the key to him becoming a millionaire and, by extension, winning this girl's affections. He lowered his voice a bit. "Are any of the machines more likely to pay out? Do you tweak the probabilities? You must know stuff now!"

I screwed my face up a bit. "I only really just started though. Also, even if that was true, I might get in trouble if I said anything, so..."

Kem nodded. "Yeah, well, you can just quietly tip me a wink."

I mean, sure, although I had no idea what it would be about.

"Post came," Kem said, handing me the small pile of envelopes he was holding. "No one was out here, so I took them."

"Thanks."

"Now you owe me one!" he smiled.

I raised my eyebrows.

He slapped me on my back. "Kidding!" He laughed, then turned serious. "You do though." Then he smiled again. "Nah, not really! Well, a bit maybe."

"I need to get on."

"I'm gonna try 'Rainbow Riches' – it's got unlimited nudges, and I lost a lot of bank on Jackpot Genie yesterday." He headed over to the row of fruit machines along the far wall. I wondered at what point Kem might be classed as having a gambling problem, and some sort of intervention should be staged. Maybe it was fine. I had no idea where he got his money from, though.

The post hardly heralded the most auspicious start to what I'd hoped would be a better day. There was a pretty aggressive letter from the bank, demanding overdue payment of a loan within five days, else they would start court proceedings. Definitely one for Maggie. And then this:

WONDERLAND = CHUNDER LAND.
YOU'RE NOT WANTED HERE. YOUR CUSTOMERS HAVE GONE. YOU'RE NEXT. LEAVE OR FACE THE CONSEQUENCES.

It was on the same thin paper with the same lunatic caps. I passed it to Ben as he walked by with a large cardboard box full of plastic golden eggs. He scanned the note, then looked at me. "*Consequences,*" he said.

"That's a threat, isn't it?"

Ben nodded. "Yeah. This one's a threat." He looked at the note again, chewing his lip as he read it. "Maybe from a different person though."

"You think?"

"Correct use of 'you're' and 'your' – when they couldn't even put an apostrophe in 'time's' in the last one. Just seems weird they're suddenly good at writing."

I nodded. "Good point." I hadn't even noticed. "We should tell Maggie."

Ben shook his head. "Nah, she's got slightly bigger problems right now." I followed his glance over towards the back office, where Maggie was facing off with a huge man in a white shirt with a police-style gilet. "Bailiff," Ben whispered.

My neck and shoulders stiffened. "Oh no."

"It's OK, Maggie was transferring some cash to their account just as I was leaving the office, but he's giving it large about them wanting more by the end of the month."

I glanced around at all the machines – and barely a single customer in sight playing on any of them. Having money by the end of the month was looking like a tall order.

Ben sighed, folded the note and stuffed it in his pocket. "We'll tell her later – got enough on her plate."

"I reckon she needs to tell the police," I said.

Ben shrugged. "I guess that's up to Maggie, but I don't think she's keen having them poke around the place." He glanced over at Drake sitting in his prize booth. "Never know what they're gonna find, right?"

"He offered me weed," I said.

"Yeah, he offers everyone weed," Ben said. "Here, you want to help me with this?" He picked up the box and led me over to the Golden Goose machine, which is basically a big plastic goose, with a see-through middle that is filled with golden eggs. You put your cash in, pull the goose's tail, and it pops out an egg, which always contains a prize. Usually, it's a pretty ropey prize, but legend has it some of the eggs contain twenty- and fifty-pound notes, and one has a Rolex watch in it.

I was dubious about the watch especially.

Ben set his box of eggs down next to the goose. "Maggie audited it, and apparently it's been popping out big-value prizes. She reckons whoever's been refilling the eggs has just whacked the new ones on top, rather than taking the big ones out first and refilling from the bottom."

I narrowed my eyes at the goose. "You mean to say, you refill it with low-value prizes to come out first, and the big ones always stay on top so they hardly ever come out?"

"That can't be a surprise to you."

"I'm a bit disappointed."

"The house always wins, you know that," Ben said, taking a key from his pocket to open the small access door on the top of the goose. "So, we need to go through all the eggs, check the contents and refill it."

"Ben?"

"Yeah?"

"I'm sorry about your mum – I didn't know."

He stopped fiddling about with the goose and was still. "Well, I didn't tell you, so how would you know?" he said, not looking at me. "You don't have to be sorry."

"Well, I—"

"I'm fine," Ben said. "I'm OK." He sniffed and prised open the access door. "Come on, let's get this done."

I didn't say anything more, I just nodded, but I knew he wasn't OK. Efia had told me as much, and his reaction now confirmed it. I wanted to hug him, but I didn't dare.

"Um . . . Ben? About the other night? When you and Efia helped me home. . ."

Now he looked at me. "What?"

"I. . ." I swallowed. "My dad tells me I said some stuff."

Ben nodded, tight-lipped, possibly trying not to smile, I wasn't sure. "Uh-huh."

"OK, so . . . I . . . I may have said some things that were out of order, and if I did, then I'm also sorry about that too."

"You were funny."

"OK."

"And like I said, you were just enjoying yourself and, OK, Efia has clearly taken it all seriously and decided to ship you and me something chronic, but we both know it was just the vodka talking. Right?"

"Huh. Sure." Except I shipped us too. *Something chronic.* I didn't think it was the vodka talking. I think it was just the vodka *helping* me talk. I broke his gaze and flicked my eyes to the floor, before remembering that Dad said I should stop doing that, so I looked back up at him again. I attempted a smile. I think it may have come out as more of a "bravely trying not to cry" sort of face.

"Don't beat yourself up about it," Ben said.

"No, I just didn't want things to be awkward, that's all."

"They're not awkward."

"No. This is fine, isn't it?" I said.

"Yes. Isn't it?"

"*Isn't it?*"

"Let's do the eggs," Ben suggested, quickly plunging

his hands in the back of the goose and pulling a heap out. "Start splitting them open and checking what's inside. Put any high value ones to one side for now." He taped an "Out of Order for Planned Maintenance" sign to the side of the goose, which seemed a little unnecessary since Wonderland was still deserted, except for Kem.

I nodded. "What counts as high value?"

"Anything more than key fobs or a stack of golden tickets."

"Cool." And I set to work prising the plastic eggs open.

"Breaking news!" Efia said, bounding up to us both in her black *Scream* outfit robes. "His name's Freddie. He's *seventeen*."

Ben's face lit up. "Is this Lemon Boy?"

"This is Lemon Boy!" Efia said.

I felt funny about how delighted Ben appeared to be at the mention of his name, but I guessed that proved how he *didn't* fancy me – he was pleased some other boy was in the picture.

"Other facts: he's a Star Wars nerd," Efia continued. "You can thank me for my excellent detective work later."

"How do you even know all this?" I said.

"Asked some people who knew people who knew people who knew him." Efia shrugged. "The info is all legit. I've corroborated it."

I went back to checking the eggs, a bit glum about

Ben's keenness on me and Lemon Boy, and feeling the burn of Efia's eyes on the back of my head.

"Oh. My. God," she said, after a bit. "That's fine, you don't need to use the information I've so kindly procured, but if you don't, I expect that's all you'll ever be doing."

"What's 'all I'll ever be doing'?" I frowned.

"*Playing with your little eggs,*" she said.

I blushed. And when I did look up, Ben was blushing too. "I told you before, I don't fancy Lemon Boy … *Freddie.*"

"You might not think you do, and maybe you don't … *yet,* but your subconscious definitely seems interested."

I couldn't deny that. Also, maybe I needed to be more into this whole idea. Maybe that would convince Ben I wasn't totally love-crazed for him and we could just get on with being mates and I'd act like I definitely didn't harbour dreams involving massages or hot tubs. "We don't even know if Freddie likes boys though," I said.

"Then you need to strike up a conversation with him!" Efia declared. "You know he likes Star Wars now – that's an 'in' right there!"

I was dreading it already.

I watched as some hipster guy with a topknot passed by with his iPhone-wielding girlfriend, as they giggled and took selfies, apparently unaware of the rough kids in the background, including the boy who licked and humped the machines, giving them the finger and an assortment of other unpleasant gestures. The couple seemed so wrapped up in each other, they didn't care about that, or anything else. Imagine that! Imagine being so in love that you didn't care about all the other stuff that normally dragged you down. I bet it would be nice. Maybe I had to take any chances that came my way.

"I owe Lemon Boy a thank-you for saving me anyway, so. . ."

Efia gave me a wide grin. "You'll speak to him?"

"Sure," I said.

As if on cue, one of the fruit machines released a huge jackpot. "Oh yeeeeeeaaah!" I heard Kem shout, as the coins continued to rain out. "I knew this one was hot! I knew it!"

I looked at Efia, who was nodding at me knowingly.

"That's not a sign," I said. "It isn't."

CHAPTER THIRTEEN

"Hey," I said, as I gingerly approached the fibreglass lemon.

Freddie gave me a warm smile that went some way to assuaging my considerable nerves. "Hey. You survived, then?"

"I did." I nodded. "I survived. But only because of your . . . heroic actions."

He laughed. He looked good in his T-shirt with a giant lemon emblazoned on the front, which was no mean feat. But then, he was pretty ripped, so a T-shirt wouldn't look anything other than good on him anyway.

"I'm very grateful," I continued.

"Well, it broke up an otherwise pretty dull day, and it's always nice to take a dip in this heat!" Freddie said. "Although when I got back here, someone had nicked off with a load of lollies. Reckon they would have had the cash too, if the till wasn't screwed down to the counter."

I shook my head. "People today."

"Right! No respect."

I swallowed and watched as he filled the juicing hopper with some more lemons, cranked the handle and pressed the button to operate the machine, simultaneously adding some sugar water to the jug beneath the machine's spout. The juicing in progress, he turned back and leaned against the counter. "What are your mates called?" he said, looking over to where Ben and Efia were sitting on a bench, further down the promenade.

This was potentially good. He might say something about one of them which might indicate his sexual preferences. "Efia, she's the girl, and Ben, he's—"

"The boy?"

"He's *the* boy. Actually just the boy. Not . . . he's the boy, yes."

"They seem nice."

I nodded. "So, I was thinking how I could repay you, you know, for the saving my life thing?"

"You don't need to."

"I kind of should though."

"It's fine."

"So, there's Comic Con happening in London in a few weeks, and I thought maybe . . . how about it?"

"Comic Con?"

The question in his tone said it all. What was I even thinking? How is Comic Con an appropriate idea for a potential first date? I should have stuck with something low key – a milkshake or something. But no, instead, I'd plunged right in with this massive trip and . . . oh god, maybe he thought a trip to Comic Con would involve an overnight stay? Maybe that was why he wasn't keen – and I wouldn't blame him, that would be *way* too much, too soon.

"You can get the train up to London and back the same day," I clarified.

"I know you can; I go up London all the time," he replied.

"Do you? Huh."

"I'm just not really into Comic Con, that's all."

"No?" I said. "Sure. I just thought maybe . . . like, Star Wars?"

"Star Wars?" He looked almost disgusted.

I swallowed and gave a nonchalant little shrug. "I just thought, 'Hey, maybe that's something Freddie is into.'"

"Who's Freddie?"

I stared at him. I was going to kill Efia. I was going to kill her using all the worst slow torture techniques I could find online. "Not you?" I said.

"Right. Not me," he said. "I don't think I ever told you my name."

I nodded. "Aaaah, maybe that's it, maybe that's . . . honestly, since the drowning, *the near-drowning*, my head's been all over the place, can't remember anything, can't—"

"It's Caleb," he said.

"That's . . . that's a nice name," I said. "Caleb."

"I'll pass on Comic Con, if you don't mind," he said. "But maybe we can do something else, sometime."

I pointed my finger at him, made a clicking noise with my tongue, and winked.

He looked mildly amused, borderline weirded out, and poured me a lemonade. "Here you are, Alex. On the house."

I smiled and made an assortment of awkward, appreciative noises, took the drink, and then stormed the twenty paces back to Efia and Ben. How could she do this? How could she have got this so wrong? If I did have a chance with him, that was surely now utterly ruined!

"Well?" Efia said as I arrived. "How'd it go with Freddie?"

"It's CALEB!" I shouted at her. "He's CALEB! CALEB!"

"Yeah?!" Caleb called over from the lemonade stand. "What is it, mate?"

I turned and waved to him.

"WHAT DO YOU WANT?" he called back.

"I just . . . this lemonade is *the best*," I said, which was a pretty quick bit of improv for me. "It's really, really excellent."

"Good, I'm glad," he shouted.

"Cheers to lemons!" I said.

He gave me a weak smile and turned away.

I turned back to Efia and Ben. "*Caleb,*" I hissed.

Efia shrugged. "So I misheard. It's similar."

My eyes widened. "On what planet is that similar?"

"It's got two syllables," she said. "And one of the letters in 'Caleb' is also in 'Freddie' – it's an easy mistake." I could tell from her face she wasn't even convincing herself. "Look," she continued, "I'm sorry for the *mild slip-up*..."

"Slip-up?" I said, raising an eyebrow. "Sure."

"But at least it gave you the confidence to go and talk to him!" Efia said. "And that, Alex, is a step forward!"

"Sure," I agreed. "I was talking to him about the fact he hates the idea of Comic Con and is not into Star Wars."

"Well, admittedly, that piece of information was somewhat in doubt – it was kind of fifth-hand gossip."

I shook my head. "Brilliant." I flopped down next to Ben on the end of the bench.

"Have you got a date then?" Ben asked.

"No. I don't even know if he likes boys."

"Well surely that's the first thing to establish?!" Ben said.

I looked at him. "It's not always that easy."

He held my gaze for a second. "I guess," he finally said.

I sighed. "It doesn't matter; it's stupid anyway." Then I remembered I was supposed to be really enthusiastic about this whole Caleb thing. "He's really fit," I said. "Look at those guns."

We all glanced over at him. He waved.

I waved back. OK, that was enough, I'd done my bit. I pulled the box of sandwiches I'd made out of my rucksack. "I made these for us all."

Ben leaned over the box. "Are these what I think they are?"

"Yeah, well, I tried. They probably won't be as good as yours, but—"

"Is this. . ." Ben had one of the sandwiches between his fingers. "Homemade bread?"

I nodded.

"You made bread?" Efia said. "You made actual bread with your actual hands using actual flour and actual yeast?"

"And actual salt, sugar and water," I added. "I actually did."

"Impressive," Ben said, taking a bite.

I shrugged. "I don't think it rose very well. You're meant to prove it for longer, but I didn't have that long." I offered the box to Efia. "Have one. Have two if they're not too disgusting."

"Alex?" I turned back to Ben, who was looking at me like the heart eyes emoji in human form. "These are really good. Proper bangin'."

"Are they?"

"They're just like—"

"I tried to do what you said – the crisp bacon, the soft avocado. I mean it's always partly luck with avocados, isn't it, because they're hardly ever properly ripe, and then they're too soft, but this one was—"

"Just right," Ben said.

"I guess it was," I said. "And the ketchup, like you said, just a streak of it, but I was nervous about the bread, because the bread—"

"Makes it," Ben said. "And the bread is great."

"He's not wrong," Efia said, between mouthfuls.

"Thanks, guys," I muttered.

We ate the sandwiches in very happy silence. And as we walked back to Wonderland, Ben hung back a bit with me, and he said, "No one's made me those sandwiches since Mum died."

"Well, I hope I did her proud," I said.

He smiled, and briefly squeezed my shoulder "Thank you, Alex."

"Happy glad you like them that total pleasure," I said.

Ben took a deep breath. "Well, that made no sense."

I took a deep breath too. "*Life* makes no sense." And I laughed, because sometimes, you just have to own the awkward.

CHAPTER FOURTEEN

Completely unbeknownst to me, my bread-making exploits had left the kitchen in "a complete scene of devastation" (Kendra's words), and, as a result, I was charged with making dinner that evening, as it was apparently "impossible" for either Kendra or Dad to cook amongst the "carnage". I'd made spaghetti bolognese, but without the spaghetti, as I find it too tricky to eat, and I prefer the little shell shapes. I swear they taste different anyway. The meal passed in silence, which I'd hoped meant that everyone was appreciating my efforts.

"Thank you, Alex," Kendra said, putting her knife and fork together in the bowl. "That was a really interesting dish."

"No worries. Thank you."

I reached across to take her plate, but she stopped me. "Did you want any feedback?"

Not especially, no, I didn't.

Kendra must have clocked my less-than-enthusiastic face. "I thought your generation *loved* feedback?" she said.

"Eugh!" Dad rolled his eyes, but with a sort of glee, because if there's one thing adults like doing, it's having a "let's bash Generation Z" session. "There's this kid at work, eighteen or whatever, he's *constantly* asking for feedback on *everything*. Drives you mad. He's written an email – wants feedback. Sneezed – wants feedback—"

"Yeah, OK, feedback's cool," I said.

"I would have simmered the ragu for a little longer – you'll find it intensifies the flavours." Kendra smiled, like she was trying to be encouraging.

"OK, but I just followed what it said on the jar."

Kendra raised her eyebrows. "*Oh.* You used a jar sauce?"

"Well . . . yes? How else—"

"Waste of money, those jar sauces. All you need is some tinned tomatoes and some herbs, maybe a splash of red wine. Plus, they're full of sugar – makes up for the lack of actual flavour, you see?"

"OK," I said, "but it was in the cupboard though."

"Was it?" Kendra said. "Must be something your mother bought."

I looked down at my empty plate. I thought it tasted nice. But then, as Kendra was fond of telling me, I did have immature taste buds.

"But it was tasty," she said, not even trying to sound convincing. "These are just some tips."

"Tips". *Plural*. Great! There were going to be more!

"Can't improve if you don't listen to criticism, Alex." Dad nodded.

I looked up at him, incredulous, but he was apparently unaware that just moments ago he had been lambasting anyone asking for feedback, so they could do just that.

"Now, this is maybe a personal thing," Kendra said, "but I would have gone easy on the pasta. Pasta is straight-up carbs, and basically contains zero nutritional value. I try to keep my body in a state of constant ketosis. Have you thought about 'courgetti spaghetti'?"

Oddly enough, *I hadn't*.

My phone bleeped. It was a text from Ben:

I'm outside your house. :)

I stood up and started clearing the plates. "Ben's just popped round," I said, trying to still my fluttering heart.

"Oh, *Ben's just popped round,*" Dad grinned.

"It's probably just about work stuff." I shrugged, quickly ramming the stuff in the dishwasher and surreptitiously having a quick armpit sniff to make sure I didn't smell.

"I'm sure it is," Dad said.

"*Dad.*"

"The cut and thrust of the amusement arcade world!"

I shook my head and walked through to the hall, stopping briefly to check my hair in the mirror and to make sure I didn't have any bolognese in my teeth.

"You look *great*!" Dad called through. "Doesn't he look great?" he said to Kendra.

"Mmm," she muttered.

I shook my head and opened the front door.

"Ben! Hey!"

I clocked the dog lead in Ben's hand and saw Artoo Dogtoo was standing next to him, wagging his tail manically. "*Heeeey!*" I said to Artoo, trying not to grin maliciously. Kendra was going to hate a dog being in the house. She'd already vetoed a guinea pig just months ago using some lame excuse about "allergies" when really she was just an unfeeling witch who hated cute animals.

"Good time?" Ben said.

I nodded. "Great time." I ushered him and Artoo Dogtoo inside. "Do you want to go upstairs?"

"I thought you'd never ask."

He winked at me and I went bright, bright red.

"Do you want the beanbag, or—"

"I'll take the beanbag!" Ben said, flopping himself down into it, while Artoo Dogtoo embarked on a sniffing tour of my room.

I perched on the edge of my bed, nudging aside the

cushions. I was doing my best to not freak out about the fact he'd just turned up out of the blue, but inside, I was totally freaking out. I'd barely known him two days – and now this? A home visit? On the other hand, that was what friends did, so I was also aware I probably shouldn't read too much into this.

"I couldn't stop thinking about something," Ben said.

I swallowed. I really, really hoped the thing he couldn't stop thinking about was *me*. I knew that was totally stupid, by the way, I'm just being honest. I was beginning to think that somewhere, buried deep in my subconscious, there was this *thing* that always made me go after unavailable boys because, for some reason, I didn't even want a boyfriend, or something. Like, maybe I was scared of it, or secretly ashamed of being gay – even if the modest shrine I have to Netflix's best Soft Boys would contradict that assertion. Although maybe that's it. Maybe that's why it's a *modest* shrine – because I'm ashamed. If I wasn't, would I have a great big in-your-face temple to the Soft Boys? Would I have life-sized cut-outs, or some of those pillows with their faces printed on them—

The sound of Artoo snuffling and snorting at something behind my bin brought me back to reality. I glanced at Ben. "What's up?" I said.

"That note we got this morning – it said, 'Your customers have gone. You're next.'"

"Uh-huh."

"Well, how do they *know* we've been empty recently? *How do they know?*"

I mulled it over for a moment. "They've looked inside – they've seen. Or..." A chill ran through me. "It's someone who's around a lot. A regular, or..." I glanced at him to check I wasn't about to say something stupid, although I really didn't want it to be true.

He nodded. "Exactly. *Or a staff member.* It's no secret how badly we've been doing amongst the staff – Maggie's told us all. And sure, if you're a regular, you would see it for yourself too." His eyes met mine. "It's someone we know," he said. Then he frowned. "Did you just *shiver*?"

"Uh-huh, this is . . . freaking me out."

Ben laughed, heaved himself out of the beanbag, plonked himself next to me on my bed, and put his arm across my shoulders. "It's OK, mate, I'll protect you from the baddie."

"OK, that's cool." I attempted a chuckle. It came out like a strangled cry. "Cool, cool. *Cool!*" I did a voice on the final "cool", like an American movie trailer voice, for some reason, really deep and dramatic. His arm was pleasantly warm and comfortably heavy across my shoulders. I wanted so badly to just pretend I was ridiculously scared, start quivering or something, so he'd let me cuddle into him. But I didn't. I just sat there, frozen, like I didn't know how to react to physical contact.

"I could be wrong anyway," Ben said. "It's just an idea."

He took his arm away and gave me a shy little smile, which just about destroyed me.

Artoo Dogtoo triumphantly trotted up to us, one of my white socks in his mouth. Ben groaned. "Huh, sorry. He's got a thing about socks. He obviously really likes you." Ben glanced at me, then looked away. "Artoo Dogtoo! *No!* No sock stealing! Give!"

Artoo Dogtoo looked pleadingly at Ben, the battle-of-wills in progress again, until Artoo dropped the sock with a little disappointed whine, then spun around in a couple of tight circles and lay down next to it.

"Good boy," Ben said.

"Uuuuumm – maybe we should speak to Maggie about all this?" I said. "Tell her the theory?"

"Maggie's just got her head in the sand about everything," Ben said. "Like, I love her, she's good to me – she's good to us all – but it's like she's just carrying on as normal, and the place is slowly going bust. You've seen the bills that come in – that's been going on for as long as I've been there, and before that as well, I'm sure. The bailiff today – that's a scary new development. She created the place, she set it all up, and it's like she's oblivious to how serious this stuff is."

"Sometimes . . . I think it's sometimes hard to face the truth."

Ben looked at me.

"And so, it's easier just to carry on like always, and kind of ignore it," I continued.

"Like, if you don't acknowledge it, it's not real," he said, looking down at his trainers.

"Something like that."

I watched him, and then he looked back up at me, and honest to god, I thought we were going to kiss.

He narrowed his eyes slightly. "Are you shivering again?"

"Huh. Guess so. Maybe I'm cold." In July. When it's still twenty-three degrees outside. But yeah, I told him I was cold.

"Maybe you've caught something? From being wet in the sea?"

"Oh, no, I feel fine," I said, not wanting him to think, in the infinitesimal chance he was planning on kissing me, that he'd catch anything.

Ben nodded and shifted back over to the beanbag, clearly not taking any chances. "Maybe," he said, flopping back down on to it, "we should do more to help Maggie turn things around. I know we're only part-time and temporary, but don't we owe her that at least?" He sighed. "If she set the place up in memory of her son, and she lost it, it'd destroy her. I know it would. Like when I thought we were going to lose *our* house."

I looked at him, open-mouthed. "Are you going to lose your house?"

Ben shook his head. "Hopefully not. But the house is

Mum, you know? It's not much, but she loved it. Memories, all that stuff. Dad fell a bit behind on the mortgage after she . . . and, well, it's OK, it's kind of why I'm doing as many hours as I can, to help out a bit. All I'm saying is, I know it's only bricks and mortar, but sometimes places and things are just as important as flesh and blood. So, I think we should help Maggie. Who else has she got?"

I nodded. "So, what like?"

"I dunno, we can think of things, surely? Little ways to increase revenue for the place, get more punters in, make them stay longer." He shifted position on the beanbag. "Like, the bingo, for example. That's usually attended by just two people at the moment. If we could reinvent it somehow, do something with it that captures people's imaginations, it might draw them in."

I pointed at him, and his eyes lit up, expectant. "*Themed* bingo," I said.

"Exactly!" he said. "But what theme?"

"Cowboys! Disney! Ahhh!" I gasped, "*Gay bingo!*"

A little smile crept over Ben's face. "Okaaaay. . ."

"So, maybe we do special gay-themed bingo calls?" I said.

Ben smiled. "Come on then, Alex," he said. "Let's hear it."

"Two cute twinks – sixty-nine!"

I admit, I wish I hadn't gone right in with something sexual and suggestive.

Ben burst out laughing.

"A twink is a kinda boyish-looking gay guy," I said. "It's just a joke."

"I know," Ben said. He was staring right at me.

"There are others, they don't all have to be about sex."

"Sex is kinda fun, though."

"Huh," I said. "Yeah."

So at that point we sat in silence for what *felt* like hours, and I seriously didn't know if I was imagining him flirting with me, or if this was actually happening. Or maybe it was all my fault for mentioning "69" where I should just have used something else completely stereotypical that gay guys might get up to or like – interior design, or musical theatre, for example.

Artoo Dogtoo made a little grunt and rolled over on to his back, paws in the air.

"I think we should make a list," Ben said, reaching over and tickling Artoo's tummy. "Brainstorm ideas – we can chat to Efia too, maybe get Eve on board with her tarot stuff, and present it all to Maggie next week."

"Good, I agree," I said, although I would have said the same thing if he'd suggested sitting here debating the use of literary devices in *Macbeth* – anything to spend time with him, basically.

"I didn't know about Comic Con happening in London," Ben said, looking up from his tickling, as I took some paper and pens from my desk for us to make notes with.

"Oh, yeah, end of August."

"Do you want to go, then?"

I looked at him, and tried not to drop the pens in some rom-com-worthy moment that awkwardly revealed my innermost thoughts and utter shock.

"Since it's not Caleb's thing," he continued.

I nodded. "Very much I'd like would that great be yes." I opened my mouth again, but no further words came out. OK, good.

Ben smiled. Argh, *dimples.* Argh, god, this was too much, too much, too much. "Cool," he said.

"Cool. So cool." I swallowed. "*Comic Con.*" I did the American movie trailer voice again when I said "Comic Con".

"It's a date."

I dropped the pens.

"Aaaand," he said, going back to stroking Artoo's belly, "talking of dates, we mustn't forget we need to fix you up with Caleb – *if* he's into guys. So we have to find that out. It's criminal for a guy like you to be single, especially over the long summer break – think of all the fun you could be having."

He looked up and winked at me.

And all at once I just wanted to scream and cry.

CHAPTER FIFTEEN

So, it turned out I *was* sick. The next morning I was shivering and wrapped up in my duvet with aching eyes and limbs. Kendra brought me what was billed as a "miracle health drink" containing lemon, ginger, Manuka honey and turmeric. It was fully gross and had zero effect. By the afternoon, Kendra was claiming my illness was "all in my head" or certainly "being made a meal of" because I couldn't hack two days in the workplace. The following day, she absolved herself of all responsibility towards me and told Dad that he'd have to take a day off work because I was being too demanding. Point of note: I had literally only asked for a throat lozenge. Anyway, in the meantime, Ben, Efia and Eve had set up a group chat with me and we had been busy discussing options to present to Maggie in our "Save Wonderland" scheme. It had started quite well:

BEN: Revamp the Museum of Curiosities?
ALEX: Hard YES.
EFIA: Eww.
ALEX: ??
EFIA: Stop talking about being hard.

But soon became a little more complex:

EFIA: Gay bingo? Why not LGBTQ+ bingo?
BEN: Good point.
EFIA: What about other marginalized people?
EVE: Straight people like bingo too.

And eventually entered the realm of the ridiculous:

BEN: Pin the tail on the donkey.
EVE: No to animal cruelty.
BEN: Pin the tail on the Eve.
EFIA: Snail racing.
BEN: Guess the length of Alex's. . .
EFIA: BEN!
ALEX: omg
BEN: Arm. What?

By the Thursday I was back and feeling much better. And we were ready to hit Maggie with all our brilliant plans.

"OK," Ben said as we stopped just outside the door to the office. "So, the key points are: it won't cost much, but the return on investment will be worth it."

I nodded. I wasn't entirely convinced that Maggie operated under the same set of principles as most other business people – why would you even bother going to the expense of running bingo when only two players ever turn up? (And one on the days when Barbara has to be at the foot clinic.)

"And I had another idea," Ben said. "Free drinks."

I frowned at him. "Really?"

"It's what all the Las Vegas casinos do: keep the drinks flowing, whatever you like, so you stay there – and spend your money." He clocked my doubtful face. "I'm only talking free sodas – the crappy post-mix stuff. It costs pennies anyway."

"She'll never go for it," I said.

"Bet?"

I shrugged. "Sure, I'll bet you. How much?"

Ben's eyes lit up. "Pizza at that new pizza place that's opened. I win, you pay. You win, I pay."

"OK." I played it cool, but I was already the winner because either way, I'd be having pizza with Ben – and that was a row of gold bars and the jackpot right there.

Ben smiled and knocked on the office door, then since it was ajar anyway, pushed it open. "What the hell?" he said, crossing his arms.

I peered around his shoulder and saw the kid who licked the machines by the desk, shifty as hell, and quite obviously caught red-handed. "Can't you read?" Ben said, pointing to the "Private" sign on the door.

"No," said the kid. "Door was open."

Ben stared at him.

"Didn't nick nothing," the kid continued, making to push past Ben.

Ben stopped him. "Empty your pockets."

"Can't make me do that," the kid said. "Get out of my way."

"Empty them or you'll be barred."

The kid laughed. "Yeah? Gonna bar one of the few customers this skanky place has left?"

The kid's eyes seemed to twinkle. I glanced at Ben, checking if he'd clocked what the kid had said and made the connection to the second note.

"Maggie will bar you," Ben insisted.

"Doubt it," the kid sniffed. He patted Ben gently on his cheek. "Be a good lad and step aside now – don't want things to get nasty."

I was getting nervous. Yes, the kid was younger, but he had a really nasty streak, you could see it in his tired, hollow eyes that exuded pain and hate. He was shorter than both of us, and skinnier, yet his confident swagger suggested he wasn't scared – he knew he could take us on, if he had to. I'd known a few boys like him at school, and they usually have nothing to lose, so they don't hold back.

"Billy, why are you in here?"

I turned, and breathed a silent sigh of relief as Maggie pushed past me and into the office. Even at my age, it's nice when an adult arrives to calm a situation down.

"Just lookin'," Billy smiled, revealing a set of teeth I was surprised hadn't all been knocked out.

"Empty your pockets," Maggie said. "NOW."

Billy rolled his eyes and removed a stapler from the pocket of his trackie bottoms.

"What you doing with that?" Maggie asked.

Billy shrugged. "Reckon you owe me something, the amount of cash I've wasted in here."

"Right," Maggie said, "get out of it, and this office is private, so if I catch you here again, you're for it, mate. Final warning."

Billy pushed past us all, back into the main room.

Maggie sighed. "Yes, boys?"

"You should lock the office," Ben said.

"Nothing worth nicking, Ben," Maggie replied.

"Maggie," Ben said, pulling me inside the office and closing the door, "those notes we've been receiving? The threatening ones? The second one mentioned that we're doing badly with getting customers in. Have you thought how they know that?"

"Because it's true?" Maggie said.

"So they must know this place well then?" Ben said. "Maybe they come here. Maybe they *work* here?"

Maggie openly laughed at him. "I think that's a huge leap to make, Ben. And anyway, there haven't been any more notes, not for a week now. Whoever it was must have got bored."

Ben sighed and looked down at the floor.

"But I'm loving the Nancy Drew vibe, boys," Maggie smiled, as Efia walked in.

"Ooh, is there a *mystery*?" Efia said. "Is it the *mystery* of Ben's missing girlfriend?"

"She's not missing," Ben replied.

"The mystery is why you're all in my office and not working," Maggie said, sitting down behind her desk.

At which point, Ben launched straight in with his pitch. And, let me tell you, Ben was really, really good at this pitching business. I'd gone through all our shortlisted ideas with him the previous night, but now, hearing them out loud, as presented by Ben, they weren't just ideas any more – they were bloody brilliant amazing solutions to all the problems at Wonderland.

". . .And the pièce de résistance," Ben said, "will be transforming the Museum of Curiosities into. . ." He swept his hands out in front of him, painting the words in the air. "*The Roswell Experience.*"

A flicker of interest passed over Maggie's face. "What's that, then?"

"*That*," Ben said, "will be an opportunity to see *up close and personal*, some of the embalmed bodies of the aliens that crash-landed at Roswell, the existence of which was covered up by the CIA, but that we've managed to get hold of and display for your horror and pleasure, here today, thanks to a rogue agent, or something like that."

Maggie raised her eyebrows.

"We back all this up with a social media campaign, getting the word out there, and watch the customers flow in. We're not even on any of the social media sites yet – but we're gonna remedy that."

"There's a Wonderland MySpace account," Maggie said sniffily.

Efia screwed her face up. "Wow."

Ben turned to me and I unfolded my bit of script and read out my lines: "With these ideas, we're tapping into multiple markets – conspiracy theorists and UFO enthusiasts with the Roswell Experience, hipsters with the retro gaming and dairy-free coffee offering, those interested in otherworldly spirits with Eve's tarot readings—"

"How much will it cost me?" Maggie interrupted.

"I haven't . . ."

"Minimal outlay," Ben said.

". . . finished," I muttered, folding my script away again, it becoming apparent no one cared.

"In fact, the Roswell Experience can pretty much

be set up with things we have now, plus a few child-sized dummies from a clothes shop," Ben continued.

We all turned to look at Maggie, who was staring into the middle distance, absent-mindedly flipping a paperclip between her fingers. And then I glanced at Ben, who had this look in his eyes, like a kid on Christmas morning, just hoping for that one present he really wants.

Maggie finally took a long suck on her electric cigarette. "Well..." She blew out a plume of steam. "Spend any more than three hundred pounds and you'll be responsible for the remainder."

Ben's eyes widened. "Is that a—"

Maggie nodded. "Give it a try, why not?"

"Boom!" Ben shouted, punching the air, then slapping my back.

"Plus, it'll be one in the eye for Carl Hudson and his manky pier." She gave us a quick smile, then turned deadly serious. "Screw it up and you're all fired. When can we relaunch by?"

"Two weeks?" Ben said.

Maggie nodded. "Done. Now get out of here."

Ben grinned, moved to the door, then quickly turned back. "Oh, one last thing – free drinks—"

"No."

"But—"

"Absolutely no way, Ben," Maggie said. "This is Wonderland, not Caesars Palace."

"But—"

"Out!" Maggie insisted.

She shooed us out the door, shutting it behind us.

"Huh. Pizza is on me, then," Ben said, sheepishly.

I smiled at him. "I think, since you did such a great job, we could agree to split it."

Efia's eyes were *gleaming*. "Are you two. . ."

Ben shook his head. "Just a lads' pizza night."

"Brilliant!" she practically squealed. "I mean, ah, lads' pizza night, that's great. Nice to have some boy time, just the boys. Good idea!" She looked like she might explode with excitement. It was kind of sweet. "*Bex!* That's your ship name. Huh? What? I didn't say anything."

Ben and I looked at each other and rolled our eyes at the exact same time. But the truth was, I loved Efia right then. I loved her and her totally brilliant ship name for me and this lovely boy who I could never be with because he wasn't gay and had a girlfriend.

Ben had written a sign (he seemed to be fond of signs), which read "Closed for Redevelopment – New Attraction Coming Soon!" and taped it to the door of the now cordoned-off Museum of Curiosities, and Efia and I sat on the floor while Ben described the vision for the place. The first room was to be an exhibition, featuring photos of the alleged Roswell incident, some dubious artefacts, like bits of an actual UFO (the plan for which was to find some likely-looking scrap metal), and a short film, which Ben was going to edit together on his laptop, which purported to show the aliens undergoing an autopsy. Like all conspiracy theory "evidence", this would all be suitably grainy and hard to verify, and any bits he didn't have, or couldn't get online, would just have a screen which would read "Redacted – Top Secret Confidential, By Order of the CIA" or words to that effect. Visitors would then be invited one by one into what was previously the "gorilla room", which was now the *alien autopsy room*, where they would encounter a dead alien on a medical table, it's stomach cavity opened up and its guts on display.

"And here's the *great* part," Ben grinned. "Hiding underneath the table is one of us, and just as the punter leans over to get a good look at the alien guts, we thrust our hand up through the secret hole in the table, up through the alien and out of the guts – like that scene in the film!"

"What film?" Efia said.

"Um . . . *Alien*?"

"Huh," Efia said. "So, our hand will be disguised in some way?"

"Yeah, as, like, a mini living alien creature. You can do a lot with latex," Ben said. "Punter screams, job done!"

"I think this is great," I said.

"So, we're using a child-sized mannequin for the alien," Efia said, "but what about the intestines? They'll need to look fairly real for this to work."

Ben grinned. "Over to Alex."

"Oh, yes, OK," I said. "So, last year, we did this play at school – well, I didn't, I don't like things like that, but some other kids did – and anyway, there was this scene where a character has to hold up some bloody animal intestines."

"What sort of school do you go to?" Efia frowned.

"Well, it is classed as 'failing'," I said. "And there were a lot of complaints about the play, which was a bit unfair because Ms Rowland really tried but—"

"Alex?" Ben said. "Tick-tock."

"Oh, right, sure. Well, guess what they used instead of real intestines?"

Efia looked blank.

"Condoms!" I said. "It turns out, condoms filled with a mixture of flour, water and red food colouring, then tied up, are really similar in look and texture to intestines. Sort of."

"How anyone would ever find that out is beyond me," Efia sighed. "So, we go condom shopping, then?"

"No need!" Ben beamed. "It turns out Alex has forty-eight in stock!"

Efia turned to me, eyes wide.

"They're not really 'in stock'," I said. "I don't . . . I don't maintain a 'stock' of condoms, I. . ." I swallowed and opened my rucksack, pulling a couple of packets out. "Huh, these ones are flavoured, for example."

"Oral sex." Ben nodded.

"Was that an offer? Should I leave?" Efia asked.

I pretended to be *very busy* putting the condoms away again.

Efia, however, was clearly absolutely loving all this. "So, let me fully understand this," she said. "I am making no judgement here, Alex, none at all, in fact, *good for you*, it's just, I'm sorry, I've only known you a short time, but you didn't strike me as being quite so . . ."

I waited in horror for her final choice of words.

". . . vivacious."

I shook my head. "Oh, no, I'm not. Definitely not. If anything, I'm probably more *listless*, I think. Not through choice particularly, more bad luck and maybe genetics, I don't know."

"We've had this chat; he bought them by accident," Ben said.

Efia raised her eyebrows and looked highly doubtful.

She heaved herself to her feet. "Right, I've had enough of this. I'm going to get us a child-sized mannequin; you two can stay here and start work on the intestines. Man, that's a sentence I thought I'd never say."

And she walked out of the door.

I set to work mixing the flour, water and food colouring in a bucket, leaving Ben to start opening the packets of condoms, which I thought was the safest way to split the work. No way did I want to fumble around with those little packets, tearing them open all wrong and revealing the full extent of my sexual inexperience. We had to put a condom on a dildo thing in a sex ed class once, and not only did all the lube make it slide out of my nervous-virgin hands, I then split it and put it on inside out.

"What do you make of that Billy kid being in the office?" Ben said as he casually and confidently plucked a foil packet from the first box and tore it open.

I stared at Ben's hands as he gently slid the condom out. My god, he'd definitely done that before.

"Alex?"

"Huh?" I looked up at him.

"The kid in the office?" Ben said again. "Like, what was he doing? Do you reckon he could be the one sending the notes?"

"The kid can't read; it seems unlikely," I said. "But if it was him, if he got someone to help him or something, then I guess it *was* just kids messing about. He said we owed him something; maybe he's just pissed off at how much money he's lost here."

Ben nodded. "Maybe." He rolled the condom out to its full length, ready for the flour mix, and plucked another packet from the box, tearing it open just as smoothly and perfectly as the first. I tried to focus on getting the mix in the bucket right, but all I could think about now was Ben and condoms.

"Let's try this," I said, giving the bucket a final stir. "See if the consistency is right."

"Righto," Ben said, picking up a condom and stretching it open.

I swallowed and scooped up a small amount of the filling, dropping it down into the condom.

Ben chuckled. "This is pretty weird, isn't it?"

"Huh. Yeah."

I dropped another spoonful in, and Ben smoothed it down to the bottom. "I think this is good," he said, stroking and coaxing the filling downwards.

"Yeah," I croaked.

"Bit like making sausages, or something."

"Yeah."

"How big should we make it?"

I looked at him, feeling a little light-headed at this point.

"Like, how thick and how long?" he said.

I think I may have just been staring at the condom he was holding, my mouth sort of open a little. "Perhaps. . ." I held my hands out vertically, making a vague measurement. "This sort of length?"

"About seven inches?"

"I mean" – I swallowed – "we don't want it to burst."

"We do not," Ben agreed. "Then we'd have flour babies!"

I emitted some sort of nervous giggle that honestly

sounded like I was about four years old and someone had just said "underpants".

My hands shaking slightly, I set back to work filling the condom, which Ben then expertly and swiftly tied off, dropped next to him, and picked up another to fill.

"Hey, Alex?" Ben said, as he tied off condom number four. "I was just thinking, you know what you said to Efia? About being 'listless' or whatever?"

I couldn't look at him. "Sure," I muttered, stirring the contents of the bucket.

"Well, I don't think you should feel bad about it. Like, I'm not saying you *do* feel bad necessarily, but all I'm saying is, if you haven't had sex yet, that's cool, I think."

Oh my god, now I had "virgin" marker-penned on my forehead. I was *so* glad it was *so* obvious.

"I haven't had sex," he said.

Now I *did* look up at him.

He smiled and shrugged. "I haven't though."

"What about Bella?"

He shook his head.

I wanted to ask, "Well how come you are *so good* at handling condoms then?" but thought better of it just in time.

"Not everything has to be about sex," he added. "I mean, I want to, one day, with someone, and I do think about it . . ."

I looked at him again.

". . . quite a lot," he smirked.

I laughed. "Yeah."

"Hey, I just think sometimes people build up the virginity thing into this huge issue, and it shouldn't be, that's all, so don't be sitting there thinking you're some sort of—"

"Sexual nuclear winter?"

"You're definitely not that," Ben said.

I smiled, because he sounded pretty confident about that, and I thought that was sweet, if misguided.

"I've never even kissed anyone though," I said.

And then I dropped my eyes again, because I should probably *not* have said that. There's failure, and there's *failure,* after all.

"Kissing's nice," Ben said.

I looked at him, and he smiled.

"Would you like to kiss Caleb?" he said quietly.

No, you stupid dork, I want to kiss you. "Maybe." I shrugged.

He pressed his lips together and nodded. "Then we gotta see if we can make that happen."

I released a sigh that was way heavier than I meant it to be. "Sure," I said.

CHAPTER SIXTEEN

I think the only reason I was going along with the whole Caleb thing was because Ben was suggesting it, and I'd dangerously reached the point where my devotion to him was such that I would have pretty much jumped off a cliff, had he wanted me to. So that's how I found myself approaching the big lemon again that lunchtime, with strict instructions to strike up a conversation and see if I could suss out if I was in with a chance with him.

"Hi, hello," I said, arriving at the counter.

"Hey, Alex," Caleb smiled. "Here for your daily dose of lemonade?"

I nodded. Despite Kendra's claim that you could train yourself into liking anything if you have it enough times, I wasn't any more enamoured with lemonade than when I started. Nevertheless, I maintained the lie, because lies are a *great* basis for any relationship.

"Nice day," I said. I had *the best* small talk.

He paused and looked at me. "Summer, I guess."

"Yeeeeeaaah."

Caleb turned his back to fix my lemonade, and it was then that this tall black guy sauntered up to the stand, dressed in a cream linen suit, with a pale blue, open-necked shirt and a matching pale blue handkerchief in the breast pocket. "Afternoon, gentlemen," he said. And I'm sorry, but I have to take a moment to recognize that this was the first time I'd ever been called a "gentleman" so this was a real rite of passage for me, you know? "How's business?" he continued.

Being British, I think it's genetically ingrained in me to immediately crumble and be completely subservient to anyone of an obviously higher social class than me, but Caleb was having none of it. He turned and looked the guy up and down, unimpressed. "Who are you?" Caleb said.

The man smiled. "Tyler Phillips. I run a business networking group for Newsands – just checking in with some of the traders to see how the season's going." He extended his hand towards Caleb, who shook it.

"Business is OK," Caleb sniffed.

"Excellent!" Tyler beamed. He turned to me, clocking the logo on my polo shirt. "Ah! Wonderland! How is the old place?"

I nodded. "Fine, sir."

Tyler winced. "Please don't call me 'sir'. Tyler's fine." He smiled warmly at me. "Summer job, is it?"

"Yes, si— I mean, yes, Mr Tyler, *Tyler*, just Tyler. Yes it is." I cleared my throat. "Actually, we're doing a bit of a relaunch."

Tyler's eyes lit up. "Now *that* is music to my ears! That's what we need more of round here – forward thinking, improvements, striving to make Newsands better!" He leaned towards me. *"I like it!"*

I nodded.

Tyler turned back to Caleb. "I'll take a lemonade, if I may?"

Caleb poured him a cup. "Three pounds then, please."

I nearly whistled. I had no idea that's how much the lemonade normally cost. Who was buying it at that price? Tyler handed him a fiver without flinching though. "Keep the change," he said.

"Cheers," Caleb smiled.

"And if you need any help with the relaunch," Tyler said, turning back to me, "get in touch. Marketing, a bit of promotion, or just some advice – whatever you need." He handed me a little printed card with his details on it. "You can reach me here."

"OK, thanks for your kindness," I said.

Tyler smiled and sauntered off, turning back briefly after he'd taken a sip of the lemonade. "Mmm! Delicious!" he beamed.

Caleb gave him a thumbs up.

"He seems nice," I said.

Caleb smirked. "Yeah? He gave you his number, man!"

"Oh, no, I didn't mean . . . he's not my type," I said. "Not that . . . I mean, it's just he's a bit old for me, that's all, he is my type in the sense that he's a . . . he's a *he*, if you know what I mean?" I swallowed. This was the moment. The moment I laid my sexuality cards on the table for Caleb and he would maybe do the same for me.

But Caleb just nodded. *Silence.* Terrible silence. Maybe I hadn't been clear?

"I'm gay," I said.

"Alex—"

I cut him off and ploughed on, because of course I did. "Yeah, I'm all about the boys. The *booooooys.* All about the—" Where was I going with this? I needed to stop. Right now. "All about the . . . um . . . when I said 'all about the boys' I didn't mean . . . that's not all I think about or anything. Like, there are more facets to my personality than that . . . it's not all boys, boys, boys . . . in fact, hardly ever . . . well, *never,* to be fully accurate, it was just a figure of speech. Which I regret." I blew out a breath. "But I am—"

"Gay," Caleb said.

I nodded. "Yup."

Caleb smiled right through the awkward pause that would have been his cue to say "Me too!"

"I'll go now. I'm sorry about the— thanks for the—" I turned and nearly collided with an old woman and her walking frame. "Arse, sorry I—" I gave Caleb a thumbs up. "Bye then!" I turned to the old lady. "Sorry, miss."

And hurried back along the front to where Efia and Ben were waiting on our bench.

"Never again," I said. "That's it, no more. I've made a total dick of myself. Let's just accept this is never going to happen. I don't even think I want it to any more anyway. Maybe I never did. The end."

"What went wrong?" Efia asked. "You can tell Auntie Efia."

I scowled at her. But also her gentle tone was comforting. "I was put off my stride by the guy who spoke to us."

Efia's eyes lit up. "We *saw* the guy! Was he deeply attractive? Were you mesmerized by his beauty and—"

"No! He's not, and I wasn't— He gave me his card."

"You are *on fire*!"

"He's just some local business club guy, and he offered to help with advice about the relaunch, if we wanted any."

"Look at you!" Efia said. "Networking, making contacts—"

"Getting guys' numbers!" Ben added.

They were both so enthusiastic about me finding love this summer, it was ridiculous. "It led to an increasingly awkward conversation with Caleb which resulted in me talking too much. But it's all over now. *Finito*."

"You give up too easily, mate," Efia said, shaking her head.

"I said, *the end*. I actually don't care. I don't care if I'm never touched by another human being, I can't talk to people, I'm a total liability. Being single's fine. I'm better alone." I flopped down on the bench.

"Maybe we're thinking about this all wrong," Ben said. "You're going to Caleb, but maybe we need to make *Caleb* come to *you*."

"Does anyone want this lemonade?" I said. "I don't even like it."

"Interesting suggestion, Benjamin," Efia said, accepting the drink and taking a big sip. "Elaborate."

I dug around in my rucksack. "Got ham sandwiches today, what about you guys?"

"We need to make Alex like a lighthouse," Ben said, simply continuing like I wasn't there, "shining his charismatic beam for all to see, guiding the straying ships safely into his port."

I nearly choked on the first bite of my sandwich. "No one is going to be guided anywhere, least of all my 'port', I mean, did you actually just say that? Seriously, I'm over it."

"A makeover!" Efia said. "Like Sandy in *Grease* when she gets that leather jacket and goes all bad girl."

"Right!" said Ben.

"Wrong!" I said. "And lighthouses may have beams, but they also tend to be solitary figures in the wilderness, surrounded by crashing waves and storms, which, you know, is where this whole analogy should really be going."

Ben laughed and ruffled my hair. "You're so funny, Alex. It's adorable."

Ohhhh, he'd called me "adorable". Code red, code red! Chances of Boy Action raised to DEFCON 4 – above normal readiness, but no need to panic.

"Aww, you should have seen the way Alex's eyes lit up when you said that!" Efia said. "Too. Cute."

I shook my head at Ben. "No, they didn't. Nothing lit up, I'm totally dead inside. Also, I really didn't like it in *Grease* when Sandy had that makeover. I actually *cried*."

Efia laughed. "You *cried*?"

"I really liked her before." I shrugged. "Pretty. And sort of . . . safe. She didn't scare me like the others did – like that Rizzo. I didn't like her."

"Rizzo's a complicated mess, that's why she's so great," Efia said. She turned to Ben and grinned. "How's Bella?"

Ben screwed his face up. "How'd you get from Rizzo to Bella?"

"Fictional girls, obvs."

Ben held his sides in mock laughter. "Amusing. Please tell me you're planning on doing a stand-up comedy course at uni."

"That's not a course," Efia said.

"I bet it is somewhere," Ben replied.

I cracked open a can of Coke, my smile soon fading as I glanced up the promenade and saw who was strolling towards us: Carl Hudson, with his horrible beast of a dog that still wasn't on a lead. He saw me, smiled, and raised his hand. "Very sorry about the other day, son! You shoulda stayed still, I did tell ya!"

I flicked my eyes away.

He stopped just next to our bench, the dog sniffing around our feet. "He's never done anything like that before, I promise. Weren't hurt, were you?" I looked up at him again, and he gave me gentle, hopeful sort of smile that looked pretty genuine.

"I'm OK," I muttered.

Carl nodded. "If I can make it up to you. . .? You kids are welcome down the pier any time – have a few rides on me, or some beers."

"We're not old enough to drink, Carl," Efia said.

He looked surprised. "Oh. Well, some Slush Puppie, then."

There was the sound of trickling water, and we all looked down to where the dog had cocked his leg and was peeing on Ben's trainer.

Ben was open-mouthed, probably caught between horror, disgust and his abject terror of the multi-fanged beast.

"Oh, Tyson! No! Bad dog!" Carl said. He glanced at us, embarrassed. "It'll wash off. It's only pee."

I didn't say anything because Ben was radiating fury

and it wasn't my place to tell Carl his dog's actions were forgiven.

"Come on, Tyson," Carl said, pulling the creature away. "Take it easy, kids," he called back to us. "Come down sometime!" He started humming to himself and plodded off down the promenade, Tyson trotting beside him.

"My. Trainer," Ben muttered.

"Don't buy that 'nice guy' act from Carl," Efia told me, ignoring the fact Ben had gone red with rage. "The rivalry between Wonderland and the pier runs deep, and Maggie wouldn't hold a grudge if he didn't play dirty." She screwed up her sandwich wrapper, threw it in the bin and stood up. "We should get on. I'm going to get back to making a hole in some poor child mannequin's stomach. Oh, by the way, there's some scrap metal in the yard out the back of Wonderland – maybe some of that could be used for the UFO debris?"

"We'll take a look," I said as Efia walked off. I turned to Ben. "Is your trainer OK?"

"No."

He was obviously really into his trainers. "Um . . . maybe you can clean it off in the staffroom?"

"I'm going to clean it off in the staffroom," he said.

I nodded. "Yes, that's what . . . good idea. You do that."

Ben got up. He looked *furious*. "I don't like things peeing on my things."

I shrugged. "I mean, who does?"

Even so, I couldn't help but smile as Ben stomped off back towards Wonderland. There was something about "cross Ben" that was somehow just as adorable as all the other Ben variants. Don't get me wrong, I loved "bemused Ben", and I certainly enjoyed "enthusiastic Ben", but "cross Ben" was also very cute. Even better, I would have all these Bens all to myself when we went for pizza together. And if I was lucky, maybe some more Bens would appear – like "romantic Ben", for example, or any number of other versions that it was bad for me to think about, like "horny Ben", or "sensuous Ben" or even "football kit Ben" because I reckoned that would probably be a *thing*.

I stopped myself because I needed to get a grip.

And no, I didn't mean *that*.

Since the others were all busy, I decided to check out the scrap metal that Efia had mentioned myself. There was a narrow alley that ran from the street down the side of Wonderland to the yard at the back, known colloquially as Piss Alley. There was an exit from the staffroom that also led to the yard, but this was the quickest route, so I held my breath and hurried down. But I stopped dead before the passage opened up into the yard because I heard voices. Low. Hissed.

"Not good enough. Where's the rest?"

"Mate, next week, I promise—"

Laughter. "Too late. *Mate.*"

The back of my neck tingled. There was something in the tone of that "*mate*" that was really *dangerous.*

"Please, I—"

And the sound of a heavy thud.

And then a sickening, soft, fleshy crunch.

I'm not proud of myself, but I ran back the way I came. I hovered by the front entrance of Wonderland, wondering what the hell I should do. Was this a police matter? Should I tell Maggie? I heard heavy footsteps tramping up the alley, so I grabbed the controls of one of the claw grabbers and pretended to play. And then, quick as a flash, a figure in black jeans and a hoodie burst out of the alley and hurried away up the street, their back to me. I didn't even see their face. They were tall, quite broad, solidly built. That's all I can tell you.

They disappeared round a corner. I shut my eyes. I mean, I had to go and look now, didn't I? If I didn't, it would be just my luck that the victim would be lying there, dying or something, and I could have saved their life if I hadn't been such a coward. I had to really force my legs to walk down that alley. There was no part of me that wanted to go down there, and I held my breath as I edged out into the yard.

Empty.

I did a three-sixty turn, but there was no one there.

And since the only way in or out of the yard is either along the alley or through the exit from the staffroom, whoever else was here was now back inside Wonderland.

I hurried in through the fire exit, but the staffroom was deserted too. I pushed through the door on to the main floor. There were a few kids playing on the driving simulators, a family having fun on the air hockey, but nothing that looked suspicious.

There was a loud bang, and I looked across to where Kem had just thumped one of the fruit machines. "Easy," I said, walking over to him.

"Gotta be rigged," Kem said. "I've been playing this one all day; it's barely paid out anything."

I shook my head. "They're not rigged."

"Know that for sure, yeah?" He lowered his voice. "Have you found out any insider secrets yet?"

I shook my head. "I'm not sure there are any to find out."

Kem rolled his eyes and opened his wallet. "Guess I'll just keep playing it then."

My eyes widened as I saw the stack of notes he had in there – a big wedge of tenners. Must have been at least a hundred quid, maybe more. "Kem, you didn't see anything in the last five minutes, did you? Like, anyone hurry past with a smashed-up face or anything?"

"When I'm playing, I only see the symbols, you get me? I see the line of cherries, or the gold bars, or whatever.

That's all. I'm in the zone, man! Focused! Why, what's happened?"

I shrugged, casting another glance around the floor. "Oh, probably nothing much."

"I did see your mate Ben stomp past. Pretty angry he was, as well. And for some reason, with one shoe off."

I nodded. "Yeah. He had an incident with a dog." I smiled. "He was pretty upset."

Kem stuck his tongue in his cheek and looked at me. "I'm getting romance vibes."

"What do you mean?"

"You and Ben."

"That's ridiculous," I said.

"I've seen the way you look at each other."

"No."

"Do you fancy him?" Kem asked.

"He's got a girlfriend."

"Do you fancy him?"

"Her name is Bella."

"Do you fancy him?"

"She lives round here and has parents."

"Do you fancy him?"

"They've been going out a while, I believe, so it sounds like a pretty solid relationship."

"Do you fancy him?"

I nodded. "Yeah. Yeah, I do."

"Boom! I knew it!" Kem shouted. "KER-CHING!"

"Kem! Sshh!" I hissed. "It's not like that. I do wish he was single, and I also wish he was into boys, but neither of those things are true. So, when we go for pizza, it'll just be as mates."

Kem grinned from ear to ear. "You're going for pizza?"

I shrugged.

"Just you and him?"

I shrugged.

"Are you going to that swanky new place that does sourdough bases?"

I nodded.

"DING! DING! DING! JACKPOT!"

I rolled my eyes.

Kem slapped his hand on my shoulder like I was very much "the man" and said, "Proud of you, mate!" then handed me two ten-pound notes. "Can you change these for me? I don't wanna lose my place and I wanna win big so I can get something special for my 'lady friend' – a diamond or something."

"She's a lady *friend* now, is she?" I said.

Kem shrugged. "I mean, define 'friend'."

"Someone you talk to, share your life with, laugh with, hang out with."

"Yeah, no, she's not exactly a friend then."

I stifled a smile. There was little chance of Kem losing his place anyway, because no one else was playing on the fruits, but I took the cash over to one of the change machines and fed the first tenner in. And it was then that I noticed Drake sitting in the prize booth, nursing a swollen lip and a cut just below his eye.

CHAPTER SEVENTEEN

"There should be a table for two of us, at seven. Ben Marshall?"

"And Alex Button," I added, although completely unnecessarily.

Ben's eyes lit up. "Your surname is 'Button'?"

"Uh-huh."

"Oh my god." Ben smiled. "That's such a cute name."

"Shut up," I said, my mouth twitching into a grin.

The waitress smiled at us both. "Right this way," she said, with a look on her face that suggested she thought this was definitely a date.

It was *not* a date. I knew that.

But I'll admit I had sort of been pretending it was in my head a bit. I'd been working with Ben a lot over the last few days, getting everything ready for the relaunch next week (I couldn't be sure, but Maggie seemed to be almost encouraging it, since she *always* assigned us to jobs together), and spending so much time with him was doing nothing for my attempts to try and not fancy him. Yesterday, he took his grey-and-navy-blue sweat top off because he was hot, and when he popped out to get us Cokes, I held it in my hands *and pressed it to my face.* These were not the actions of someone who is in control of their feelings.

And then there was something potentially more dangerous.

I'd started to question if Bella was indeed real, or whether there might actually be something in Efia's teasing that she was made up. I'd composed elaborate fantasy sequences in my head, where Ben explained how he felt pressured into saying he had a girlfriend because of a heteronormative society's expectations, but that really, he was GAY, GAY, GAY!

And yet I knew the reality was much simpler: Alex "I only fall for unavailable straight boys" Button had only gone and fallen for an unavailable straight boy. Well done, me.

I trailed behind Ben and the waitress as she led us through. It was a rustic sort of place – a hotchpotch of different tables with random chairs that didn't match, peeling plaster falling off exposed brickwork and, in one corner, a lively kitchen area with a huge pizza oven and several chefs shouting at each other in Polish. There was none of the identikit finesse of the high street chains here, but with the low-level lighting, the little candles and the huge cured meats they had hanging up by the kitchen, you knew this place was as cool and sophisticated as they came.

"Can I get you some drinks?" the waitress said as we sat at a small table by the wall. She indicated the bottom right-hand corner of the menu. "All the soft drinks are here." She smiled knowingly, like we might have tried it on and attempted to order several bottles of vodka.

"Coke for me," Ben said. "Alex?"

"Coke." I nodded.

The waitress made a note. "OK, just so you know, we don't serve regular Coke here, it's an organic cola, infused with herbs and a blend of botanicals."

Ben's eyes flicked to mine. "Maybe just some water, then, for now?" he said.

I nodded enthusiastically.

"Or we have some delicious fresh Sicilian lemonade?" the waitress suggested.

The ability to finally be honest was liberating. "Oh, god no," I said, enjoying being able to wince. "I hate the stuff!"

"Water it is, then!" the waitress smiled. "I'll be back to take your order in a minute."

Ben looked down at his menu, which gave me a chance to look at Ben, without it seeming weird. "Concentrating Ben" stuck his tongue out a little bit, gently biting it between his lips, which made me thankful I didn't go to school with him, because I would get zero work done if that were happening around me.

He glanced up and found me staring at him. A little smile crept over his face. "All right?" he said.

I nodded. "Nice shirt." Which it was. Red and black checks. It really suited him.

"Thanks. I like yours too. What's that print exactly?" he said, squinting at it.

"I dunno, it's some sort of floral thing. I'm not very good at fashion – if something looks OK on me, it's really just an accident. . ." I stopped myself before I plunged any further into negative mode.

"I think it's nice," Ben said.

"I got it in the sales."

"You look good in it."

He smiled at me, and I smiled back.

I glanced down at the menu, which boasted sourdough pizza bases and a range of topping options which were somewhat more exotic than I was used to. I'm not being funny, but pizza should be topped with some combination of tomato, ham, mozzarella and yes, *pineapple,* because I am that person. This place was all artichokes, goat's cheese and courgette, although there was clearly a market for it because the restaurant was rammed.

"They've got some live jazz tonight," Ben said.

"Really? A live band? That's cool."

Ben nodded, and must have clocked the look of slight horror on my face as I continued to scan the menu, because he said, "And the pizzas here are pretty good."

"I don't think I've even ever *seen* an artichoke," I said.

"Yeah. Don't have that one. Have the cured meat one, but ask for no chilli, unless you like a bit of heat?"

"Garlic bread?"

"*Obviously*."

I put the menu down. "It's nice here, I like it. Thanks for sorting it out."

"You won the bet, and I'm good to my word."

The waitress reappeared with a carafe of water, poured two tumblers for us, then lit the little tea light in the middle of the table. "That's better, isn't it, boys?" she smiled.

In the sense it was ridiculously romantic, *yes*, it was better.

We both ordered the cured meat pizza (with really strict instructions for no chilli on mine), and after the garlic bread had arrived (which had *rosemary* on it, but OK), the jazz band start playing on a small stage behind me, towards the rear of the restaurant. And you know what? For the first time in my life, I didn't feel like a kid any more. I was having dinner with a nice boy, in a nice restaurant, with a fricking *jazz band* playing, and I suddenly had this vision of what life *could* be like. And I saw it could be *good*.

"Pretty cool, right?" I heard Ben say.

I met his twinkling eyes and smiled. "Yeah."

"Are you having an OK time?"

"Ben, oh my god, I'm having *the best* time!"

He nodded. "OK, cool. Because sometimes I think you look like you're about to burst into tears, and I just wonder if I shouldn't give you a hug," Ben said. "But then, you probably wouldn't want that."

I think my mouth fell open a bit. I swallowed. Pulled myself together. "No, I do. *Would*. I wouldn't mind."

Ben nodded. "Better look out then, next time you're a bit sad! I'll be like, 'Hug, incoming!'"

I half gasped, half giggled. Oh my god, I could not wait for that. Would it be too much to start weeping right now?

I actually nearly *did* start weeping when the pizzas came. They were so big we struggled to fit them on the table. I had never seen this much pizza in my life. Pizza really is *the best thing*.

"How about some desserts?" the waitress said, when she came over to clear our plates.

"Let me pay for dessert," I told Ben.

"No way. This is my treat, and you won the bet fair and square," Ben replied.

"But . . . are you sure?" I didn't want to mention what he'd told me about his dad, and how tight money was for them, but him paying was making me feel bad.

"I'd like to," he said. "But maybe you can get the bill next time."

I smiled. There was going to be a next time. That was epically excellent news. "OK, well, I'm pretty stuffed though – shall we share one?"

"Sure. What'll it be? Your choice."

I scanned the blackboard menu of desserts on the wall and opted for the cheapest. "Um . . . the tiramisu?" Ben nodded, and the waitress jotted it down. "As long as you're OK serving us that with the alcohol in it?" I grinned at her and she gave me a wry smile.

"Good job you're sharing it," she said. "Don't want you two getting hammered and making trouble."

"Are you giving the waitress *sass*?" Ben said, when she'd gone.

My eyes widened. "Oh god, do I need to apologize?"

He laughed and I got full-on dimples shimmering in candlelight with a jazz accompaniment. Frankly, it was a miracle I'd managed to hold it together this long, but that tipped me over the edge and I actually *groaned*.

"Are you OK?" Ben said.

"Uh-huh. Just had . . . too much to eat."

"You liked the pizza, then? You weren't sure."

"I wasn't sure at first," I agreed, "but I love the pizza. And I *love* the jazz." And you. I love you.

Ben shifted his chair across to the wall a bit. "Shuffle round here, then you'll be able to see the band properly."

I moved my chair around and tried not to think about the fact I was now sitting right next to him, in the low-level light, about to share a creamy dessert, whilst the band played a slow, bluesy cover of "Your Song" by Elton John. Tingles danced through my spine as his leg brushed mine, and then I held my breath as it actually came to rest *against* mine. I didn't dare look at him, just kept my leg where it was, pressed next to his, like our little secret. Was this OK? What about Bella? But I guessed that we weren't doing anything wrong. Or at least, he wasn't. He was just being normal, nice, Ben. It was me who was probably making the rest up, in my head.

"Oh, wow," I heard him mutter.

I glanced at him, and he had tears in his eyes.

"Mum loved Elton," he said, wiping his eyes with the palms of his hands. "Sorry. Sorry, Alex. I don't mean to bring a downer to the whole evening."

My stomach plunged with heaviness. There I was, thinking naughty stuff about Ben, and there *he* was, hurting about his mum. I was the worst sort of person.

"Don't be sorry, Ben. You really don't have to be sorry." I looked at him, doing his best to hold it together, but the pain bubbling through, and I wondered whether *he* might appreciate a hug, or anything similar. So I did it. I put my hand on his. I didn't mean anything romantic by it, it just felt like the *right* thing to do. I squeezed. And he looked down at our hands, then turned his palm to face upwards and laced his fingers through mine. And suddenly it felt like something different.

"Thanks," he said.

"No worries." I glanced at him. I wanted to keep this normal, and not act like this was my first time holding another boy's hand, although that is in fact what it was. My heart was pounding. Actually *pounding*. "I, um . . . I don't really know many Elton John songs. I've heard this one before. And I know that 'Candle in the Wind' one—"

"Which we had at Mum's funeral."

"Oh, *shit*, I'm so—"

Ben chuckled.

"Honestly, Ben, I'm such an idiot, I'm so sorry. That was completely thoughtless of me."

"It's fine."

"Sometimes my brain just isn't connected to my mouth."

He squeezed my hand tighter. "Hey, it's *fine*."

I looked at him, and he was looking right back, deep into my eyes, lips slightly apart.

"One tiramisu, two spoons!" the waitress said, putting the plate down in front of us. We instinctively unclasped our hands, but she saw, and she had a look on her face that said, *Oh yes! My job here is done.*

"Thanks," I gasped. "It looks great. I like the sprig of mint, that's a . . . nice touch."

"Enjoy," she said, giving me a little wink and walking away again.

"Now she thinks we're a *thing*," Ben said, carefully slicing his spoon into the tiramisu.

I focused on scooping up some of the dessert. "Yeah." I glanced at him. She's thinking it, I'm hoping it, but where do *you* stand?

"Good tiramisu," he said.

". . .*Very* good," I agreed.

We both got down to the business of eating the dessert, but I was wishing like hell that two boys being affectionate didn't have to always attract knowing looks and little winks, like it automatically had to be front-page news. And I resented the fact we'd both snatched our hands away, like we'd been caught doing something dirty and wrong, when all it had been was letting someone I cared about know I was there for them. And even if it had been something other than that, I should be able to hold a boy's hand and not feel guilty about it, or like someone is going to say something nasty. I should be able to.

Later, we stood outside the restaurant, the night air still warm, shifting about on the spot, home being in different directions, but, certainly on my part, and I think maybe on his, not quite wanting to say goodbye yet.

"I had a really nice night," I said. "Thank you."

He turned to me. "Yeah. Me too." And he turned

away again, then turned back, sort of restless.

"I guess . . . tomorrow we'll crack on with the alien experience?"

Ben nodded.

"Maybe make a start on Eve's fortune-telling booth."

He stepped towards me, took my hands and rested his forehead against mine.

I didn't know what to do.

Did he want to kiss?

His breath, hot on my face.

My heart, somewhere in my throat.

The only sound, for a few moments, our breathing.

"Oh god, I'm sorry," he muttered, breaking off and turning away again.

I stared at him.

He turned back. "Sorry, Alex, I . . . I think I'm in a weird place tonight."

I nodded. "It's fine."

He nodded back. Swallowed. His eyes, almost pleading for . . . for *what*? Forgiveness? *For me?*

"It's OK," I said.

And just as I was starting to dare to think maybe Ben was gay, or maybe he was bi, or maybe he was confused and didn't know what he was but he *liked* me and didn't know how to deal with it, *just as I let myself actually go there,* probably the most beautiful girl I've ever seen in the world ran up to us and said, "Ben!"

And he turned to her, and his face broke into this wide, beautiful, *loving,* mega-dimpled smile, and he said, "Bella?!"

And my stupid make-believe world, that I had no business inventing anyway, just fell apart.

CHAPTER EIGHTEEN

"How come you're back early?!" Ben said. "I thought it was next week?"

"Ahh, Rachel's grandad had a heart attack," Bella said. "I couldn't let her come back by herself. Plus I wanted to surprise you!"

Ben broke the hug and stepped back from her a bit. "Is he OK?"

"I think it's touch and go."

"Poor Rach," Ben said. "Although it's really good to see you." He gave her a smile, one of his ones with extra dimples, then went back in for more hugging. "You should've let me know though!" Ben continued, rocking Bella from side to side in the hug.

I stood on the sidelines, kicking the suede high-tops I was wearing especially for our pizza date on the ground, hands in pockets, waiting for Ben and Bella to *stop hugging,* and trying to look at least semi-happy because I didn't want to be rude.

The truth was, right at that precise moment, I hated Bella.

But of course it wasn't her fault. It was all me. I'd misread everything, the *signs*, or whatever it is that supposedly tells people how other people feel about them.

Plus, she really was real! Ben had never been anything other than totally honest about having a girlfriend. I'd just allowed myself to be persuaded he might not have.

"I would have texted, but I wanted to see that smile when I just appeared out of nowhere," Bella grinned.

Great. She liked his dimples too. They were *my* dimples. Now I was sharing them.

"I went to your house and your dad told me you were in town with your mate," Bella added.

Mate. Bloody *mate.* Although I don't know what I was expecting. Ben was hardly going to have told his dad he was going out with his "red-hot gay lover". I certainly didn't tell my dad that. In fact, I said I was "meeting a *mate*", now I thought of it, even though the knowing look he gave was as if I had said "red-hot gay lover". So why was I cross that's also what Ben had probably said?

"Bella, *this* is Alex!" Ben said, breaking away from the hug and pulling Bella over to me.

"Hey," I said, attempting a smile and extending my right hand. "Nice to meet you, I've heard so much about you." Obviously that wasn't true, she was a complete enigma, but hey, *small talk.*

Bella ignored my hand and went right in for a hug. "Likewise! Great to meet at last!"

"Yeah," I said as she squeezed me tightly. She smelled lovely. Fresh and floral.

Bella stepped back from the hug a bit, but kept her hands on my upper arms, looking into my face. Then she broke into a smile, dropped her arms and said, "How was the pizza, boys?"

"Lovely," we both said, in unison.

Bella laughed. She had a nice laugh. I was really annoyed that there was literally nothing annoying about her. Most people who came back from "travelling" were usually eminently slap-able. Every year, the kids who've gone off for a gap year come back and they'll have dyed their hair a stupid colour because they've "discovered themselves" or be walking barefoot because some yoga guru told them to, and they'll set up a lifestyle blog and Instagram their new life, decrying material possessions and capitalism, but still uploaded *from their iPhone.* But Bella didn't seem to be any of those things.

She was the worst.

There was an awkward silence, which I suddenly realized was probably my cue to wrap things up and leave because . . . well, it made my throat go tight, but I guessed Ben and Bella probably wanted to be alone.

"So, I'll probably head home," I said, doing my

absolute best to keep everything normal and light. "Thanks again, Ben. Nice to meet you, Bella. Welcome back."

Ben put his arm around Bella's waist. "You sure you don't want to come back to mine for a bit?"

I looked at them both, smiling at me, so happy. "Aah, *no*, no, I should . . . and anyway, you two probably have so much catching up to do, so."

"Come back for a bit, Alex," Bella said. "It'd be really nice to get you know you properly."

I shook my head. "No, I really—"

"Come on, Alex," Ben insisted.

"I have schnapps," Bella smiled. "Butterscotch flavour."

Man. This was a total nightmare. If I did go round, it would only extend the awkwardness, and we might well have a nice chat for a few minutes, but then they'd just be wondering how long I was going to stay for so they could get round to. . . I swallowed, because the thought of Ben doing *that* made me feel sick. And really anxious. My chest was tight, my throat was tight, everything was—

"I feel a bit funny," I said.

Ben raised his eyebrows. "Are you OK?"

"No, yes, I'll be fine, I think I just. . . I should maybe go home and have a lie-down, that's all." I sounded so lame. I glanced at Bella. "I nearly drowned the other day."

"And he knocked himself out the day before that,"

Ben added.

"I know, you told me," Bella said. "*Oh, Alex.*" She smiled at me and shook her head. "What are you like?"

"Huh," I said. "Bit unlucky, I suppose."

She laughed and I honestly thought she was going to ruffle my hair like I was a cute toddler.

"Are you OK getting home?" Ben asked.

"I'll be fine," I said. "You two go and..." For a horrible second I came this close to saying "shag" and then couldn't think of any other words at all to finish the sentence with. "*Have fun.*" Ben's eyes widened. "You know, *catch up* and everything. Together. Talking."

Bella laughed. "You're hilarious."

"Right?!" Ben said.

"Ha!" I said. "Sure, I'm all about the LOLs, that's . . . me."

"All right," Ben said, giving me a little fist bump on my shoulder. "See you tomorrow then."

And we did all the goodbye business and off they went. I stood, watching as they walked away, hand in hand, chatting. But this was no more than I deserved. Would I ever learn, or was I doomed to continuously repeat the same basic mistakes, until the end of time?

If you're into betting, I would put money on the latter.

I lay under my duvet, staring up at my ceiling, doing my absolute best to stop my stupid brain thinking about exactly what Ben and Bella might have been doing *right then.*

Their lips gently brushing. . .

Stop it.

Tongues exploring each other's mouths. . .

Stop it.

Hot and frantic, and ripping clothes off—

OH GOD, STOP IT!

What did he mean when he was resting his forehead against mine? "*Oh God, I'm sorry.*" Was it just the case that he was missing his girlfriend, he was feeling horny, and for a split second, just in that moment, he felt like he needed someone, *anyone,* to be close to?

I closed my eyes. Remembered the feeling of him close. His hot breath. The rise and fall of his chest. Then I imagined what kissing him would be like. *Yes, I'm an idiot.* But let me tell you, it was *wonderful.* I imagined him pulling me closer, I imagined no Bella turning up, and I imagined him taking *me* back home, and *our* lips brushing, *our* tongues exploring, shirts off, his fingers sliding down my boxers—

No.

No, no, no. I couldn't do this to myself.

Goddam it all to hell!

I flung the duvet off, jumped out of bed, darted across the room and tore down my shrine to Netflix's Soft Boys. "I hate boys!" I screamed, tearing a poster in half. (I know, I know, I'm a *monster.*) I started hunting for a match, because I just wanted to burn everything down, burn all the boys down, but then my mobile started playing its ringtone, which it never does, because who actually *calls* you any more, so what the hell was this? I thought about ignoring it and just finishing what I'd started, but it's kind of distracting, having "Everybody Hurts" by REM playing while you're trying to violently destroy everything you hold dear to you, so, breathless and angry, I grabbed it, because I was probably just going to silence it anyway, but it was Efia, so now I'm . . . I'm pretty . . . well, my finger slipped so I accidentally answered it anyway.

"Hi!" I gasped, the fury still pumping round me.

"Oh *god*," she said. "Seriously?"

"What?"

"*What are you doing?* Actually, you don't need to say. I'll call back."

"No! What?" I sat down on my bed. "I'm just destroying ... things."

Silence.

"I'm sending you a link. Read it and call me straight back," Efia said, after a pause.

She hung up.

I just stared at my phone, because I had no idea what was going on, and then her text pinged through, with a link to an editorial on the local newspaper's website:

IS THE WONDER OVER FOR WONDERLAND?

With its glittering lights, jaunty music and the promise of winning one of the many cuddly toys or trinkets on display, Wonderland has been a stalwart of Newsands' promenade for over three decades. But look beyond the razzmatazz and all that glitters is not gold.

Our undercover journalists paid a recent visit to Wonderland, posing as members of the public, and encountered gangs of youths who hang around the premises, engaged in illegal gambling that the young, inexperienced teenage staff seem powerless to do anything about. More concerning was the blatant drug dealing they observed, particularly when you take into account the young age of the impressionable clientele.

We have passed our concerns to the local police, who have promised to investigate, but it's time we asked a wider question: what sort of town do we want Newsands to be? Wonderland is a symbol of a bygone era, a near-derelict eyesore on the increasingly smart promenade. And as we all begin to see the positive impact of investment from new businesses, and the influx of house buyers who are keeping the property market buoyant, is it time to say goodbye to the old, and welcome the new?

By the time I'd got to the end of the article, I was shaking, not least because of the photos. There was a picture of some of the troublesome kids, hanging around and giving the finger to the photographer. I remembered it clearly. The two hipsters who came in when I was sorting through the Golden Goose game with Ben, looking like they were having fun and harmlessly – seemingly harmlessly! – Instagramming it. They did this, right under our noses. I felt sick.

I called Efia back. "It's lies," I said, when she picked up.

"It's not though, is it?"

"What?"

"Maggie *does* let some of the kids play games she shouldn't, and we all know Drake *does* ask people if they want to buy weed. It's not inaccurate, Alex."

"Well, OK, but it doesn't say anything about all the good things."

"That's not really how newspapers work."

"Well, newspapers are stupid, then," I said. "I never thought I'd say it, but this is *fake news*."

"Look, I don't know how Maggie's gonna take this, but let's hope she doesn't call the whole relaunch off."

"Why would she do that?"

"I dunno, maybe she'll think there's been enough attention drawn to us, and want to lie low for a bit," Efia said. "We might need to convince her it's still a good idea – that the perfect time to relaunch is when everyone's eyes are on us anyway."

"Sure."

"I tried to call Ben but he wasn't answering," she said.

"Oh. He's with Bella."

"Excuse me?"

"Bella came back. She's real. He's gone home with her."

"Oh my *god,*" Efia finally muttered. "What's she like?"

"Seems nice," I said. "I mean, she's actually *really* nice. She's a really lovely person. She has nice blonde hair, lovely eyes, I mean, you would describe her as beautiful, for sure, with a very appealing personality."

Silence from Efia. Then, "Are you OK, Alex?"

". . .Yes?" I swallowed and tried to relax my rapidly constricting throat. "I'm OK. I'm fine!"

"*Oh.* You really do like him."

I attempted a little laugh, like I could just wave this one away. "Yeah, I mean, he's a friend, so—"

"You *like* him, like him," Efia said. "*You know what I meant.*"

"No! God, no, that's not true, Efia."

"I can hear it in your voice, Alex." She sighed. "And, honestly, I did think there was a chance you two might. . ."

"You did?"

"Yeah. I really thought you two would be cute together. And my gaydar, it's normally—"

"It's fine!" I said, my voice randomly using a whole range of octaves.

"Oh, Alex." There was a tragic sadness in her tone, a tone that most people tend to use when saying my name. "Still, it's not necessarily over yet."

"No, it's over, Efia. I can't take much more of this."

"But I really think—"

"It doesn't matter! It doesn't matter what anyone thinks. If he's not, or he doesn't want to, or he's not ready, it doesn't make any difference. He's with Bella. He's happy to be with her. You should have seen his face when she turned up – it . . . it's what 'love' looks like." I sighed. "I'm happy for him. For *them*. It's nice, I guess."

She didn't say anything.

"We should focus on Wonderland, anyway," I continued. Having something to take my mind off Ben would definitely be a good thing. "We can't let those stupid journalists get away with this. I just don't understand why anyone would have it in for the place."

"Or, more importantly, *who*?" Efia asked.

CHAPTER NINETEEN

Efia was waiting for me on our bench on the promenade, fifteen minutes before we were due to start work. She had a new hairband, in shades of burnt orange, white and black, and her lips seemed more defined, and were a deeper red than usual. She looked . . . fresh and perky and *together*. How did people manage that? Efia raised an eyebrow when she saw what I was wearing, but must have thought better than to say anything right then. Since working practically full-time, I was catastrophically behind on my laundry, although, in honesty, this was less to do with not having the time, and more about wanting to steer clear of Kendra, in case I somehow got the washing machine all wrong again. Anyway, this all meant I was not only running on emergency clothes reserves, but had also failed to wash my uniform polo shirt, so I'd been forced to resort to shorts with a Hawaiian shirt, which I was no way confident enough to pull off. Efia was all sophisticated and coordinated, and I was a mess. A *hot* mess. It wasn't ten yet, but it was already baking, and everyone else was taking advantage of that on the beach, with donkey rides in full swing, a load of the sun loungers already taken up, and the water sports guy zipping a load of kids across the water on the back of an inflatable banana, attached to his speedboat.

Nice to see some people having fun, I'm sure.

"Cheer up, mate," she said, handing me a takeaway cappuccino. "And, yes, I did put three sugars in it. You should really cut down, you know?"

"I feel like wrecking myself anyway," I muttered.

Efia laughed. "And you're doing it with over-sugared coffee? You're such a *bad boy*."

I flopped down next to her on the bench, and showed her the text Ben had just sent me:

> Tell Maggie I'll be late – didn't get much sleep last night. 👍 x

Efia blew a breath out.

"Exactly!" I said. "Talk about rubbing it in. Also, why the thumbs up emoji? Are we going to be celebrating him losing his virginity all day?"

"How do you know he—"

"He told me," I said, before realizing he probably told me that in confidence. I took a sip of coffee. "Let's talk about something else."

"It doesn't mean he had sex necessarily," Efia said, totally ignoring me because that's what people do. "Like, maybe he was up all night with indigestion, after your pizza?"

"And the thumbs up emoji?"

"*Is sarcastic.*"

I shook my head. "Let's talk about something else."

There was an excited scream from the kids on the inflatable banana as the speedboat guy took a sharp turn and flipped them all into the water. If I could swim, I would *so* be in there right now.

"We need to think about who might hold a grudge against Wonderland," Efia said. "That seems like a sensible place to start. Who would want to cause trouble for the place?"

"I mean, have I just been imagining that he maybe liked me? Did I get it completely wrong?" I turned to her. "Efia?"

"Hand on heart, I did think he liked you."

"Yeah?"

"Just the way he acts around you sometimes. I got romance vibes. But maybe I'm wrong."

"Huh."

I wanted to tell her about him resting his forehead against mine, outside the restaurant, but I knew I shouldn't. That was a private moment, just me and him, and it wasn't mine to share, however much it felt like it might be relevant.

It was my one glimmer of hope, albeit one that was being rapidly extinguished by all his bragging about the red-hot porn-style sex he'd been having *all night long*. OK, I didn't know that *for sure,* but what else are you going to be doing when your really nice, beautiful girlfriend who you haven't seen for weeks suddenly comes home? Playing *Jenga*? That game is good, but it's not *that* good.

"Let's talk about something else," I said.

"Don't bottle it up, Alex."

"I'm good at bottling things up, Efia. I'm great at it. I've made it my life's work, to be honest. And there's a water-tight seal on these emotions, you won't ever notice."

"Oh, right? So all this doom and gloom since you've arrived this morning, that's—"

"I'm just a bit tired!" I snarled. "I didn't get much sleep!" I gave her a thumbs up and a grimace. "What about the kids who hang about the place? What about Billy? He was actually in the office, for a start, and he's always causing trouble."

"But why would he tip off the local paper that kids like him are causing trouble? It makes zero sense."

"OK then," I said. "What about *Drake*?"

"I know he's stupid, but you think he's actually stupid enough to grass up his own weed dealing up to the press?"

"Okaaaay, what about an *associate* of Drake's then?"

"What are you getting at?"

I quickly glanced up and down the promenade like this

was Cold War espionage, lowered my voice, and recounted everything I heard the other day as I cowered by the wall of the alley that led to the back yard of Wonderland.

"Drake's in trouble," Efia said.

I nodded. "Drake's in trouble."

"So it's possible someone is turning the screws to pile the pressure on? The person who supplies his weed, maybe?"

I hadn't thought of that in all honesty, but I nodded anyway, like that was *exactly* what I'd been thinking.

"Good work, Alex."

"Yes," I said. "Thank you."

"MORNING, CAMPERS!"

I looked up, seeing Caleb jangling his keys next to the fibreglass lemon. "Hey." I waved to him.

"Mercury's set to reach thirty today," he said. "Gonna be a good day for lemonade."

I nodded. "And associated lemon products," I added.

"You bet!"

I didn't know how he could be so permanently cheerful, but I was happy for him. He smiled at us, then busied himself starting to open up the lemon.

"I think he's into you," Efia whispered.

"He is not."

"You have banter."

"That wasn't banter. It was awkward lemon-based small talk."

Caleb flung the shutters of the lemon open from inside. "Hey, Alex?"

I looked up at him.

"Loving the Hawaiian shirt!"

My cheeks started to flush. "Thanks."

"Oh. My. *God,*" Efia said, under her breath. "He's *so* into you. He's complimenting your shirt."

"So what?" I hissed.

"Your shirt is a shitshow, and you know it. Oh my actual god."

Efia and I braced ourselves as we hurried across the darkened gaming floor, towards the staffroom and whatever terrible Maggie mood awaited us within. We'd rehearsed a hundred things to say to calm her down, and reassure her the relaunch was still a good idea, but this was Maggie, and she was completely unpredictable.

And we hadn't predicted *this.*

Maggie was standing in the middle of the staffroom, and greeted us all with a large plate of bacon butties – the best sort: crisp bacon, soft white buttered rolls, and heaps of ketchup. "Little treat for you all!" she beamed.

At first I thought it was some sort of joke.

Or maybe a trick.

I was glad for the bacon roll though. I'd been so miserable, I hadn't been able to eat my Coco Pops that morning, but thirty minutes later, I was beyond starving, and the gloom would have to wait.

"What's all this in aid of, Mag?" Drake said, biting down on his roll.

"In times of trouble," Maggie said, "I've always refused to give in to despair. Now, we could all drag our feet around today, worry about the stupid newspaper article, and fret about the future – or we could have a good time, and get on with what we do best – creating a bit of magic so other people have a good time too."

Drake shrugged and took another bite.

Maggie smiled at him. "Deal any more weed from the prize booth and I'll cut your balls off."

Drake stopped eating and stared at her.

"So!" she said, all brightness and light. "Where's young Benjamin?"

I suddenly felt less hungry again. "Oh, he's sorry, but he'll be late. He didn't get much sleep last night," I said.

"Bella has come back," Efia added.

"Who?"

"Bella. Ben's girlfriend."

Maggie's face dropped, and she flicked her eyes to me, with this look on her face that basically said, *Oh, you poor, heartbroken creature.*

"I'll get on with the cleaning," I muttered.

"My office, *now*," Maggie said.

"But—"

"*Alex!*"

I sighed and followed her into the office, shoving the rest of the bacon butty in my mouth. This was all I needed. I didn't need any more advice. I didn't need anyone trying to make me think there was any hope. Everyone was so full of it. They just all needed to admit defeat and leave me alone.

"Have you told him?" she asked.

"*Told him?* You mean—"

"You should tell him."

"There's . . . no. *No.*"

"*Why not?*"

I put my hands in my pockets. "Because I'm fully unlucky in love, Maggie. I'm actually *the unluckiest*. Fact."

"And what did I tell you about luck?"

I sighed. "Sure, *you make your own*, but in this case, all I'll be making is a big awkward mess and I'll have ruined another friendship because I can't stop falling for straight boys."

"What if he feels the same?"

My eyes widened. "He's. Got. A. Girlfriend. Her. Name. Is. Bella."

"*What if he feels the same?*"

I didn't know what else to say. I flopped down on the plastic chair and put my head in my hands. "He doesn't feel the same. He likes girls and the only indicators that he might not, or might not exclusively, have all been in my stupid head. Also, even if he was into boys, which as I say, I doubt, you really think he'd like me, specifically?"

"And your pizza date?" Maggie said.

"How did you know about that?"

"Alex, I may look like I could rarely give a damn, and granted, that is true most of the time, but I know what's going on around Wonderland."

"Oh. Well, pizza was just because he lost a stupid bet about you being willing to give away free soft drinks, like the Las Vegas casinos."

Maggie snorted. "Seriously? He *knew* I'd say no to that. He's only asked me three times before."

I looked up at her while I computed this new information. "He *knew* he'd lose the bet?"

"Almost certainly."

I took a deep breath. "Oh."

"Mmm. That muddies the waters a bit, doesn't it?" Maggie smiled, like this revelation was somehow conclusive. But I knew it wasn't. I had the weight of history on my side:

"Boys don't like me. Not like that. They just don't. It's one of the laws of the universe, like what goes up, must come down: *who Alex likes will never like him back.*"

"All right, boo hoo," Maggie said, "but here's what you need to understand, Alex: people don't always behave how you'd like them to, or how you expect them to. Everyone's a mess. It isn't just you. Everyone's trying to work it out, Alex. Everyone's confused, at least some of the time, if not most of the time. You could do worse than cut the poor lad some slack."

I shook my head. "Ben's so . . . *sorted* though. He's a sorted-out person. He has it together."

"Does he?"

"Doesn't he?"

Maggie shrugged. "If he's anything like the rest of you, I'd say that's a resounding no. But sure, you throw him to the wolves just because he hasn't bounded up to you with his rainbow flag and whistle."

"Oh my god."

"Advice session over. You're going to change that shirt, right?"

"I'm behind on laundry."

"The uniform isn't optional. There's a spare polo shirt in the staffroom; you can't wear that monstrosity, we'll be liable for inducing epileptic fits."

I stood up. "Maggie, Efia and I were wondering about who told the press about everything. . ."

She was busy looking through some papers and didn't look up. "Uh-huh?"

"Like, do you think someone could have a grudge against us?"

"Maybe. . ."

"So, Efia and I were thinking about looking into some suspects, you know—"

She held her hand up. "Alex? Sort your own mess of

a life out, then come and help me. We're fine. People write crap about things all the time. TripAdvisor have built an entire business on it."

"But—"

"Ask yourself, *is it true?* Are we an 'eyesore' on the town's landscape?"

"No?"

Maggie nodded and got back to her papers. "Next time, try answering without intoning it like a question."

I walked out, still mulling over this idea that Ben *knew* he was making a bet with me that he would lose. What did this mean? Did he just want someone to have pizza with?

"Hey."

I looked up and straight into Ben's eyes. Ben's tired, slightly red eyes. Ben's tired from *all the sex* eyes. He was carrying his laptop under his arm and had knee-length denim shorts on, because the universe clearly wanted to make my pain as terrible as possible. I took an unsteady breath. "Hey. How's things?"

"Pretty tired," Ben said. "Literally only got a couple of hours' sleep, I reckon." He nodded at me, like I should maybe be impressed.

I attempted an appreciative murmur. "Pretty cool."

He waggled his eyebrows. I was pretty sure he was standing differently. Like, in a "not a virgin" sort of way. Had an extra air of confidence or swagger, I don't know, but it was *there*. "Bella's coming over in a bit."

I nodded. Obviously that was brilliant, and by "brilliant" I meant "a complete disaster and I wished Bella would resume her travels".

"You saw the newspaper article?" Ben continued.

"Yes, I chatted to Efia about it last night," I said, realizing there was more than a hint of jilted lover in my voice, so adding, "I think she tried to get hold of you, but couldn't, so that was the only reason."

"Put my phone on silent for our little. . ." He looked at me, mouth frozen in what looked like he was about to say a word beginning with "D".

"Do?" I offered.

"Dinner?"

"Yes, that's what it was," I said. "On silent, huh? That's good. Good not to risk disturbing the jazz band with phone calls. I think that's considerate."

He blinked at me.

I thought it best to just continue babbling. "Maggie's taking it well, doesn't seem worried at all. Efia and I were thinking about doing a bit of detective work, maybe see if someone has it in for the place. . ."

Ben nodded. "Good idea." His eyes drifted down. "Interesting shirt."

"I know. It's horrible. Pretty much everyone hates it."

"Who doesn't hate it?"

"Caleb . . . he was pretty positive about it. But then he's positive about everything. I could've been wearing a bin bag and he'd be telling me how great it was."

"He's a happy boy."

"He is. He's a happy boy."

Ben gave me a sad sort of smile. "I was just gonna see Maggie, but you want to help me finish off the alien afterwards?"

I did, I so did, but it was a terrible idea. Despite everything, I was already like butter being gently melted in the presence of Ben's warmth and goddam utter cuteness. And knee-length denim shorts *and* dimples – together, on one person – I would explode. And like an addict who craves something bad, I knew I mustn't give in. I had to be strong. It was for my own good. I would thank myself for it – one day. "Actually, I was going to help Eve and rehearse the fortune telling." I nodded. Firmly. I firmly nodded because that was definitely what I was going to do.

Ben's eyes softened into full-on sad puppy dog. "Aww, but I need help too!"

"OK, then."

"Cool, see you in there in five minutes."

He knocked on the office door and went inside.

God, I was so weak. He was the boy equivalent of Cherry Coke, and I was powerless to resist, even though he would probably end up rotting my insides.

Efia sidled up to me. "Have you heard of the term 'playing hard to get'?"

"I'm not into playing games," I told her. "Games are

for the school playground." This was probably the most intelligent and wisest thing I think I've ever said.

"It's not a game, it's *psychology.* People always want what they can't have, or what they think other people want."

I shrugged. "He can have me if he wants me; *he doesn't,* but he can. And no one else wants me, I'm pretty sure of that."

"Jesus," Efia said. "That's the problem, right there. This . . ." She looked me up and down. ". . . constant downer you've got on yourself. You're like that mule from Winnie the Pooh."

"He's a *donkey*!" I couldn't believe the disrespect. "And there's nothing wrong with Eeyore."

"'Eeyore', huh? Role model, is he?"

I shrugged. "I may have had a poster of him when I was younger. Perhaps a stuffed toy too."

She dragged me away from the office and over to the stools by the fruit machines, forcing me down on one, next to where Kem was playing. "Listen up. If a boy requests your presence, you don't just roll over and let him tickle your belly."

That sounded perfectly fine to this boy.

"He has to *work* for it. Play the game, Alex."

"But I don't know the rules!" I bleated.

"She's talking sense!" Kem said, not looking at me, but focusing on the machine.

"Precisely," Efia said. "I am going to be your wingman. Wing*woman*. Your kick-ass caped love-crusader. And this . . . *Bella*, whoever she is, is not going to stop us."

She looked into my eyes, then followed my gaze as I looked over towards the entrance, where Bella had just walked in, looking all radiant and graceful and like she'd just stepped out of a woodland glade, with pretty birds still fluttering around her head, chirping sweetly.

Efia looked back at me. "Is that Bella?"

I nodded.

"*Damn.*"

Exactly. If this was a competition, I wasn't even going to make it through the heats.

"Any danger of you two doing any work today?" Drake said, as he walked by.

"That's a nasty bruised eye you've got there," Efia said.

Drake stopped and looked at her.

"How'd ya do it, Drake?" she said.

You could see the cogs in his head turning, then he sniffed and said, "Knocked over someone's pint in Wetherspoon's and they clobbered me." He turned and headed over towards the cash booth.

Efia blew out her cheeks. "It's plausible."

"It's a lie," I said.

"OK, well, we'll talk to him," Efia said, watching Drake as he flopped down behind his counter and started counting coins. "Later."

I nodded, then did my best to look happy and welcoming as Bella spotted me and came over. "Hey, *you*," she said.

"Hey. Hello. This is Efia. Efia, *Bella*."

"Ah!" Efia said. "So *you're* Bella! Ben . . . has mentioned you."

Bella laughed. "All good things, I hope?"

"So good, I was beginning to wonder if you were actually real!" Efia grinned.

Oh yeah, we all had a good old laugh about that.

"I have *pain au chocolat*!" Bella said, holding up a large paper bag. "Thought it might help keep everyone going."

"I actually love you," Efia said.

Huh. Didn't take long for *her* to be won round! Still, it was a nice gesture. And they did happen to be my favourite type of pastry, except for those Portuguese custard tarts.

"Well, I baked them myself, so I hope they measure up," Bella added.

I mean, FFS, *really*?

"Ben's request – he's a sucker for my baking," Bella continued.

"He's in with Maggie," I explained, sensing she was about to ask where Ben was.

She shook her head. "I have to give it to him, that boy has some stamina."

My expression froze in a fixed smile. This was not the friendly small talk I was looking for.

"He's like the Duracell bunny – he's just keeps on, and on!" Bella laughed.

She was talking about his work ethic, right? I told myself that was *definitely* what she was talking about. This wasn't about his *sexual* stamina. I mean, of course it wasn't. I was going mad. I was reading all the wrong things into everything. I was a wreck.

I needed to take five minutes to sort my head out, but matters took their own course, because that was the moment a little kid opened the plastic egg she'd just got out of the Golden Goose, and screamed as a half-decomposed mouse and a load of hypodermic needles fell out of it.

CHAPTER TWENTY

Bella was frozen to the spot.

Efia was completely silent.

Even Kem was staring, wide-eyed.

The screaming child's mum, however, did what any sane person would do when a loved one was in danger and was filming the situation on her phone, zooming in on the rotting mouse and huge needles on the floor, as Maggie hurried over with the biggest stuffed animal Wonderland possessed.

"We're so sorry," she said, offering the giant lion to the crying girl. "Are you OK? Not hurt?" She looked at me. "Alex? Can you clean this away please? *Quickly.*"

"This is disgusting," the mum was saying, still behind her mobile, her kid still wailing.

"We can only apologize," Maggie repeated. "I've no idea how this could have happened. *Alex!*"

I flapped about, looking for some quick way of cleaning away the needles and mouse carcass.

"Dude, scoop it up in your hands!" Drake hissed.

I didn't really want to do that, I mean, they were *needles*. What sort of lunatic picks up random needles with their hands? Never mind the manky rodent.

"It must be a faulty batch, I'm sure we can sort this out," Maggie was saying.

I headed off to the office, muttering about "health and safety" and "dustpan and brush".

"What's going on out there?" Ben said, looking up from his laptop.

"Some kid opened an egg from the Golden Goose, and a load of crap fell out."

"*Crap* as in, one of our usual prizes?"

"*Crap* as in a load of needles and a decayed mouse." I took in Ben's horrified expression. "Yeah, it's not good."

"But we were the last people to fill the goose up," Ben said.

I nodded. I was well aware of the implications of all this.

"Well, did you notice any eggs had been tampered with?"

I rolled my eyes. "Yeah, but I thought we'd put them in anyway – all adds to the fun, right?"

"All right, Mr Sarcastic!" Ben said. "Since you're here, come and take a quick look at this."

I was meant to be hurrying back with something to clean the dangerous mess up with, but he nudged up on his chair so that I could sit on the other half, right next to him, so naturally I did just that. He tapped on his laptop and a video starting playing on the screen – black and white, grainy, with lots of "covert" style shots and some pretty scary images of the Roswell aliens, with their child-like bodies and big heads with massive black eyes.

"That's really excellent," I said.

"Thanks. Took me all night, but I got there in the end."

I flicked my eyes to him. "All night? All *last* night?"

He nodded, fiddling around with the volume on the soundtrack in the editing programme.

"Wow, that's . . . I thought you'd be busy catching up with Bella?"

"Yeah." He shrugged. "We caught up, I got on with this, she got tired, and anyway, she wanted to get home and see her folks, catch up with them too." He shifted round in the chair to look at me. "Is … something the matter?"

I swallowed. "Matter?" I shrugged. "No."

"OK, but you're being weird."

"Am I? How?" I said.

"On edge, I dunno."

"Well, the golden egg thing—"

"With me, I meant. Ever since I got here. What's up?"

I looked him in the eye. "Nothing."

"Nothing?"

"Nothing," I confirmed. I mean, actually, everything. Maggie suggesting Ben knew he would lose the bet – what did that mean? Ben nearly kissing me? Last night? Were we going to acknowledge any of that or just pretend like it didn't happen? But then, maybe it didn't happen? Maybe it was all in my head? Maybe I was unreliably narrating my entire existence? I cleared my throat and looked down towards the floor. "I mean, um … maybe just—"

He leaned towards me. "What?"

"Huh?"

"You're mumbling, I can't hear you," he said.

"Oh, um, sorry." I cleared my throat again. "I was just saying, maybe, you know, last night. Right?"

I glanced at him, and he was staring back, eyes darkening.

"ALEX!"

It was Maggie, red and furious, in the doorway.

"I was just getting it!" I bleated.

"Getting what?"

"Something to clean the mess up with."

Maggie threw her hands in the air. "Well, try the cleaning cupboard, not the office!"

"Oh."

"Oh." Maggie said, in a mocking sort of voice. "NOW!"

I scrambled to my feet and hurried out of the office, but still heard her mutter a despairing "Boys!" as I left.

Worse, I'd left the awkward conversation with Ben hanging. He clearly hadn't liked what I'd started saying, and I hadn't had time to make it better, backtrack, or gaffer tape my mouth shut so I could never speak again.

I hurried across the main floor, aware that Maggie was making a beeline back towards the fuming mother, whom Efia and Drake were still trying to persuade to calm down and put her phone away. The light switch in the cleaning cupboard was one of those little toggle ones that look like they've come straight out of 1940. In fact, it probably had, come to think of it. A very low-powered single light bulb came on, accompanied by the faint buzzing sound of dodgy electrics. I poked around the shelves, eventually finding a dustpan and brush amongst the old mop heads, bottles of bleach and assorted rags that should have been thrown away last century.

I hurried back over to the "crime scene", where a full-blown slanging match was now in progress. As the kid's mum shouted obscenities – "Shithole! That's what this place is!" – and Maggie finally flipped – "Try sayin' that to my face!" (to which the mum replied, "I am sayin' it to your face, you stupid cow!") – I got down on my knees and did my best to scrape up the mouse corpse and assorted needles, using what must have been the world's crappiest brush, which was missing most of its bristles. As Maggie and the kid's mum circled around me like boxers gearing up for the first punch, I scurried out from between them, holding the dustpan at arm's length, and wondered what the hell I was meant to do with it all now. Putting a dead mouse in the staffroom bin didn't seem hygienic, and I was pretty sure needles were classed as clinical waste and were meant to be disposed of carefully.

"ALEX!" Maggie hissed. "Get that *thing* out of my sight!"

I stared at her and opened my mouth to speak—

"NOW!" she barked.

I jumped and headed straight back towards the cleaning cupboard, by default. At least there the mouse would be out of Maggie's view, just like she'd asked, and I could have a moment to decide the best course of action. Although, once inside, I realized there was no solution to the body disposal issue and I'd just have to go out again, cross the gaming floor – *in full sight of Maggie* – and take the mouse somewhere else. I put the dustpan on the floor because I couldn't have it near me any longer, and tried to decide what to do.

I jumped as the door creaked open behind me.

"Oh, it's you," I said, relieved it wasn't the crazed killer I'd been expecting, since I was in a dimly lit cleaning cupboard.

"*What are you doing?*" Ben asked.

"I don't know," I said.

Ben glanced over his shoulder, then nudged the door closed behind him. I froze in panic. This was it. We were going to have a "chat" and he would tell me I seriously needed to stop being obsessed with him and back off. The look in his eyes in Maggie's office had said it all. He'd looked horrified. He sighed. "Look—"

"Nice cupboard!" I blurted out.

Ben's eyes widened a little, whilst I mentally slammed my head repeatedly into the wall. Of course, I wasn't done yet. "Haven't been in here before. Quite big, really."

Ben nodded, slowly.

"What's this?" I said, desperately turning and grabbing the first thing I could find so that I could talk about it. "Cillit Bang. Ha! Multi-surface spray. Pretty … cool."

"I don't think that's what you're looking for," Ben said, inching towards me.

I shook my head but clung on to it anyway, completely forgetting what it was I was looking for.

He took the Cillit Bang out of my trembling hands and placed it gently on the shelf behind me. But he stayed facing the wall, head bowed a little, and sighed again. "Look, if … if all this is anything to do with last night … I'm sorry, yeah? I was … I'm sorry, anyway, so, can we just—"

My breathing was jagged. "No! It wasn't! Dinner was great!" I grimaced. I knew he wasn't talking about dinner.

He smiled, shook his head, and turned to glance at me. "Good. I'm glad. I enjoyed dinner too."

I swallowed and tried to read his face. So, he was saying he enjoyed dinner, but the thing in the street afterwards was a mistake? It felt like something important was slipping away from me. "We could do it again!" I added, trying to sound breezy and light.

"Maybe," he said, sounding less than keen.

"We don't have to…"

"No."

"But … we could?"

Ben nodded.

I was sounding desperate. I needed to backtrack. "Bella could come too," I added, just to make it clear I was happy with just being mates.

Ben flicked his eyes to mine, holding contact for a second or two. "Sure."

"OK," I said. "That would be … nice."

And then there was this terrible silence where it just felt like I'd somehow said everything wrong.

The door flung open.

"ALEX!"

It was Maggie.

I grabbed the Cillit Bang and held it out towards her. "This?" I said.

She was silhouetted in the doorway, but I could tell she was quivering like she was about to explode. "What the actual frig use is a bottle of multi-surface spray?! What are you doing in here? Where's the frigging mouse?"

"I wasn't sure where to put it," I pleaded.

"Sling it in the dumpster in the back yard!" Maggie screeched, giving me a hard scowl.

"Dumpster in the back yard." I nodded. "Yes."

She stormed back out, muttering and cursing under her breath.

"Ben?"

But he was gone before I could stop him. *Way to go, Alex.* I wasn't sure how, but I knew I'd messed that one up.

"I think we should look at what's staring us right in the face here," Drake said as Maggie ushered us all into the staffroom for an emergency meeting, about half an hour later.

"Not now, Drake," Maggie said.

"Why not now?" he replied. "We all know it, so I'm gonna say it. Ben and Alex were the last people to run maintenance on the Golden Goose."

I looked at Ben, but he didn't look back at me.

"We checked all the eggs," I said. "We didn't see anything."

Drake gave a contemptuous chuckle. "Sure you did."

"Shut up, all of you," Maggie said.

We all stood in silence, feeling the burn of her glare as she looked us all up and down.

"All right," she said, finally. "I'm aware that Ben and Alex were the last people to reload the goose, but you all know the keys to the goose are in this office, so if we're really going to throw stupid accusations around, let's be honest and say any one of you could have booby-trapped one of the spare eggs and slipped it in."

I looked between by fellow suspects. My god. *Any one of us!* Well, except for me. I knew I hadn't done anything. Not deliberately, anyway.

"However," Maggie said. "There's also quite a few of our regular punters who probably know that too, so as a precaution, the office is now going to be locked, twenty-four seven, and if you need to get in, you'll have to see me. No one's going to touch anything unless I know about it. Get it?"

We all nodded.

Maggie sighed. "I know I don't pay much, but I do the best I can. You all know I'll do anything to help you out; you've always got a home here, whatever else is going on. I hope . . . I hope you all know that. None of you had better be mixed up in this, or as God's my witness, I will serve time for what I'll do to you!"

I looked at Ben again, but he was looking down at his trainers.

"Now, I want all these new ideas to be up and running ASAP," Maggie continued. "So it's all hands to the pumps."

Ben looked up. "Bella's offered to help, if you like? She wants to hang out with me anyway and she told me she doesn't need to be paid. It'll mean we get some of the stuff done quicker."

Now it was my turn to look down at my trainers.

"Fine," Maggie said. "You, her and Alex can go through all the eggs in the goose again. Check every single one. Efia – rehearse the fortune telling with Eve. How long until the Roswell Experience is ready?"

"I reckon tomorrow?" Ben said. "Bella's putting out teasers on social media about it."

Of course she was. Probably in between brokering a peace deal in a war zone and singing lullabies to orphans.

"So we'll make the relaunch date in three days?" Maggie said.

"For sure," Ben replied.

Maggie nodded. "Get on with it then. *No more screw-ups.*"

We shuffled out of the staffroom, the unpleasant stench of suspicion hanging in the air. Efia came up close alongside me. "My money's still on Drake," she muttered.

"Yeah?"

"Trying to deflect attention on to you and Ben – absolute classic," she said. "What were you doing with Ben in the cleaning cupboard?"

"Ruining everything," I said.

Efia grimaced. "Well, now Maggie has put you with Ben to work on the goose, the universe has granted you a chance to put it right."

"Maybe."

"Don't mess it up."

She patted me on the shoulder and walked off to join Eve in the fortune-telling booth. I took a deep breath and strolled over, super casual, to the damn goose, where Ben and Bella were already pulling all the eggs out of its backside.

"We can probably manage this, if you want to do something else?" Ben said, *not even looking at me.*

I just stood there, mortally wounded.

"We'll get it done quicker if Alex helps," Bella said, giving me an encouraging smile.

Ben actually shook his head. "There's so much else needs doing though, but whatever."

Bella looked at me, like *what the hell is his problem?* At least I wasn't imagining it. I shrugged. "That's OK, I'll . . ." I looked around for something else to do. ". . . I suppose I could help Eve with the fortunes then."

Ben sniffed and started cracking open the eggs.

I seriously considered saying, "Just in case it's this, I loved the fact you nearly kissed me!" but how could I, in front of his girlfriend?

"Sorry to have troubled you," I said, quickly hurrying off towards the booth where Efia and Eve were. I ducked under the curtain and into the candlelit space where Eve was sitting (dressed in a velvet robe, virtually indistinguishable from her usual garb), behind a small table with a crystal ball and some tarot cards on it.

Efia sighed. "Did you mess it up?"

"I messed it up. By doing *nothing*. Just by *existing*, I messed it up."

I flopped down on the chair next to Efia, and she pulled me towards her, giving me a little cuddle. "It'll be OK," she said.

I doubted it would be.

"Anything I can do to help?" I said.

"Sure," Efia smiled. "Why don't you be Eve's first customer? She'll do a reading for you, and I'll observe and take notes for feedback."

Eve smiled at me from beneath her hood. Maybe she meant it to be friendly, but she just looked like a demonic monk that was after my blood for a sacrifice.

"Cool," I said. "So this is, like, a load of Barnum statements, right? General statements that sound very specific and personal, but actually pretty much apply to anyone? *I see myself as a very creative person*, that sort of thing?"

Eve's face dropped to a frown.

I swallowed. "No?"

Eve leaned towards me, across the table. "Non-believers anger the spirits, who put curses on the heretical ones, before carrying them off to the nether."

I nodded, trying to look enthusiastic, and definitely like I shouldn't have any manner of curse placed on me. After all, things were bad enough as they were, without the intervention of malicious spirits.

"Eve suggests you close down your prejudice and open up your mind."

And now she was also taking about herself in the third person. Was she possessed, or simply in character? I felt like I couldn't ask. Eve thrust the pack of tarot cards into my hands, then clasped hers over mine, closing her eyes and seemingly channelling some sort of energy, or spirit, or something.

I didn't really believe any of this stuff but I have to admit, I was too much of a wuss to really call out the bullshit, you know, *just in case,* which is why I'm also agnostic, rather than atheist.

"Shuffle," she commanded me.

I moved the cards around a bit, then handed them back to her. Eve took a deep breath, then picked off the top ten cards, which she arranged face down on the table between us.

"Let us consider your past," Eve said, turning the first card over, to reveal The Fool.

"That's me!" I chirped.

Eve ignored me. "Someone who is just beginning. An innocent."

Read: *virgin.* Oh my god, even the tarot cards were trolling me.

Eve turned the card next to it over, revealing The Hermit. "You were lonely, withdrawn and isolated," Eve said.

So, I was a virgin who was a total loser with no mates. I mean, sure, it was accurate so far.

"We have two major arcana cards right here, suggesting these are fundamental elements that are maybe hindering your spiritual journey. Eve will now interpret your present and then look to your future."

I nodded.

"Here we have the Knight of Cups, who indicates the arrival of romance."

"Ah!" I said.

"But next to it, we have the Seven of Cups, suggesting elements of fantasy, illusion and wishful thinking."

"Oh."

"And next to that, we have the Nine of Wands – courage, persistence and resilience . . ."

"Ah!"

". . . *except* this card is reversed, so it paints more of a picture of paranoia, defensiveness and being on edge."

"Oh."

"Eve will now seek the cards' guidance on your future."

Her hand hovered over the first card and she looked up at me, eyes full of worry.

"What is it?" I swallowed. "Something bad?"

She didn't answer, just turned the card over, and from the way she gasped, I gathered it wasn't good news. "The Tower!" she muttered.

I waited for her diagnosis.

"*Disaster!*" she said, finally.

Well, she certainly told it like it was and didn't mince her words. I admired straightforwardness in a person. *Still.* "How bad a disaster?" I asked.

Eve shook her head, and turned the next card. "Ten of Swords – some sort of betrayal. You're being stabbed in the back."

"Great."

"And then. . ." She turned the next card. "The Hanged Man!"

"Oh god. . ."

"The sacrifice, the scapegoat. . . Five of Cups, *loss, regret, despair. . .*"

I swallowed. "Now all we need is—" I stopped as Eve turned the next card over, and I was actually staring Death in the face. "And there it is," I said.

"*Endings,*" Eve said. "Not necessarily a bad card," she added.

I rolled my eyes. No, I loved a bit of death, who doesn't?

Eve turned the final card over. "Judgement," she said. "*Rebirth.*"

I was screwed. I'd always suspected it, but now the tarot had confirmed it. "Is there anything I can do?" I asked, thinking maybe I could make some sort of sacrifice, or burn some herbs, to please the spirits and improve my lot.

Eve shook her head. "The cards have spoken. They don't make the future, they merely foretell it."

I looked helplessly at Efia. "It's just a bit of fun," she said, giving me a not remotely convincing smile, like everything was fine. *Fun?!* At this rate, next thing you know, we'd be opening a clinic at Wonderland to tell people they had STIs, or running a stand selling funeral plans.

"Ignore the cards at your peril," Eve said.

"See?!" I said. "*Ignore the cards at your peril.* It's real, Efia. It's all real. My life is basically ruined. What did I ever do?"

We all sat in silence for a few moments while they tried to come up with something soothing to say to me, I've no doubt.

"The answer lies in the major arcana cards that underpin your past," Eve finally said. "The withdrawn, isolated, innocent. You must correct that, learn from that, to change your path."

"Otherwise I'm going to be stabbed in the back and hanged from a noose?" I said. "Huh."

Eve blew the candle on the table out. "We'll ask the cards again soon."

I could barely wait.

I still don't believe in this sort of thing, but the funny thing is, knowing what I know now, it's scary how accurate the predictions were.

CHAPTER TWENTY-ONE

Ben spent the rest of the day making sure he was so busy he didn't have time to so much as look at me. He didn't even eat one of the freshly fried and sugar-coated doughnuts I had bought for everyone to share, in my attempt to out-nice Bella. *He didn't even have a doughnut*. How bad is that?

As I stood under the steaming shower the following morning, I'd got round to thinking that maybe what I needed to give Ben was a bit of space. I realized I was gay when I was thirteen, but there was a year either side of that where I was confused and scared by it all. Maybe Ben was going through that now? And the last thing you need when that's happening is someone trying to force you into a corner, demanding answers. Maybe Ben needed to go at his own pace, and maybe the best thing I could do was just to be there for him. Be his friend. And if he ever wanted to be more than that, then let him drive it.

Or maybe he was straight and I needed to stop all this wishful thinking.

I tied a towel around my waist and emerged from the bathroom to find Kendra on the landing, waiting. "You've been in there forty-five minutes!" she scowled.

I hadn't. It was half an hour.

"You know we're on a water meter? We get charged for all your rampant water use! And that aside, you know the reservoirs are at historic lows?"

Sure. You thought it was the oil companies, or the destruction of the rainforests, but here I am – the cause of the environmental apocalypse.

"I'm meant to have a meeting with the planning committee and I'll be late now," Kendra continued as I dripped on to the carpet. "If I miss the slot, the project will get pushed back, and that'll add several thousand on to the budget. You're dripping on the carpet; can't you dry yourself properly before you leave the bathroom?"

"Sorry."

"Why *do* teenage boys take so long in the shower?" She looked at me with *that face.* The one that people use when they're implying we're doing something else in the shower other than showering.

"Sorry, Kendra, I'll try to be a better person."

She narrowed her eyes at me. "Don't take the piss."

"I wasn't!"

She pushed past me into the bathroom. "I'm going to speak to your dad about putting an en suite in the master bedroom, this is ridiculous."

She slammed the door.

And good morning to you too.

The haunting and melancholy strains of REM's "Everybody Hurts" filtered through from my bedroom. Another phone call! That was two in the space of this whole month. Madness! I padded across the landing and into my room. Obviously it was Efia, like that girl just didn't understand how intimidating phone calls are and simply couldn't bring herself to message.

"Meet me in ten minutes," she said when I answered.

"Efia, I've only just got out of the shower!"

"It's half past ten."

"Exactly?!"

She sighed down the phone. "OK. Fifteen, then. We've got a meeting with one of the journalists who ran the Wonderland story – I told her we had some information and she took the bait. Their office is on Castle Street. I'll meet you outside."

She hung up before I could protest. I pulled on some boxers and shorts, sniffed a T-shirt that I figured would be passable, and whacked that on too. Then I grabbed two handfuls of Coco Pops from the kitchen and hotfooted it over to Castle Street, whilst eating my breakfast.

"I'm going to use this to try and find out who might have tipped them off," Efia said as I raced up to her. "Don't know how willing they'll be to reveal their source, but it's worth a shot. Something's going on – the threatening notes, the article, the tampered golden egg – *someone* is behind all this." She picked a Coco Pop off my T-shirt. "Is this yours?"

"Thanks," I said, taking it off her and putting it in my mouth.

Efia shook her head. "Just go with me on everything, OK?"

I nodded, pleased she didn't expect me to do anything too taxing which I would invariably mess up. "Do I have Coco Pop breath?" I asked.

"That's not a thing."

"No, but—"

"Alex, you're not going to be snogging the journalist, you're just accompanying me, OK?" She sighed and handed me a Tic Tac from her bag. "Here, if you're worried." She pressed the intercom buzzer on the wall. "I spoke to Ben last night."

The intercom crackled. "Hello?"

"We're here to see Helen French – it's Efia Adomako and Alex. . .?"

I leaned in. "And Alex Button!"

"Aw, sweet!" Efia grinned.

The door buzzed and Efia pushed it open, leading

us through into a small hall, the floor covered in flyers for takeaway food and junk mail, with a set of stairs leading up to the first-floor offices. "So, you spoke to Ben?" I said as we climbed the stairs, trying not to sound too interested. "OK."

"He wasn't in a good place."

My heart skipped a beat. "What?"

"Turns out it's the anniversary of his mum's death."

I stopped dead halfway up the stairs. Oh god. Maybe this wasn't about me at all. That poor boy had so much else going on in his life. OK, maybe him thinking I was being weird about what happened after our pizza didn't help, but when you've other stuff happening, if you're feeling sad, or low, it's easy to blow all sorts of things out of proportion. You can get so wrapped up in your own story, you forget other people have theirs, and sometimes those stories aren't nice ones.

"He's not coming in today anyway," Efia added. "I think he just needs to be at home."

I nodded. "Sure."

Efia looked at me, reading my face. "So, maybe that explains some of how he's been, right?"

I broke her gaze. Maybe it did. And maybe this was exactly the moment Ben needed a friend, not some romance-obsessed boy chasing after him.

"Come on, let's get on with it," Efia said, pulling me up the stairs.

*

A blonde woman in her late twenties, whom I recognized as the "hipster woman" who came into Wonderland, and whom I supposed was Helen French, was standing on the landing on the second floor. "Efia?" she said. She looked at me. "Hello."

I nodded at her but played it cool, the snake that she was.

Helen led us through into the offices, which were a ramshackle bunch of desks and old computers and several people on telephones who were shouting things like, "I can do you five hundred for a ten by two and run it in two editions and a month on digital."

It all sounded very high pressure and awful.

She sat us down in a small and dingy back room that smelled of stale cigarette smoke. "So, what have you got to tell me about Wonderland?" she asked.

"Mainly that you got it wrong," Efia smiled. "And we think you should give the place a second chance."

Helen crossed her arms.

"We've got a relaunch in a few days, and we'd love it if you'd come along and cover it. You know, in the interests of balance?"

"We'll see if we can make it," Helen said.

"It'll be good," I added.

Helen smiled at me. "I'm sure."

I nodded because I was indeed *sure.*

"Who tipped you off about Wonderland?" Efia said.

"I can't tell you that," Helen said.

"Well, someone must have pointed you in our direction."

"Oh, they did," Helen replied. "It's just I can't tell you who."

Efia nodded. "Some sort of journalistic integrity thing, is it?"

"No," Helen said, getting up and pulling a file out from a set of drawers. She flipped it open, took out a letter and handed it to Efia. "I can't tell you because it's anonymous."

I leaned over Efia's shoulder, reading the anonymous letter about the Wonderland. Five paragraphs detailing everything that was wrong with the place – including the stuff that was mentioned in the article, like the supposedly out-of-control customers, and the fact it encourages gambling from a young age, as well as things that didn't make it in, like the apparent fire hazard the entire place was. It was a devastating diatribe – but my fury was all the greater because, however eloquently it was worded (and it *was*), and however forceful and aggressive the arguments (and they *were*), whoever had sent this was not brave enough to put their name to it.

Efia handed the letter back to Helen. "Please come to the relaunch. We're changing and we're proud of what we've done."

When we got outside, Efia said exactly what I'd been

thinking. "OK, if the previous notes were 'kids pranking us' *that* letter definitely isn't."

"Too well written?"

Efia nodded. "It was . . . eloquent. *Serious*."

"So what are we dealing with?" I asked. "Different people? All of whom hate us?"

"I honestly don't know." Efia sighed. "It feels like the haters are circling, and all we're trying to do is save Wonderland for Maggie so she doesn't lose everything she's ever worked for. Why can't whoever it is just leave us alone?"

"Maybe we need a bit of extra help," I said. "Maybe I should contact that Tyler guy who gave me his card – he said he could help out with publicity. Can't do any harm, right?"

"Good plan. See what he can do." She checked her phone. "What time do you start?"

"Not until after lunch. I'll see you there. There's something I need to do. For a friend."

Efia nodded and gave me a little smile. "I'm sure he'll appreciate it."

There wasn't time to make my own, but I bought the nicest-looking crusty loaf I could find in the supermarket, along with a pack of bacon and an avocado. I made the sandwiches just like he'd told me, cut them into triangles and wrapped them in brown paper, tied with string. His dad answered the door, but I didn't ask to see him, I just handed his dad the package and asked if he could pass them on.

And on the front I'd simply written:

For Ben. Love from Alex. X

CHAPTER TWENTY-TWO

"Oh my goodness, this brings back memories!"

Tyler Phillips gave me a wide smile as he took in the surroundings of Wonderland. No linen suit today, but he looked just as smart in a checked navy number featuring a waistcoat and one of those pocket watch chains. I admired his ability to regulate his body temperature wearing that outfit in this heat, as much as his sense of style. "I used to come to these sorts of places a lot as a kid," he continued.

"With the relaunch, we're hoping to appeal to as wide a market as possible," I told him. "Kids and families, obviously, but also hopefully a young, trendy crowd too."

Tyler nodded. "Diversifying your market – *excellent.* These days you have to adapt to survive. Tough market, am I right?"

I nodded. "Things aren't easy, I guess."

"How can I help?"

"We really need to get some good PR on relaunch day," I said. "You kind of said you might have some contacts?"

Tyler smiled at me. "I didn't 'kind of' say, I *did* say. And of course, it would be a pleasure."

"Really?"

"Leave it with me. I'm sure we can get Breeze FM here, plus I've got some good contacts in the blogger and influencer community – online buzz is just as important these days."

"We tried the local paper," I said. "They said they'd try to come."

Tyler flashed me his bright, white smile. "I think I can turn that 'try' into a 'will'. I'll speak to them too. And let's see if we can get some local dignitaries too – maybe the mayor."

I didn't know what to say. This all seemed so easy. Nothing was ever this easy. Not in my life, anyway.

Maybe Tyler read my mind, because he said, "Hey, I admire what you're doing. Too many people sit around, not taking positive action, and wonder why things don't improve. So it's a pleasure to help out in this small way."

"We appreciate it," I said. "Thank you."

Tyler patted me on the shoulder. "I'll be in touch. Give my regards to Maggie."

I watched him as he walked out, so confident and assured.

"Should have asked him for a thousand pounds and a holiday to somewhere fancy whilst you were at it!" Kem said, not turning around from his fruit machine of choice for that day.

"Guess there's some nice guys left in the world after all," I said.

"Hey!" Kem said, looking at me over his shoulder. "There's plenty of nice guys! One sitting right here, for starters!"

"Sorry, Kem."

"And I'm talking to one right now!"

I smiled at him. "Flirt."

Kem tutted and rolled his eyes. "*Flirt.*"

"Hey, hey, hey!" Bella bounded up to me. "I've been looking for you!"

"I had stuff." I hadn't, I'd just been keeping out of the way all morning because I didn't know what Ben would have made of my little sandwiches gift. I only wanted to cheer him up, and let him know someone was thinking of him, but it's possible he might have seen it differently.

Bella smiled. "Why don't you come and see what we've done to the Roswell Experience?"

"Where's Ben?"

"He's in there, with Efia. He's just getting the lighting

right in the alien lab section. Thinks it'll be better if it's a bit darker."

I sighed and glanced over towards a couple of kids pointlessly trying to win a toy from one of the claw machines.

"I'm sure he'll appreciate your thoughts," Bella continued. "*Plus,* I've bought a twelve pack of Krispy Kreme, in case you need any more persuading."

"Do it!" Kem said, jabbing his palm on the "nudge" button. "Krispy Kreme? Why you even hesitating?"

I sighed. "Yeah, OK then. Um. . . Is he OK?"

Bella nodded and lightly touched my forearm. "Yeah. He had a little wobble yesterday, just couldn't face anyone, but he's OK."

I exhaled. "Good."

"Are *you* all right, Alex?" she asked.

I nodded, grimly. There was too much on my mind to really be OK. And it wasn't just The Ben Issue – it was the identity of the person with the vendetta against us, and the nagging fear of those damn tarot cards. In the sense that I was imminently about to be stabbed in the back and be hanged, yes I was OK.

She led me through into the exhibition room, which I had to admit did look pretty cool. A projector had been rigged up at the far end and was playing the film Ben had made, and there were some benches for people to sit on and watch. Along the other wall, there were big photos of the supposed UFO crash site, along with "copies" of classified documents, with certain lines blacked out. In the middle of the room, a piece of twisted metal was displayed on a wooden pedestal, with a sign telling visitors it was an actual bit of UFO. Only those of us "in the know" would recognize the tailgate of a Renault Clio.

It was looking really good, but when Bella opened the door into the "lab" it actually took my breath away. Dry ice billowed over the floor and green lighting illuminated a solid stainless steel plinth in the centre of the room, with a cordon around it made from biohazard tape. And on the table was the alien. And my god, it did look like it could be real. The thick, leathery skin I knew to be made from condoms, split open and stretched over the plastic moulding of the mannequin, and painted grey – simple, but really effective. But that was nothing compared to the intestines that were proudly on display – red and bloody, and completely gross. I leaned forward to get a better look at our handiwork, and BAM! A mound of gore burst straight out at me, blood shooting in the other direction.

OK, I knew it was coming, sort of, but I screamed.

Bella laughed.

"*Shit!*"

Efia emerged, laughing, from under the table, pulling off a long rubber glove that was adorned with bulging lesions and bulbous growths. "We got you good, Alex!" she said. "Did you wee yourself a bit?"

"Goddam, *nearly*," I said.

Ben walked out of the shadows. "Reckon we're good to open, then."

"It's really good, Ben. Really excellent—" I attempted to catch my breath. Wow, he looked cute. Aside from his uniform yellow polo shirt, he was wearing grey jersey shorts and was just in his white socks, for some reason, no trainers. "I really—"

Ben nodded, flicking his eyes shyly down to the floor. "Well, team effort."

He glanced back up at me, but quickly looked away again when he caught my eye.

"We're gonna need extra condoms," Efia said. "The guts keep splitting when I thrust my hand through them."

"No worries, I've got some," Bella said. "And I can go and buy some more."

I watched as Ben raised an eyebrow at her. Did he smirk a bit too?

"Stop it!" Bella said, clocking Ben's face and smacking him on his bottom.

"Didn't say a thing!" Ben chirped.

I glanced at Efia. "Well, I should. . . Maggie wanted me to clean the Mirror Maze."

The door to the lab pushed open and I gasped as Caleb poked his head round. I really can't deal with seeing people out of their usual context. I screamed when I once saw Ms Willow, my English teacher, rounding the dairy aisle in the supermarket, for example. Like, why the hell wasn't she at school? Why was the natural order of things in such disarray? "Knock, knock," Caleb said. "Oh . . . *wow*. This is cool."

"We're not open yet," Ben told him.

"Yeah, no, I know, sorry to barge in." Caleb nodded. "That guy at the prize booth told me you were all in here, and I just wanted to give you all one of these. . ." He held a bunch of flyers out. "*Aqua*-cadabra!"

We all looked blank.

"That's . . . what they're calling it this year. It's the end-of-season pool party at Splash Down! My mate works there and he asked me to spread the word. There's a DJ and all-you-can-eat street food in with the ticket price, *and* they're opening all the rides this year too, so it'll be like a private party for all the summer season workers in Newsands. It's gonna be . . . moist."

"How appealing," Efia said.

Caleb grinned as he handed each of us a flyer. "Does that guy in the booth offer weed to everyone who comes in?"

Efia rolled her eyes. "Pretty much."

Caleb handed me a flyer. "Hey, Alex. You gonna come along?"

"I dunno." I shrugged. "Pools make me nervous. As you know, I can't really swim."

"I can teach you," Caleb smiled.

I stared at him for slightly too long as I tried to work out if that was a good idea or not.

He narrowed his eyes slightly. "What part of that was tricky to understand?"

"Oh, no, none of it, that's great," I said quickly.

"I got a membership at the leisure centre, so we can go sometime," he said.

I nodded. I really didn't need to embarrass myself in front of a load of other people from the town. And the idea of being in a pool made me so anxious, even the smell of chlorine made me feel sick.

Ben crossed his arms. "I used to be a lifeguard there for a bit."

"Oh right?" Caleb said. "Small world, I guess."

Ben nodded. "I guess so. How much are Splash Down! tickets this year then?"

"Twenty quid."

Ben whistled.

"*But*," Caleb said, "everyone's gonna be there, and you guys *know* it'll be the party of the year, so what else you gonna do with your hard-earned cash?" He looked between us all. "Efia? You gonna come?"

"How do you know my name?" Efia said.

Caleb's eyes widened. "*Wow*. Alex told me."

"Huh," Efia said. "I don't know, it's a lot of money."

"Ben?" Caleb asked.

"It's a lot of money."

Caleb blew out a breath. "OK. Tough crowd. Well, it'd be nice to see you all, but no pressure."

I felt even worse about Ben paying for pizza now. How bad is it when you can't even use the money from your summer job to go and have a good time for one night?

"Seven at the leisure centre," Caleb said to me, backing out of the door.

Oh, OK, that was definitely happening, then. But I supposed I ought to learn to swim sometime. If we did end up at Splash Down!, I'd want to be in the pool, and inflatable armbands are never gonna get me a boyfriend.

"I'll be the guy in Speedos!" Caleb told me.

"Ha!" I said. "And I'll be the guy in the knee-length, baggy swim shorts."

"You should definitely get some Speedos," Efia said, once Caleb had gone.

"I may not be sure of much in my life," I said, "but I'm positive you will never see me in Speedos."

Efia laughed. "Aw, Alex. . ."

I held my hand up. "Stuff to do!" And hurried out.

No sooner was I back on the main floor than I walked straight into Carl Hudson and his stupid dog, which was finally on a chain.

"Um, Tyson can't be in here," I told him. "Dogs aren't allowed."

Carl looked apologetic. "Sorry, son, I had no idea."

"There's a sign on the door," I said.

"My eyesight isn't what it was," Carl said. "One of the curses of old age!"

I nodded and looked at him expectantly. Why exactly was he here?

Carl cast his eyes over the fruit machines, then over past the driving simulators, the Mirror Maze, and finally the Roswell Experience. For a man with bad eyesight, he was certainly doing a lot of *looking*. "Heard you folks were having some sort of makeover?" he said.

"Sure," I said.

Carl nodded. "Be good for the place, I expect. Lick of paint. Bit of TLC."

"Uh-huh."

Carl sighed, clearly picking up on my hostility. "Listen, son, Maggie and I may have had our differences in the past, but it's time to bury the hatchet. Am I right? There's plenty of trade for both my pier and Wonderland to coexist, and hey, a little healthy competition never did any harm, did it?"

"Healthy competition?!"

I whipped round and was faced with Maggie, brandishing a fire extinguisher. "Get out of it!" Maggie hissed, pointing the hose at Carl "Spying on us, are ya?!"

Carl raised his hands in submission. "Just dropping by to offer my good wishes!"

"Like hell you are!"

"I'm seventy-five this year, Mag," Carl said, backing

towards the exit. "Just looking for a quiet life, no trouble, I promise you!"

"I will pull this pin out and hose your sorry OAP arse unless you leave *NOW*!" Maggie bellowed.

Carl shook his head, pulled Tyson out with him, and hurried away.

Maggie stared after him. "Scum."

I cleared my throat. "I mean, he seems . . . OK?"

She turned to me. "That man would steal the shoes off my feet if he could. Mark my words, Alex. Do not trust him."

CHAPTER TWENTY-THREE

I was polishing the smudges off the mirrors and glass panels in the Mirror Maze, mulling it over. What exactly was the deal between Maggie and Carl Hudson? Other than his dog (and maybe that was just an accident), he seemed pretty . . . old and harmless. And Maggie refused to elaborate on their history, so I only had her word for it that he couldn't be trusted. Fine, I wouldn't let him in again, but I felt bad, being mean to an OAP.

I jumped as I saw Ben looking at me from the other side of the glass panel.

He smiled and held his hand up in a little wave, then pushed through the panel to his left and worked his way round to where I was.

"What's with the socks?" I asked.

Ben rolled his eyes. "Guess who had another dog-based trainer accident?"

"Oh no. Worse than last time?"

"Much worse," Ben said, grimly. "Just what I needed this morning."

"Never rains, it pours, huh?" Man, I knew what that felt like.

Ben nodded and sighed. "Anyway. . ." He held up a paper carrier bag with "RAW" printed on the side in bold black writing. "I bought you this."

"What are you talking about?" I said.

"Dropping those sandwiches off at my house was really sweet of you. I mean . . . it was such a nice thing, Alex." He looked a bit sheepish. "I actually cried."

My eyes widened. "Oh god, I'm so sorry, I'm such a—"

"No, just because it was so lovely, that's all!"

"Oh. And . . . how are you doing?"

He gave me the smallest hint of a smile. "I'm OK."

He handed me the bag and I pulled out the T-shirt inside. It was a distorted chequered design, in black and lime green. Not my usual thing, because I'd never be brave enough to pick out something like that, but I loved it. I looked up at Ben. This was from RAW. It would have cost loads. "This is so nice of you, but I can't accept it—"

"Do you like it?"

"Yeah, I love it. Thank you. But—"

"You said when we went for pizza that you found it hard to find anything that looked good on you – well, I reckon this will. I'm also kind of sorry for being weird in the cleaning cupboard."

"That's fine, you weren't. I think it was me. Sometimes I … it doesn't matter. I enjoyed our dinner. I loved it. *All* of it."

"Yeah, it was really nice."

He flicked his eyes down to the T-shirt in my hands. "You could wear it for your date with Caleb."

I snorted. "Well, (a) it's not a date, and (b) we're swimming, and you don't usually do that in a T-shirt."

Ben smiled. "I think it's a date."

"It's not a date."

"Alex, he came in here on the flimsiest of pretexts and arranged to go swimming with you. *Swimming*. There will literally just be some Speedos between you and him."

"And my swimming shorts too," I added.

He ignored me. "Factor in the free lemonade and all the little chats you've been having, I think the writing's on the wall. I'm happy for you."

He didn't look particularly happy. There wasn't a dimple in sight.

"Do you want to come with us?" I suddenly blurted out, like an idiot.

He stared at me. "Alex—"

"Sorry."

"*No.*"

"It was just an idea."

"It's *your* date."

"Yes. I mean, *no*, I'm still saying it isn't a date, but OK."

He rubbed a little smudge off one of the mirrors with his sleeve. "So. Mates?"

I took an unsteady, shallow breath. "Definitely."

He pressed his lips together and nodded, then backed away through the Perspex door and disappeared into the mirrors.

I'd meant to tell him about all the weirdness with Carl Hudson and Maggie. I'd meant to say to him, "Hey, did we nearly kiss, or what?!" And also, "So, Maggie said you *knew* you'd lose the bet, so what gives?" but that boy makes my brain turn to mush and all I can think about is AAAAARRGGGHHHHH!

"AAAARRGGGHHHHHHHH!"

Efia brought over two glasses of Coke and sat down next to me in the Bellevue Café next door, whilst I repeatedly banged my head on the Formica table. "That boy has led me right down the rabbit hole! I'm so confused! This is such a nightmare! I've no idea if he likes me or not and anyway he's with Bella, so all of this speculation is utterly pointless!"

"And yet here you are, *speculating*!" Efia said, sipping

her Coke through a straw. "Did Ben say anything else during your amazing maze conversation?"

"No. What like?"

"Did he seem . . . *jealous*?"

"Of what?"

Efia lowered her voice. "*You and Caleb!*"

"Right. I've already had this discussion with Ben, and it's not a date. It's just swimming."

"Two boys swimming."

"Yes. That's just . . . factual. We're two boys, swimming."

"Sounds like the title of a gay porno to me."

"Well, I wouldn't know about that."

That was sort of a lie, because I did know, but that wasn't the case here. I sipped my Coke.

Efia shook her head. "He's jealous."

I sipped my Coke again.

"For a start, did you see how he got all defensive when Caleb was talking about swimming? Mentioning how *he* used to be lifeguard? That's classic male posturing during a courtship ritual, as the boys try to impress the other boy, hoping he'll pick them for mating season."

"*Mating season?!*" I spluttered. "We're not . . . antelope!" I don't know why I picked "antelope".

Efia waved my objections away. "Animal, human, gay, straight, it's all the same principle. The interested party will always try to do things to impress the quarry."

"Can you quit with the weird animal and hunting

references? It's really off-putting."

I sipped more Coke.

"Anything else you haven't told me?" Efia asked.

I avoided her eyes and sipped more Coke.

"Maybe he bought you something? A small gift? Some little trinket or love token, perhaps?"

I sighed. "He bought me a T-shirt."

Efia beamed. "*I knew it!* Actually, I did know it, because I saw him heading to the Mirror Maze with the bag from RAW, and when I asked Bella, she told me what he'd done. That's so sweet. Isn't that sweet?"

I sipped my Coke.

"The boy has mixed-up feelings, that's my diagnosis," Efia said. "But this little date that's not a date with Caleb might work in your favour. If he thinks there's a chance he's going to lose you, it may spur him into action."

"AAAAARGGHHHH! He's got a girlfriend!"

"And he might not have by next week!"

"I can't split them up!" I said. "Bella is literally the *nicest* person in the history of humanity. If I wasn't already, I would go straight to hell for doing that."

"Alex, people change their minds! OK? Sexuality is fluid. It's not all, 'That's it, I'm straight and always will be!' – what do you think this is, the twentieth century?"

I shrugged.

"OK!" Efia chirped. "Let's take your mind off it all with

something else." She glanced over towards the entrance. I was just about to ask what could possibly be more interesting than my massive boy obsession, when Drake walked in.

"What's *he* doing here?" Drake asked as he ambled over, looking about as shifty as anyone can look.

"*He* has a name," Efia said.

"*Alex,*" I added.

"Thought this was just gonna be me and you, babe," Drake said.

I immediately stood up. "Oh my god, I'm so sorry, I'll—"

Efia pulled me back down. "Sit down, fool! *Really,* Alex?"

I shrugged. How was I supposed to know?

Efia cleared her throat and smiled at Drake. "Drake, I don't know why you thought that."

Drake cocked his head. "Said you wanted to chat. *Privately*, you said!"

"And that is true," Efia replied.

"And, I dunno, just with the party at Splash Down! coming up and everything. . ." He stuck his tongue in his cheek and gave Efia a little wink that made a bit of sick come up in my mouth.

"Oh, Lord!" Efia muttered. "You thought I was up for some fun in the back of your Fiat Panda, did you? Drake, are you *high*? Actually, don't answer, of course you are. No, Drake. I am flattered, but no. No."

"Your loss, babe."

"Yes, and I'm feeling it deeply."

Drake kicked one of the chairs out and slouched back into it. "So, what's this about then? I've got things to do."

Efia leaned towards him across the table. "What do you make of all the stuff that's been going on at work?"

Drake stared at her. I was just glad she hadn't told me the plan was to quiz Drake this afternoon. There's no way my nerves would have taken it, especially when he was still the most likely suspect.

"You know," she continued. "The notes, the newspaper article, the tampered golden egg. . ."

Drake gave a little shrug.

"Looking like an inside job, don't you think?" Efia continued.

"Oh! I get it!" Drake stood up to leave. "No idea, but it wasn't me."

"What about the guy who hit you?" Efia blurted out.

Drake turned his head sharply back towards her, sizing her up for a second, probably wondering how much she did or didn't know. "Keep yourself out of my business," he hissed.

"Well, maybe if your business didn't infringe on everyone else's, that would be fine," Efia said. "But since you're still dealing weed, even though Maggie expressly told you not to, and since you're clearly in some sort of trouble with someone, because *you were overheard in the yard*—"

I tried to look like it wasn't me who'd overheard him by putting a look of mild surprise and interest on my face.

"Then I think it *is* our business to ask, especially when stuff is happening that shouldn't be happening."

Efia sat back, satisfied.

Drake glared at her and sat back down. He looked at us both, curled his lip and shook his head. "So easy for you lot, isn't it? Working here over the summer, earn a bit of cash, and in a few weeks you're back at school, forgotten all about this place, and then, couple of years, you're off to uni or whatever. All works out nicely, doesn't it? Just a little game for you lot. Little story to tell your posh uni friends one day – have a good laugh about the time you worked in a crappy amusement arcade with all these useless wasters. Well, guess what? Some of us have to live in this town because there's no chance for us to get out. So some of us have to do what we gotta do. And you little bed-wetters have *no idea* about what's really happening in Newsands. All you see is your own little lives, in your own little bubble." He sneered at us, then adopted a mocking tone, at least an octave higher than any of us actually spoke. "Oooh, I've got an essay deadline, oooh, I fancy someone, oooh, Kayleigh isn't talking to Chelsie because Amy snogged Adam."

Who the hell were Kayleigh, Chelsie, Amy and Adam? Maybe they were mates of Efia's. They sounded *awful*.

Drake made a contemptuous little snorting noise.

"You think I'd hurt Maggie?"

"We don't know, Drake," Efia said. "Maybe you wouldn't. But maybe someone else would? Someone who was trying to get something out of you, using Wonderland as leverage."

Drake shook his head. "We all know how much Wonderland means to Maggie. We all know about her son, how she built the whole place in his memory. I get that you have a low opinion of me, but really? You think I'm *that* low that I'd do that to a heartbroken woman who's only ever been good to me?"

He got up abruptly and stormed out of the café.

Efia watched him go, crunching thoughtfully on a piece of ice from her glass.

"I mean, I think he seems genuine," I told her.

Efia rolled her eyes. "You do understand that people lie, don't you?"

"*Yes.* I'm not that much of an innocent!"

Efia raised an eyebrow.

"So where does this leave us then?" I asked.

"Still looking for our culprit, Alex."

CHAPTER TWENTY-FOUR

I hadn't been back to a public swimming pool since Mum and Dad chucked me into the deep end, aged five, in what I'm pretty sure was in direct contravention of all the guidelines about how to teach people to swim.

"Kick your legs!" Dad had shouted. "All the other kids are doing it, why can't you?"

"I don't think . . . I'm like . . . other kids!" I had gasped, paralyzed with fear and slowly sinking.

Of course, a childhood nightmare is something that can grow in the imagination over time, but I'm pleased to say that my trip with Caleb lived up to every terrible expectation and every fear I had. For a start, the session we were joining was called "Family Fun Time" and that meant it was chock-a-block with screaming kids.

Luckily, I had pre-empted the first horror of swimming pools by pre-dressing in my swimming shorts, so all I had to do was take my T-shirt, socks and shoes off, and I was basically good to go. I took my stuff to the locker, then stood barefoot and vulnerable, waiting for Caleb, my arms crossed up over my chest, like how they do with corpses in coffins. It was less to do with my expectation of imminent death, and more because I was modestly shielding my nipples from public view, although boys' nipples are less of a "thing" than girls' nipples, for some reason, so it probably wasn't necessary.

Caleb snapped the waistband of his Speedos. Those carved abs, tapering down in a perfect "V" and his smooth, rich brown skin radiating warmth and health were in stark contrast to the shivering, goose-pimpled pasty wreck that was my own body. "Ready?"

I nodded, then stepped in a small pool of tepid water on the floor, at the exact moment a father shouted to his passing son, "Arthur? You've forgotten to put your verruca sock on!"

"Now," Caleb said, putting his hand on my shoulder. "I know you're nervous about this, so today's lesson is just about getting comfortable in the water, OK? We'll just splash about, have some fun, get you feeling happy and relaxed."

I nodded, tense as hell.

"I said, 'Relax!'" Caleb smiled, patting me on the stomach. "Good to go?"

"Absolutely *buzzing*," I lied.

Caleb led the way through to the main pool, my heart rate increasing in direct proportion to the smell of chlorine.

I wanted to go home so badly, but I was here now, and I supposed that learning to swim was just one of those rites of passage you have to grin and bear, like drinking your first pint of beer (gross) or learning to drive (*me*, in charge of a dangerous machine – *really?!*). We went down into the shallow end and sat on the floor, our backs up against the side of the pool, and the water lapping over our legs and up to our bellies. I glanced over at some ten-year-old boys, splashing about with some inflatable hammers, across the other side.

"Where's Jake?" one of them shouted.

"He's havin' a piss," another said, cocking his head towards a boy (presumably Jake), standing perfectly still in the middle of the water, with a vacant look in his eyes.

I took a deep breath, feeling immediately sick with the chlorine fumes. "Um, so, how long is this all happening for?"

"For as long as you like," Caleb laughed.

"Oh, I didn't mean—"

"We can get out whenever you want to," he said. "No pressure."

A used plaster floated by. "Sure," I said. "Thank you."

"Wanna try the inflatables?" Caleb said, nodding

towards the huge range of blow-up creatures floating in the middle of the pool. "Or there's the water slide?"

"Let's not run before we can walk," I said.

Caleb cracked a smile. "Wise words."

"Maybe an inflatable," I said. "I guess that would minimize my chances of drowning?"

"Exactly," Caleb nodded. "You can just have a float."

We waded out towards the inflatables, and since my feet could still touch the bottom of the pool, that was basically fine.

"You good?" Caleb asked.

"I'm good."

"Holler if you need help."

I nodded, then screamed as a man suddenly burst up from beneath the surface, literally a metre from me, showering me in water. The man glared at me like I was the one at fault, put a finger over one nostril, and blew water and snot into the pool from the other one. Then he sniffed, turned, and dived right back in, swimming back towards the deep end. I looked at Caleb, checking to see if he'd registered the full horror, but he was laughing at me.

"It's just water," he said.

That pool was so much *more* than just water.

Caleb commandeered two huge inflatable animals – a big shark, and a unicorn with a rainbow tail, mane and horn, which he pushed in my direction. "Is this how you see us both?" I said. "*You're* the big, powerful, majestic sea creature—"

"And *you've* got a big gay horn."

I went red.

"Alex, I just thought the unicorn looked more stable, and you can kind of sit *in* it, whereas you have to straddle the shark."

I nodded. "Yes, it seems sensible."

"Do you want me to help you up into it?"

"No, I've got this," I said, except I hadn't because every time I tried to grip on the gay unicorn, it slid away from me.

Caleb waded over, and held on to the unicorn. "Flip yourself in," he told me.

So I launched myself at it, landing half in, half out, my middle sort of beached across the sides of the inflatable ring that formed the body of the unicorn. I dragged myself forward with about as much dignity and allure as some barely evolved creature crawling out of the primordial soup.

Anyway, I was in.

Caleb climbed aboard the shark, straddling it with his strong legs, gripping the fin with his hands. He paddled his feet and shifted around so we were next to one another, but facing different directions. "Having a good time?"

Across the pool, an angry-looking mother was dragging a sobbing kid across the tiles, shouting, "Well, I told you not to come if you had diarrhoea!"

"Yeah, it's lovely," I said.

"OK," Caleb said. "So now that I've got your full attention and you basically can't go anywhere, I need to talk to you about something."

I looked at him, wide-eyed. *Oh no.*

"Don't look so scared," he told me.

"I'm sorry, I think it's that phrase, *I need to talk to you about something*. It's just, every time someone has said it to me, something bad comes after it. My parents said it before they announced the divorce. Mum said it before she told me about the cat's accident with the electric fence—"

"OK, this is not a bad thing, Alex. At least, I hope it isn't."

He gave me a little smile. I swallowed. My stomach was full of lead.

"But it's maybe a bit *delicate*."

I stared at him.

"'Cause love *is* a bit delicate, isn't it?" He gave me a sort of cheeky, slightly shy grin.

If this was going the way I thought it was going, I had to stop him before he got to the bit where we both ended up embarrassed and awkward. Maybe this was my fault. He'd basically asked me on a date, albeit a pretty crappy one, I'd agreed, and I *had* been flirting with him a bit over the last few weeks.

"Caleb," I said. "Let me stop you a moment."

"Okaaaay. . ."

I took a breath. "I really like you—"

Now it was Caleb's eyes that widened. "No, mate, I like you too, but not like that!"

"Like *that*? Like *what*?" (I knew perfectly well what he meant.)

"I . . . don't fancy you, Alex?" He looked mortified.

I nodded. "No. Good. I mean, not good, but that's fine because me neither."

Caleb was just staring at me.

"I'm glad we can be mates," I added, glancing at him. "We can be mates, right?"

"Yeah. I sort of thought we already were."

"That's good, because we were. *Are*. Excellent."

Caleb gave his face a brisk rub with his palms. "Ah. Yeah. OK, this feels awkward now."

"I'm really sorry."

"No, *I'm sorry*. Have I completely given you the wrong impression?"

"You've done nothing wrong," I told him. "Everything turns awkward when I'm involved, that's all."

He didn't look convinced. He looked like he was feeling bad for me and my stupid, unrequited feelings for him that actually didn't even really exist.

"Look," I said. "I'll be honest, Efia and Ben thought it would be a good idea if I maybe tried to flirt with you a bit mainly because I knocked myself out at Wonderland and when I came round, I was muttering your name.

Well, not your name, I was muttering 'Lemon Boy' because I didn't know your name, but I knew you were a boy who was involved with lemons. To the unknowing eye, it would appear I had some sort of subconscious crush on you."

He furrowed his brow. "*Efia* suggested it, did she?"

"Well, she certainly encouraged me to. . . *Oh,*" I said, finally realizing. "*Oh*. You like Efia, don't you?"

Caleb dropped his eyes shyly away.

"Aw, well, maybe I can help get you together. I mean, matchmaking is really not my thing, due to a staggering lack of experience on my part, but I could *try*. . ."

"You don't have to," Caleb said. "I just really wanted to know if I might be in with a chance with her. Like, does she have a boyfriend – or girlfriend – already? Is she into boys?" He dropped his eyes again. "Might she be into *me*?" he added, quietly.

"I will subtly and covertly gather that information for you, Caleb."

"Whoa! Hold up there. Maybe it's best just to leave it. I just thought you might know."

"I'll find out. I'll be your *wingman*. I've always wanted to be one of those."

He chewed his lip for a second. "OK. But . . . keep it cool, yeah? I don't want her thinking I'm all obsessed with her. Which I'm not, by the way! I'm take it or leave it."

I laughed.

"Yeah, OK, maybe that's not completely true," Caleb said. "But gotta play it cool."

I nodded. "Is that a thing?"

"Apparently."

"Efia told me the same thing."

"Yeah? OK, that's good to know," Caleb said. "She'll be playing the same game then." He nodded, thinking it through, then looked back at me. "She was telling you to play it cool with me, then?"

"No. Not you." I looked down. "Someone else."

"Spit it out."

"Ben, maybe?"

My cheeks started burning just by saying his name. That was not an example of "playing it cool".

"Ah, yes!" Caleb beamed. "You two would be *so cute*!"

"Well. . ." I shrugged. "He's got a girlfriend, so. . ."

"Really? Who?"

"Bella."

"Bella?!" Caleb spluttered. "As in, really nice Bella who's just come back from travelling?"

"Uh-huh."

"Err . . . you sure about that?"

I looked at him, his face a picture of confusion. "Yeah? I mean, that's what he *said*. And they're . . . always together and stuff, and they. . ." I looked away because this was all pointless. "I mean, yes, she's his girlfriend. Do you know her?"

Caleb nodded. "Maybe I got it wrong then."

I flicked my eyes to his, scared to let the hope build up inside me too much. "What did you get wrong?"

"She came to get a lemonade from me yesterday and we got chatting about how she was helping at Wonderland, and I asked how she ended up doing that, and she said her 'mate' Ben was working there, and that was how."

I blinked at him.

"*Mate,* Alex. That was the word she used."

"Not boyfriend?"

Caleb shook his head.

"Huh."

"*Mate,*" Caleb repeated.

I still had my doubts, because my life is never going to be easy, and that's a fact. "OK, but what if she's one of those people who refers to their partner as a 'mate'. You know, like I went to my aunt's wedding this time, and her husband gave this speech where he said he was so lucky to be 'marrying his best friend' and I thought, "Cool! I'm not the only gayer in the family, David's actually marrying Paul, that's amazing!' but it turned out he just meant my aunt." I nodded at Caleb. "It made me feel a bit sick, to be honest. But maybe Bella meant that?"

Caleb sighed. "God, you're good at pissing all over good news."

I nodded. "I'm trying to change."

Caleb's face grew into a wide smile. "Time to get out

of the pool, lover boy. You're gonna help me, and I'm gonna help you. We're gonna see if we can get you a boyfriend."

I did my best to smile at him, in a really positive, grateful, excited way, but inside I was like, "Really? More help? How many people are going to attempt this before everyone finally realizes I'm a total *lost cause*?"

CHAPTER TWENTY-FIVE

"Do you want to get some food?" Caleb said as we walked out of the leisure centre. "I've got a voucher for two-for-one on pizzas at that new place that's opened." He nudged me, conspiratorially. "We can make *plans*."

It sounded good to me. Now I was working at Wonderland I had actual money of my own to do things with – I didn't have to go and beg Dad or Kendra, both of whom would usually make me jump through hoops like a championship show dog, just for a few quid. I didn't mind mowing the lawn, or doing the dishes, but they had me up a ladder sawing a branch off a tree in the garden a few weeks back, and it took me three hours, *and* I nearly broke my neck. *For a fiver.*

There was no live jazz at the pizza place that night,

but it was still buzzing. The exact same waitress who served me and Ben greeted us, and gave me a knowing smile when I walked in with Caleb, like I was some sort of modern-day Casanova.

"Table for two, please," Caleb said.

"We have *vouchers*," I added.

"No problem, lads," the waitress said. She led us over to a table in the corner, turning to me as we approached it. "Your *other friend* is here too."

She cocked her head towards the other wall, where Ben was sitting with Bella, a large wine bottle with a big candle stuck in it sitting in the centre of their table. Ben was leaning forward, staring *really intently* at Bella as she spoke, which means I'm ninety-nine per cent certain he'd already seen me with Caleb, and was now doing his best to ignore the situation. The waitress nodded at me, to make sure I'd clocked him, like she was an accessory to my two-timing antics with the teenage boys of Newsands.

Caleb raised an eyebrow. "Aha! The game is afoot. And sooner than I'd thought."

"Should we go somewhere else?"

"Definitely not," Caleb said, sitting down, then noticing the little tea light we had on our table. He smiled at the waitress. "May we have a big candle in a wine bottle too?" he said.

"Sure." The waitress shrugged.

I took a deep breath. I could see what Caleb was

doing. He was doing exactly what Efia had advised. He was trying to make Ben jealous. Surely he knew such a plan would end in tragedy?

"Actually, make that *two*," Caleb said.

The waitress looked at him. "You want *two* candles in wine bottles?"

"Uh-huh."

"Okaaay," she said, reaching out to take the tea light away.

Caleb stopped her. "We'll have that as well," he said. "I like candles."

She nodded, like he was weird. "Some drinks?"

"Champagne!" Caleb said, loudly.

The waitress rolled her eyes.

"No, but can I have cider?"

"No, you cannot," she said, patiently.

"*Damn.* OK, just a glass of milk then," Caleb said. "What? I like milk!" he said, in response to the waitress's disbelieving look, and mine, which would have been one of disgust because I'm not a fan of milk just by itself.

The waitress made a note, then looked at me. "And *not* a lemonade, right?"

My eyes went wide.

"Why *not* a lemonade?" Caleb asked.

"He hates the stuff," the waitress chuckled.

"Ha!" I said. "Water's fine. Thank you!"

The waitress went. I ran my tongue over my lips and

tentatively glanced back at Caleb, who had his arms folded across his chest, staring at me. "I'm waiting," he said.

"She's got me mixed up with someone else," I said. "Must be. Because I *love* lemonade."

"Good." Caleb nodded, like it would be a personal affront if I didn't. He glanced over my shoulder to where Ben and Bella were sitting. *"Huh,"* he said.

It was driving me crazy that I couldn't see them, but maybe that was for the best. "What is it?"

"They are sharing dough balls. Well, two can play at that game."

The waitress came back over with two candles in wine bottles, which she placed on the table.

"We'll have the *charcuterie platter,*" Caleb told her. *"To share."*

She made a note and headed off again. Caleb winked at me. "We're gonna out-romance them."

"It'll never work."

"FYI, he has seen the candles and now he's *feeding* her dough balls."

"I think we should admit defeat."

"We will retaliate. I'm gonna feed you prosciutto. We are not gonna lose this thing."

"Do you think we should just go over and say hi?" I said. "This is kind of ridiculous."

Caleb shrugged. "Be my guest."

I glanced over my shoulder, just in time to see Bella

feed Ben a dough ball dripping in garlic butter. They both giggled as the butter dripped down his chin. I turned back to Caleb. "Well, I don't want to interrupt anything," I muttered.

"Ben has cute dimples, right?"

"Can't say I've noticed."

Caleb hooted with laughter, then his face dropped. "Ugh. Don't look, but they're sharing a milkshake. One glass, two straws. *Such a cliché.*"

"Well, that's very romantic," I muttered. Half of me wanted to go home and be sad with a mug of hot chocolate and a Radiohead album, but the other half was echoing with Maggie's words of wisdom: *you make your own luck.* Maybe I did need to be a bit proactive? Maybe I needed to fight for Ben! The waitress arrived with the charcuterie platter and I glanced over the selection of different cured meats, along with various pickles and some olives. "OK." I nodded. "Pork me up."

The waitress looked mildly amused. I gave her an awkward smile. I'd only been in there twice and I already had a reputation.

Caleb dangled a slice of Parma ham from his fingers. "Open wide," he said.

I leaned forward, and Caleb popped it in my mouth. "Oh, *mmmmm*!" I said, as loudly as I dared. "Oh, *yes*!"

Caleb laughed and flicked his eyes over my shoulder and back again. "Yeah, he saw that."

"Do it again!" I hissed.

"Try my salami!" Caleb said, also quite loudly, folding a slice in half and pressing it into my mouth as I cracked up with laughter. "Caleb!" I snorted. "This is a family restaurant!"

The waitress came over. "Boys, just to remind you, this is a *family restaurant*?"

We both nodded solemnly, then collapsed in giggles. "Do you want to sample my little cucumber?!" I gasped, holding up a gherkin. I was totally creasing up, I think maybe because I was slightly hysterical about the whole situation, rather than any of this actually being amusing, although as Kendra often says, guys never really grow out of fart jokes or willy gags, and I think on that one point, she might be right. I had full-on tears rolling down my cheeks about all this anyway, so it took me a few moments to realize that Caleb wasn't laughing any more, but was sort of looking serious and sitting more upright on his chair. So I followed his gaze, and Ben was standing by our table.

I immediately stopped laughing and sat up. "Hey!" I said.

"Having fun?" Ben said.

I nodded.

"All lit up, I see," he said, indicating all the candles.

"Who are you here with?" I asked, trying to play it innocent.

Ben gave me a mildly unimpressed look and folded his arms. "Bella. How was the swimming lesson?"

"Cool." I nodded. "Yeah, it went OK."

Ben looked between me and Caleb. "Bella and I were going to go to the fair on the pier after pizza, do you want to join us?"

"Yes!" Caleb said, before I could reply.

"R-really?" I said. "The pier though? The *rival* pier?"

Ben nodded. "Undercover research mission. Always need to keep tabs on your competition. We won't mention it to Maggie, obviously. She'll go ape on us. Wanna come?"

I nodded. "Sure."

"OK, then," Ben said. He seemed wary. Cautious. Like he was trying to work us out. "Have a nice pizza."

"Have a nice pizza," I replied.

I watched him go back to his table, then turned to Caleb. "How did it go?"

"Fine. He came to you. We broke him."

I flinched. "I don't want to *break* him!"

"But he's chasing you, so that's good."

"The other interpretation is that he just saw us and is being friendly."

"Let's go with my interpretation," Caleb said. "I like that one better."

"So do I," I agreed.

*

Legitimate spying mission or not, I still had reservations about our trip to the pier – not least because if Maggie got to hear about it, I wasn't sure she would ever forgive us. But this whole feud between Wonderland and the pier was stupid anyway. The pier (and its fair) were in direct competition with Wonderland only in as much as they were both cheesy. Yes, you could win massive stuffed toys at the various sideshows, but all of the pier games were manned individually, and were the sort where you had to shoot a pellet gun, or aim an arrow, and we didn't have that type of thing anyway. And other than that, there were dodgems, a big wheel, various waltzers and a ghost train that was about as bad as our Museum of Curiosities used to be. Point was, you wanted rides, you went to the pier, you wanted arcade games, you went to Wonderland. Two different markets, in my humble opinion, but hey, who was I to be the voice of reason?

"How's the lemonade trade this year?" Ben asked Caleb as we passed the fibreglass lemon, swung a left and headed straight into enemy territory.

"So so." Caleb shrugged.

"Gonna look for something different next year?" Ben said.

"Gonna have to," Caleb replied. "They're closing it at the end of the season."

My ears pricked up. The lemon was closing?! That was devastating news. The lemon might be a total joke, but it was part of the town. It was part of my childhood. "How come?" I said.

"You know it's owned by the people who run the Bellevue Café?"

I nodded.

"Well, they're selling up, and the lemon goes with it."

"Selling up? To someone else, though?" I said. "Someone else will run it instead?"

Caleb shook his head. "Nah, I asked about that, in case I could work for the new people instead, but they're closing it all down and getting out. They had an unexpected offer on the premises apparently, so they're taking the cash and retiring. This place is changing, man. All sorts going on. We've just had *sourdough pizza,* I mean, *come on*!"

Oh my god, someone was probably going to change the Bellevue into an Avocado Den or something similarly hipster-y. They couldn't. I had so many memories tied up with that old café, grim and tired as it may be. It's where I first met Will . . . or, more accurately, accidentally squirted him with a gummed-up bottle of ketchup I was applying too much pressure to. But then, I hadn't seen or heard from Will since that day in the chemist's at the start of summer. I thought me and him were going to be mates for ever, but we're not. Things had changed. We had changed. And so perhaps it's normal if the things around you change too. Especially when you're also part of that change. Like Caleb said, *we'd just had sourdough pizza.* Maybe that made us complicit.

Ben was eyeing up the stall on our left. "I really want to win one of the stuffed elephants."

"Ben. We're here undercover," I reminded him.

"I want an elephant though. Knock down the cans – it looks easy."

"It won't be."

"Just one go. *For research,*" he grinned.

He'd already fished the pound coins out of his pocket and was handing them over, so it was happening anyway. He narrowed his eyes at the set-up of tin cans that you had to knock down with balls. Three balls, six cans – knock all six cans off the shelf and you win the big prize, with some consolation prizes for fewer cans.

I tugged at Ben's shirt.

"What's up?" he said.

"Don't bother with the bottom cans," I whispered. "They usually weigh them down, so it's almost impossible to knock them over. Just aim high, go for the smaller prize."

"But then I won't win the elephant."

I shrugged. "Maybe the cuddly ferret will do?"

"I think that's meant to be a meerkat. And no, *it won't.*"

I blew out a breath. It was his choice. I'd said my piece.

Ben set his focus on the cans, then hurled his first ball

at the bottom row, slamming it right into the middle can, sending it clean off the shelf, with the three cans on the next two tiers exploding off the shelf too, like he'd just put a bullet between them.

My mouth fell open. Oh wow. *Wow.* This was the hottest thing ever.

There were just two cans left. Ben tossed the second ball in his hand a few times, winked at me, then shot it at the left-hand can. THWACK! Right off the shelf.

Everyone applauded.

It's well documented how certain people are drawn to strong, powerful partners who can provide for them – you know, it's basic survival and evolution. *That's what this was!* If we were cavemen, Ben would be killing bears and dragging them back to the cave to eat, and lighting fires and stuff. It was only because it was the twenty-first century that it was tat from a funfair instead, but the principle definitely still applied.

"Come on, Ben," Caleb said. "Final ball!"

"Go, Ben!" Bella shouted.

I couldn't speak, I just wanted him to win so badly.

He fired his last ball at the final can, and we all held our breath as it clipped the edge of the far right can, wobbled . . . wobbled . . . and fell on to its side and. . .

ROLLED OFF THE GODDAM SHELF, OH YES IT DID!

I can't remember exactly what I did, but there was a

lot of screaming, and I was jumping up and down and I threw my arms around Ben and I think I kissed him on the cheek and called him a "god".

I was definitely a bit overexcited, but you must understand I'm incredibly easily pleased. I get excited by a fortune telling fish in a Christmas cracker, so this whole thing was a pretty big deal.

The lad running the stall grabbed one of the big elephants and handed it to Ben. "Nice one, mate."

Ben was grinning. He was totally pleased with himself.

And I was so proud of him. "That's so cool!" I told him, giving the elephant a squeeze. "Look at his cute ears!"

He looked at Bella, who smiled and sort of rolled her eyes at him, and then he turned to me and. . .

I'm almost choking up telling you this. *He handed me the big elephant.*

My mouth was just hanging open.

"Have it," Ben said.

This was the best day ever. "Ben," I managed to say. "Really?"

Ben laughed.

Bella smiled.

Caleb said, "Aww, man!"

"I mean, if you like elephants so much." Ben shrugged.

"It's lovely, thank you," I said.

I held it close to me. I would call the elephant Ben.

"Dodgems?" Caleb suggested.

OK, it was meant to be a research mission, but I was having a good time, so I didn't really care. We decided to get a car *each* (because who really wants to be the passenger in a bumper car, and besides, I had a passenger now, and it was Ben the Elephant). The siren sounded, and we were off. My usual strategy for bumper cars is really just to have a nice drive around, carefully avoiding any conflict. But Ben's was apparently to pursue me whilst giggling, and continually ploughing into me at any and every opportunity.

"Oh my GOD!" I squealed, ricocheting in my seat as Ben hurtled into me again. "Be careful of Ben!"

"What?" Ben said.

"Nothing. Who?" I replied.

Ben grinned and swung his car around in a big circle as I tried to steer away from the side of the arena, which is always hard when the damn things won't actually reverse. Out of the corner of my eye, I could see his car looming about ten metres away, and then, like in those films where a car suddenly turns its headlights on and massively accelerates towards a victim, he started coming at me like a bloody bullet.

The impact catapulted me forward. Ben's eyes were ablaze with mischief as he came around and slammed into me again.

OK. OK, two can play at that game.

I finally steered my car away from the wall and zipped away just as he swept in for another smash, then did a hard right and came back at him, careering into the side of his car and knocking him sideways. Breathless, I steered immediately away, sweeping around in a three-sixty loop, giving him another good smack, and then zooming off to the other side of the arena, cackling like some sort of lunatic, before he could retaliate in any way.

And then there we were, at opposing sides, suddenly facing one another, the huge expanse of space between us. Our eyes locked across the abyss. This was it. All or nothing.

I floored the pedal.

He did the same.

Fast and furious we were shooting towards one another, distance shortening, still accelerating, impact imminent, faster, closer—

The siren sounded and the cars went dead as the power was cut. We ground to a halt about half a metre apart, both of us breathless, shaking with adrenaline, and laughing.

We both struggled out of our cars, then he walked up to me.

"You're a dangerous driver!" I gasped.

Ben laughed. "You're a *bad* driver!"

I snorted, because he wasn't wrong.

Ben lifted Ben out of the car and handed him to me.

"So, how was swimming with Caleb?" he said.

I shrugged. "It was OK, I guess. The leisure centre pool, on the other hand. . ."

"Grim?"

"Grim."

Ben nodded, like he knew it only too well. "You should learn somewhere else. Not that old cesspit."

"Yeah?"

"Uh-huh. Like . . . I could teach you, if you wanted? And we'd go somewhere different." He looked down at his shoes, kind of shy.

"That'd be great," I said.

He looked up and nodded. "OK then."

I nodded back.

"Are you seeing Caleb?" he asked.

I looked him right in the eyes. "We're just mates."

Ben swallowed and nodded again.

"We're getting candyfloss, do you want candyfloss?!" Bella called over from the side of the arena.

"Err – yes?" Ben smiled. He gave me another nod, then walked off towards Bella.

Bella.

His girlfriend.

And I wasn't a hundred per cent sure, but he'd just asked me out on something that sounded a lot like a date.

Bella did not deserve to be cheated on. I couldn't let that happen.

But Ben...

And yet, Bella...

I hurried off the arena, trying to work out whether I needed to not go swimming with Ben, or find out what was happening with Bella first, or just speak to her myself and admit all my feelings. And as if things couldn't get any more anxiety-inducing, I then saw Carl Hudson grinning at me from over by the entrance to the ghost train, and putting his finger to his lips in a "Ssssh! Secret!" kind of way, and then it felt like I was cheating on Maggie as well.

CHAPTER TWENTY-SIX

"Morning!" I said to Kendra as I headed out of the front door the following morning. It was relaunch day, the sun was shining, and despite my Bella-based guilt (which I was definitely going to deal with), things were looking up. "How are you?"

"Shattered," Kendra said. "I was just drifting off to sleep last night when you slammed through the door at god knows what time."

Eleven p.m. to be precise. I mean, really?!

"I'm very sorry."

Kendra looked me up and down. "Relaunch day, isn't it?"

"Uh-huh!"

"I admire how you've thrown yourself into this project, Alex."

I smiled. Finally! A compliment! "Thank you!"

"I mean, it's futile, but I still admire it."

Oh.

"Not everything is worth saving, Alex," she told me. "Wonderland, that greasy spoon café—"

"My parents' marriage."

I wasn't sure why the things I normally only ever *thought* were now things I was actually *saying* out loud, but there we were. And besides, she *was* pissing me off.

Kendra took a deep breath and stared at me. "Hope it goes well."

I nodded. "Thanks." And made a swift exit.

"Oh my actual god, are you *smiling*?!" Efia said as she walked up to our bench on the promenade.

"For you," I said, handing her a takeaway cappuccino. "And I have muffins too."

Efia's eyes widened. "Did you get laid or something? What the hell is wrong with you?"

"Perhaps Ben is taking me swimming . . ."

"Yes?"

". . . to some secret spot he knows. . ."

"Oh my god!"

I shrugged. "I mean, it's probably nothing. Plus, he's

still seeing Bella, so it definitely isn't a date or anything. Still, it has made me very—"

"Horny."

"Happy," I corrected her.

She raised an eyebrow.

"OK, and what you said too, I guess," I added. "I went for pizza with Caleb, and Ben and Bella were there as well."

"Ben got jealous," Efia said. "I knew it!"

"I dunno, maybe a bit. Caleb laid it on pretty thick." I chuckled. "He's hilarious."

"Caleb seems like a nice guy," Efia said.

My ears pricked up. I had offered to do some digging for Caleb, and here was my chance. "Yeah, *he is*. Really nice. Top bloke!"

"Why are you being weirdly enthusiastic? That's very unlike you."

"Huh? No. I'm just saying. So you think he's nice?"

Efia stopped in her tracks. "What's going on?"

I blew my cheeks out. "Nothing."

"*Alex*. What is going on?"

It took three seconds of her staring to break me. MI5 material, I am not. "I think he likes you."

Efia rolled her eyes. "Oh my days."

"He's a nice guy, Efia. Really nice. He's really sweet and romantic and quite caring."

Efia shook her head. "I don't need the distraction. I want to focus on my studies for the next two years."

"Everybody needs somebody," I said.

"No, they don't, Alex. Some people are quite happy by themselves. And me, I don't really mind either way. I'm not against it, per se, but I'm not actively pursuing."

"OK," I said. "What shall I tell him?"

"Has he asked you to ask me out?"

"Hmmmm – not exactly. More to test the water. Dip my toe in, and report back."

Efia's eyes narrowed. "You keep your toes to yourself, mister. I'll take it from here."

"Oh no, don't say I said anything!"

"I won't!" Efia chirped. She ushered me off the bench. "Come on, we've got a relaunch to make happen."

Walking past the Bellevue Café reminded me. "Caleb told me something else last night."

"This'll be good."

"No, Efia, seriously. The people that own the Bellevue are selling up and apparently it's not even going to be a café any more. Caleb doesn't know who too, but what's the betting it's going to be super fashionable and high end?"

Efia grinned. "Maybe it'll be another fancy restaurant you can wine and dine Ben in."

"What about the café though?"

Efia shrugged. "Alex, it's not that great. They can't even make good coffee. And if Caleb needs a new job, maybe he can come and work at Wonderland next year, with us. Assuming we get this relaunch right."

"Oh, that'd be nice," I said.

"There you go. Not all change is bad."

"Caleb looks good in Speedos, by the way," I muttered, trying to subtly plant good things about him in Efia's mind.

"Oh wow. . ."

"*Exactly*. That's kind of what I wanted to say, but it would have made things weird."

Efia gave me serious side-eye. "Alex, can you just please *not*?" She nodded towards the entrance of Wonderland, where a number of people were already waiting to come in. "That's what I was 'wow-ing' about. An actual *queue* of people waiting to come in! I think this scheme of ours might just pay off!"

We knocked on one of the locked glass doors at the entrance and Ben emerged through the unlit gloom the other side to let us in.

"Hey," he said, holding the door open for us, then locking it back up.

"A queue of people!" Efia beamed.

"Right?!" But something in Ben's face didn't look so excited or pleased.

"What's up?" I asked him.

Ben glanced at me, then handed Efia an envelope. "*This*."

Efia pulled a scrappy piece of A4 paper out of the envelope and unfolded it. It was blank, except for one typed sentence right in the middle:

Sounds like there's a BAD EGG at
Wonderland

My throat tightened. The business with the golden egg wasn't actually public knowledge. In the end, the mother had been placated through Maggie giving the child armfuls of free stuff and Bella stepping in to calm everyone down with her gentle, measured voice. The only people who knew what happened were the staff and any customers who were around at the time.

"Oh my god," Efia muttered. "It's the same person, isn't it? Whoever sent this note planted the egg?"

"Looks that way," Ben said. "I'm taking this to Maggie. I know she wasn't interested before, but I think this changes things."

"Mm, fascinating," Maggie said, after we'd finished relaying the evidence to her. She shut her eyes and was perfectly still, a look of serenity of her face.

"Um . . . Maggie?" Ben said, after a long-enough awkward pause.

She opened her eyes. "Hm? Oh, sorry, I was just imagining myself on a Spanish island, away from all this crap." She smiled at us.

"Maggie, you do see that this almost certainly means the culprit is someone who works here?" Ben said. "It's someone who *knew* the booby-trapped egg had already been, well. . ."

"*Laid?*" I offered.

She took a long drag of her e-cigarette.

Ben held his hands out, palm upwards in a gesture of *Well?!*

Maggie blew out a plume of menthol steam. "Is everything ready for the relaunch?"

I think we all nearly screamed in frustration and Efia definitely did.

"Listen," she said. "I hear what you're saying, but right now, the relaunch is what matters. Let's bring the punters back and see the money start rolling in. That's what we need. Whichever little joker is behind these . . . *pranks,* I'll find them, and then I'll deal with them. Let's all get on. *Now!*"

We all turned and started filing out, it being perfectly obvious that Maggie wasn't up for discussing any of this.

"Oh!" Maggie suddenly shouted. "One last thing for you all – a little something by way of a thank-you – I've taken the liberty of buying you all tickets to the pool party at Splash Down! tomorrow night."

Everyone turned back. "Really?!" Efia said.

"The least I can do for all your extra work. I do appreciate it. So, this is me, saying thank you. I hope you all have a great night – relax, let your hair down. Don't drink or do drugs. Actually . . . do what you like, what do I care?"

We all moved forward to hug her at the same time,

which she tolerated for about four seconds, before pushing us all away. "All right, get on with it!"

We all headed back out again, buzzing with excitement that we'd be going to the party.

"Alex?" Maggie said. "A word."

I sighed and closed the door behind the others.

"Well?" she said.

I assumed she was asking about Ben. "He's taking me swimming."

Maggie nodded. "Progress."

"Maybe." I shrugged. "But it took such an extraordinary effort to get to this point, I'm really not sure things can go much further. And like everyone says, I shouldn't push it by appearing too keen, so I don't know what to do."

"You have to *feel* it, Alex."

I looked at her like, WTF?

"You'll know, when the moment comes," she said.

Since I'd never even kissed anyone, I really wasn't sure I would. As it turned out, like so many of the things Maggie said, she was bang on the money.

When I walked out on to the main floor, it had all come alive. The lights, the music, and considering it was only ten a.m., the place was buzzing. It looked like the relaunch plans had worked. My phone vibrated with a message from Tyler Phillips:

Hi Alex, Breeze FM have confirmed they'll attend, plus assorted bloggers, and the local paper guys who are bringing a photographer too. Will try to drop by myself at some point. Best of luck for today! Tyler.

"We've got plenty of press coming, thanks to Tyler," I said as the others came up to me.

"Ah, brilliant," Ben beamed. "Nice one, Alex." He gestured for everyone to come round. "So, guys, this is it. . ."

Oh good, Ben was going to do one of those team pep talk things. I'd never been part of a team before, so this was pretty exciting for me.

Ben huddled us all closer together. "Charm the pants off the journalists, make the punters happy." He lowered his voice. "We know there's an enemy in our midst, so keep your eyes peeled. Anything looks off, anything at all, we make sure we tell each other. I'm assuming there's more of us than there is of them, we can manage this."

"GO, TEAM!" I said, because I thought that was the appropriate time to say that. Sadly, it wasn't.

"This is for Wonderland. For Maggie," Ben said. "She's a tricky old thing, but we love her, and I think, in her own peculiar way, she kind of loves us. So let's make this work."

"GO, TEAM!"

"We can show everyone that Wonderland *does* have a place in Newsands," Ben continued, ignoring me. "And Maggie deserves that, after all the years of work she's ploughed in."

I nodded, solemnly.

"GO, TEAM!" Ben shouted.

"YAY!" I replied, giving everyone a high five. I liked this team business very much.

Efia and Bella scooted off to intercept the journalist and photographer from the local paper, and Ben went to man the Roswell Experience. Kem emerged from Eve's tarot booth as I passed by. "Reckon this tarot shiz is true?" he said to me.

I shrugged. "I mean, I kind of hope not, because if it is, I'm doomed."

Kem laughed, even though I wasn't joking. "Apparently 'my fortunes do not lie in the place I've been looking' so I'm ditching the fruits today and I'm off to play Storm Racer instead." He glanced around at all the customers. "Whilst I can still actually get on it. Never seen so many people in the place, man!"

I smiled, because it was true: the place had never been so busy. Happy people, spending money, enjoying themselves. It made my heart full. And then it sank a bit. Over by the main door, Efia was gathering the invited journalists and bloggers for a tour, just as resident troublemaker and machine-licker Billy, and his obnoxious mates, walked in – one of them with a Super Soaker strapped across his back. One thing we didn't need on relaunch day, with so much riding on remedying our bad reputation, was some kid squirting water all over everyone and all the electronics.

I took a breath and walked up to them. "Gentlemen," I said.

That stopped them in their tracks.

I gave an incredibly courteous smile. "A fine morning for a contest, wouldn't you say?"

"Yeah, whatever, mate," Billy snarled.

"You and me, Billy, on the game of your choice."

"Got no money," Billy sniffed.

"I'm paying."

"What do I get when I win?"

"The satisfaction of knowing, once and for all, that I'm a total loser." I grinned at him. "Unless, of course, you're worried I'm not?"

What looked like an evil grin played on his lips. "Dance Fusion X-treme," he said.

OK, I knew why he'd go for that. Dance Fusion is a two-player game where you compete to hit the correct pads on the base of the machine, in time with the beats of a music track. Billy had me down for a total dork with no eye-foot coordination and was making the assumption that because I was awkward and pretty quiet, it meant I couldn't bust a move or two.

Billy was wrong.

I was much worse than that. I could barely coordinate my hand and mouth whilst eating.

"Deal," I said. "Best of three. No rematches."

Billy shrugged. "Won't need a rematch, *Bambi*."

I grimaced, because I was pretty sure that was a direct reference to when I fell flat on my face every single time I tried to stand up on the ice rink last Christmas, and annoyingly, that's something he clearly saw and remembered.

His mates crowded round as we both stepped on to the machine and I let him scroll through the song options on the screen. I froze as he hovered over Paranoia Survivor Max, which is pretty much the toughest song in existence, coming in at around 290 bpm and over six hundred arrows. Luckily, the kid wasn't that much of an idiot, and he scrolled past it, selecting "Move Your Feet" by Junior Senior instead. I inserted two pound coins in the slot, and I gripped the back bar with my hands, before noticing he wasn't and taking them off again. OK, he was a pro with great balance, I was probably screwed, but I was just gonna go through with this. We were off.

We both mucked up the first few moves, but within a few seconds he'd found his rhythm and his feet were darting over the platform in pretty much perfect synchronicity with the arrows. Every time I glanced across, his life bar was topped up and the screen was ablaze with "PERFECT!" and "GREAT!" messages. Meanwhile, I was literally clomping around like Frankenstein's monster. Zero grace. Nothing nimble or swift about me. I was a mess. But I dug in, and by halfway through I was marginally better, although that might just have been a hallucination based on lack of oxygen reaching my brain. Point was, I was still in the game, and I was actually now getting a few "PERFECT" and "GREAT!" messages myself. Billy's mates were really into it – like, it's a full-on competition, and they were cheering and shouting his name, and a couple of them actually took *my side* and were cheering *me,* and in the midst of all this, out of the corner of my eye, I saw Efia pass by with her little group of journalists and bloggers, and all they saw was a group of kids having *the best time* on the Dance Fusion machine. No one was swearing, no one was causing trouble, we were all just laughing and cheering and enjoying it. And I'd done it, I'd actually resolved a situation by myself, and it didn't go wrong. I didn't care that I was blatantly going to lose this match, and the next two – I had sorted this. Me. For Wonderland.

He won the first one, by some margin. "Need a piss," he said, heading off towards the customer toilets.

"Be back soon!" I called after him. "Best of three!"

"Sure, sure." He shrugged.

I had a quick flick through the song choices whilst

he was gone – if I picked something I was at least vaguely familiar with, and with fewer steps, maybe I could win the next one.

Moments later, this piercing, crazy-loud bell started ringing, and beating Billy became the least of my worries.

CHAPTER TWENTY-SEVEN

All the customers we'd worked so hard to get into the place were streaming back out again, as the fire alarm continued to ring. On the plus side, there appeared to be no obvious signs of smoke or flames. But on the bad side, the invited journalists were observing all this. Still, these things happen and hopefully—

"HELP! HELP US!"

The strangled, plaintive cries were coming from the Mirror Maze.

"WE CAN'T GET OUT!"

I locked eyes with Ben and we both darted over to the maze entrance. We'd only entered the first section when the problem became clear. Ben was pushing one of the doors that was meant to open, only it was stuck. "What the hell?" he muttered.

Ben gave the door another couple of firm shoves, then rammed it with his shoulder, the door splintering open into the next section. "WE'RE GONNA GET YOU OUT!" Ben shouted to the trapped customers.

But then Ben tried the next door that was meant to open, and that too wouldn't budge. When he glanced back at me, he was pale. "Alex? This isn't right," he said.

A cold shiver ran through me. I knew it wasn't. One door was not entirely unlikely, given how ramshackle Wonderland was. Two was looking like it was deliberate.

Ben shoulder-barged the second door, which also splintered open into the third section. The doors weren't hard to open if you knew which sections were doors, but no way would a customer know that. Ben turned to me. "Those two sections are the ones that lead out of the maze – if you can't get through them, you're basically stuck in here," he said.

We found the trapped teenagers in the next section and led them out the way we came, trying to play down what had gone wrong. But when we walked out of the main entrance with them, it was straight into the path of at least four cameras, belonging to the invited journalists and bloggers.

"It's OK, everyone, it's a false alarm!" Maggie announced. "We're just resetting the system now."

But it didn't matter. If that had been a real fire, we

would just have had several kids trapped in the Mirror Maze, and no obvious way to get them out. I was no journalist, but even I could see the story here – and it wasn't a good one.

Meanwhile, Carl Hudson was standing in front of the crowd, looking very sombre about the whole situation. "Folks, this is obviously terrible, but we are offering FREE CHICKEN NUGGETS on the pier today, and all rides are half price, so come on over while they sort this mess out!" The fickle crowd started drifting off towards the pier and he turned his attention to me. "I'll keep them entertained for you. I'm sure they'll come back when you're ready, son," he said.

He gave me a little wink that made me realize Maggie had probably been right all this time. He might come across as a sweet little old man, but Carl Hudson knew damn well what he was doing.

Ben pulled me away from him and we walked across the road and over to the wall where Efia was standing with Caleb, who had left his lemon to check what was going down. "Christ," she said. "Didn't you ever learn not to run back inside burning buildings?"

"Wasn't burning," Ben replied.

"Don't you ever do that again," she said. "You didn't know what was going on, not for sure, and one thing I could do without is losing all my mates in some—"

"Efia," Ben interrupted. "The doors in the Mirror

Maze had been tampered with."

She froze and stared at him. "How?"

"I'm not sure." Ben shrugged. "Like, stuck with something, so they wouldn't easily open."

Efia nodded, slowly. "This was a set-up?"

"I reckon," Ben said. "And I'd guess that whoever gaffed the maze also set the fire alarm off. And planted the bad egg in the goose. And is behind all the notes and the newspaper tip-off."

Caleb was all ears, looking between us all like WT actual F?! Since he didn't yet know about any of this, I guess it sounded like he'd just walked into a Scooby Doo episode.

"Could have been any one of them," Ben said. We all followed his gaze, over the road, towards Wonderland. He was looking at Billy, and sure, Billy would cause us trouble, or might be more than happy to take some cash from someone else to cause us trouble. But so would Drake, depending how much debt he was in. Carl Hudson was still shepherding our punters towards his pier – would a long-standing rivalry push him to engineer all this?

"But why?" I asked. "What's the point? What are they trying to achieve?"

We watched as all the journalists swarmed around the trapped customers, getting the story that was going to damn us.

"More bad PR," Ben muttered. "This is gonna force

us bankrupt at this rate."

Efia closed her eyes and took a deep breath. "Oh my god, *of course*. We've been so stupid. That's exactly what this is all about." She shook her head. "Cover for me, I'll be back as soon as I can." And made off down the street.

"Wait, Efia!" I said.

She turned back. "Yes?"

"What if it's dangerous?" I had no idea, but it seemed like it could be.

Efia laughed.

"If you need some help..." Caleb said. "I'm good at . . . helping."

I stifled a smile. That was the first time I'd seen Caleb be even slightly awkward. It was cute.

"It's not dangerous," Efia told him.

Caleb nodded. "And what's the one thing we've all learned from horror films?"

"I've no idea, but this isn't a horror film, Caleb."

"Yeah?" Caleb said. "Well, from what I'm hearing between you guys, something's going down, and when it's going down, you never split the squad up, do you? Rookie error. That's when the killing starts."

"Oh my god," Efia said.

"Just sayin' – safety in numbers." Caleb stuffed his hands in the pockets of his shorts. "Plus, I can always get you refreshments or whatever. I have uses."

I had to give it to him: between suggesting she was in

danger of being chopped up by a crazed killer and offering to ply her with drinks and food, he was hard to refuse.

"OK," Efia said.

"Yay!" I said. I couldn't help it. Efia glared at me and I cleared my throat. "I mean, that seems sensible. In the circumstances."

"But this isn't. . ." She trailed off, thinking better of it.

"Not what?" Caleb asked, a picture of innocence.

"It's nothing, you're just helping me."

Caleb nodded. "Yeah. That's what I just offered to do."

Efia turned and strode off down the street, giving Caleb just enough time to give me a thumbs up and a grin, and then scamper off after her.

We were all allowed back in the building ten minutes later, but the damage had been done. Half the customers had wandered off to the pier for their free chicken nuggets, and the journalists had all got their story now – of how Wonderland was basically a death trap. Only time would tell if this was the final nail in the coffin.

It was during my afternoon break that I cornered Bella. Ben was busy manning the Roswell Experience (which the customers were loving, by the way), so I had her to myself.

And I had cupcakes.

I'd already nipped out to get a couple of red velvet

ones, which I offered up to her with a hopeful smile as we sat with our tea in the staffroom.

"Alex, I love you," Bella said, taking one.

I nodded. I hoped she would still "love me" when I'd told her what I was about to tell her.

"Ben's offered to take me swimming," I said, thinking it best to just get it out there, straightforward and honest.

She smiled at me. "Yeah, I know."

"Oh."

"He said."

"He did? OK. Well."

"He's a good swimmer, and he taught some of the kids when he used to work at the leisure centre, so you're in good hands."

I nodded.

She ate some of her cupcake.

I glanced at mine, but I didn't feel like it.

"You two are cute together," she said, after a dreadful silence.

I stared at her until she glanced up.

"What?" she said.

I didn't know what to say.

A smile spread across her face. "Well, you *are*. I'm just saying."

I jolted myself into action. "Yeah, but we're not, we're not . . . are we? We're not."

"Well, why not?" she said.

I swallowed. "Um..." I mean, *you*, Bella. That's why not. Did I really have to point out the obvious to her?

Bella put her cupcake down. Oh no. *Serious talk*. "Ben and I aren't..."

"What?"

"Maybe he should speak to you about..."

"What?"

"We're not going out, right?"

"*What?!*"

Bella sighed. "I mean, we kind of were. But only kind of. For a bit."

"How kind of? What bit?"

"We ended up going to Leavers' Prom together because neither of us had a date, and, well..." She sighed and shook her head. "You know, have this chat with Ben. I'm just saying, he's not my boyfriend. He's my friend. Best friend. But that's it. So this swimming thing..."

"Which is *just* swimming!" I protested.

Bella laughed, and I must have looked horrified because she then stopped laughing and said, "Yeah, no, I know it is."

I nodded. I had so many questions. Like what the actual hell? And if he wasn't with Bella, did that mean he was gay?

"But thanks for the guilt-cake," Bella grinned, finishing it off.

"It's not a guilt-cake, it's just a . . . cake-cake."

"And *have fun*."

And she ruffled my hair and walked out of the staffroom.

We ended up being a bit busier than usual that afternoon, and the new attractions had been well received – people had properly screamed at the Roswell Experience, we'd sold a surprising quantity of coconut milk lattes, and an entire hen party had turned up for Gay Bingo, albeit no actual confirmed gays – but the whole fire alarm thing had definitely put a downer on the relaunch. It was also *so* hot, and there was no relief when I walked out of the main entrance at five p.m., straight into the oppressive afternoon heat, airless and stagnant, and the crowds of holidaymakers who were starting to make their way back to hotels and self-catering flats, but just seemed to want to get in my way as I tried to cross to the road. When Newsands was this busy, I just wanted to shower it all away, then lock myself in a dark, cool room until late September, when everything went back to normal. "You're weirdly quiet," Ben said as he caught up with me.

"No..."

"Er . . . *yes*!"

The truth was, I *was*. There was all this stuff I wanted to talk to Ben about, but I didn't know where to begin.

Luckily, I was saved by Efia as she scooted up to us, with Caleb in tow. "Walk and talk, boys, walk and talk!"

"Where have you been?!" Ben said, as we both

jumped into a (completely unwelcome in this heat) speedy stride to keep up. "You've been gone all day!"

"What did you tell Maggie?"

"Said you had tummy troubles," I told her.

"OK," she said. "Now look, there's still a chance this is all some scheme by Carl Hudson to keep custom at the pier, and I still believe there's someone, either a staff member or customer, at Wonderland who has been carrying out all the stuff that's happened. But I've been looking at the bigger picture. Like, who's the puppet master here?"

"I'm listening," Ben said.

Efia stopped us in our tracks and we turned to take in the row of shops along the front. "Behold, the seafront businesses of Newsands," Efia said, sweeping her hand along the vista.

"Inspiring," I said.

Ben snorted in amusement.

"I present item one of my evidence," Efia continued, ignoring us. "The Bellevue Café. A stalwart of the Newsands promenade since . . . well, it's always been here. Except, as we now know, the owners sold it, on the quiet, six weeks ago."

I clocked the look of smug satisfaction on Efia's face. "Oh my god, do you know who to?" I said.

Efia nodded. "A company called 'Develop Newsands'."

Something about that name sounded familiar.

"Who are they?" Ben said.

"No idea, but I can confirm they are one of a number of companies that have been buying up properties right along the front." Efia pointed at the pick 'n' mix shop a couple of doors up. "Sweet Treats was purchased by Foresight Properties recently too, and in both cases, planning permission has been lodged to demolish, and rebuild with retail units on the ground floor and apartments above, including penthouses at the top that will probably be worth nearly a million."

Ben whistled. "Still don't quite get the appeal of the place."

"Like Drake told me and Alex, the place is changing, Ben," Efia said. "I spoke to one of the estate agents, and she told me that people from London are cashing in their properties there and buying bigger places for half the price in Newsands, whilst still being able to commute back to London for work if they need to. Others are just going for a lifestyle change – living the good life by the sea, going self-employed, slower pace. . ."

"Snail's pace," I added.

"Yeah, but older people like that," Efia said. "But you're missing the point. Two properties near Wonderland have recently changed hands – and I think that leaves two possibilities—"

Ben opened his mouth to speak, but Efia put her hand on his arm. "Don't ruin my moment," she told him.

He shut his mouth.

"Number one," Efia said, "the developers don't want a place like Wonderland dragging down the area, acting like a magnet for 'feral youth', and damaging the asking price of their new apartments."

I nodded. It sounded reasonable.

"Number two," she continued, "the developers want Wonderland too – they want to demolish that as well, and rebuild, just like the other units."

That also sounded reasonable.

"Either way," Efia said, "my money is on one of the developers trying to either force Wonderland bankrupt through bad publicity, and close it that way, or force Maggie to sell, and get hold of the property to redevelop."

I blew out a breath. If that was true, this was a lot bigger than I ever imagined.

"So what happens now?" Ben asked.

"I need to dig around a bit," Efia said. "See if I can find any paperwork from any developers. Apparently you can find out who the directors of companies are through something called Companies House – they keep some sort of register. But find that out, and I reckon we've good chance of unmasking who's really behind all this."

"So, this isn't about someone with a grudge at all?" Ben said. "It's probably not even Carl Hudson being stupidly competitive. It's..."

"I reckon it's business," Efia said. "Underhanded business."

"Can we do anything to help?" Ben asked.

"Boys, boys," Efia said. "I don't want anything to get in the way of your little get-together tonight!" She grinned at us both.

"We're just swimming," I said.

"Yeah, it's just swimming, Efia," Ben added.

"It's not a date," we both said at the same time. We looked at each other. We both went red again.

Efia rolled her eyes. "Oh, this is *painful*. OK! You enjoy your 'not a date' and meanwhile, Efia will continue her investigations. And yes, I am talking about myself in the third person, because I think Efia's done rather well and I appreciate her. I'm going to treat Efia to an entire bag of doughnuts." She put one hand on each of our shoulders. "I'm shipping you so hard, *Bex*. Aubergine emoji, banana emoji, winking tongue man."

Ben rolled his eyes. "Really?"

"Circus tent emoji," she continued.

I screwed my face up.

"Erection," Ben clarified. "Apparently."

"Hand job emoji."

"That's just a fist," Ben said.

"Volcano, splashing water emoji."

"Got any more?" Ben asked.

"That's *quite enough* for a first date!" She laughed, then headed off down the promenade, a definite spring in her step, Caleb scampering after her.

I didn't know what to say. I was mortified.

Ben scratched the back of his head. "Seven o'clock, OK?"

"Sure."

"You OK to cycle?"

"Uh-huh. Where are we going?"

"A little spot I know." He smiled, and his dimples broke me again. "If that sounds all right?"

"Sounds awesome."

"Bring your swimming shorts, a towel. . ." He lightly tugged at the hem of my T-shirt, like he was checking the quality of the fabric or something. He flicked his eyes up to mine. "See you in a bit then."

And I couldn't speak because I was all fireworks emoji, love hearts emoji, two boys holding hands emoji.

CHAPTER TWENTY-EIGHT

We rode our bikes out of town, until the roads became country lanes. Ben wouldn't tell me where we were going, except to assure me it "wasn't too far" and, alarmingly "he wasn't going to murder me in a remote location and bury my body in an old drain", which sounded way too detailed and thought-out for my liking.

In any case, I was merrily peddling along after him anyway because I honestly think, when it comes to cute boys, any common sense I might possibly possess just goes right out of the window.

Ben looked back over his shoulder, presumably to check I was keeping up, then swung a left off the lane, on to a dirt track that led towards a wooded area. If it had been a gloomy, chilly night, this probably would have been serial killer territory, but with the warm glow of the sun starting to set between the trees, and the fact it was still insanely hot (but at least now with a very gentle breeze), it was actually really beautiful. We cycled fast, standing on our pedals and hovering above our seats over the dips and bumps in the track, until we pulled up by the side of a lake just inside the wooded area.

"Wow," I said.

"My secret spot." Ben smiled, lying his bike down on the ground.

I dropped my bike next to his. "Um . . . is this where we're going to swim?" I'll be honest, that really alarmed me.

"It's a great spot to swim," Ben said.

"Is it . . . *safe*?"

Ben smiled . . . but didn't actually answer my question. "Get your shorts on."

"Oh, they're on."

Ben nodded. "Oh. Me too."

I smiled. I liked the fact we'd both put our swim shorts on before leaving home. Ben smiled too. "Forward planning, saves time!" he said.

I nodded, swallowed, and hoped Ben couldn't see my hands were shaking.

Ben kicked his trainers and socks off, and then pulled his T-shirt up over his head.

His stomach was smooth and flat, with a tantalizing hint of abs. His chest, also smooth, with the beginnings of some pretty lovely pecs. Lean and taut, those deep brown eyes, the little freckles on his nose, those dimples. . . He caught me looking.

"Alex?"

"Huh?"

"T-shirt off would help."

"Oh!" I pulled it off. "Yeah."

I dropped it on the ground next to me and he smiled. "The water's not too bad, once you get used to it." He walked towards the edge where the water rippled up against the ground.

"Do you come here a lot?"

He nodded. "It's a nice place just to think."

He was right. It seemed like it would be. Peaceful. Just the birds gently chirping in the trees.

"Come on!" he insisted.

I padded over to him, so we were both standing with our feet just in the water. "It gets deep pretty quick," he said. I felt his warm hand suddenly on the small of my back. "It's OK though, it won't go up further than your chest, and I've got you."

I nodded.

"Best thing is just to run in," he said.

I exhaled unsteadily.

He grabbed my hand, and before I knew what was really happening, he pulled us both into the lake in one swift tug, and we both tumbled and splashed in. And just as I lost my footing and was about to suck up a lungful of lake water, his hands were around my waist, keeping me upright. We both gasped with the shock of the cold water, but laughing too, breathless and exhilarated. Then his hands found mine as we bobbed in the water, feet occasionally brushing the silt and stones on the bottom. "OK?" he said.

"That was . . . surprising," I said.

"You'd have taken half an hour to get in otherwise." He squeezed my hands in his. "I've got you though."

We stayed like that as our breathing settled down and slowed, and the water started to feel beautifully warm.

"Come on," he said. "I want you to hold on to my shoulders with your hands, and just let yourself float up."

I didn't really want to let go of his hands, and he must have got bored of waiting for me to do it, because he just moved my hands himself, placing them on his shoulders. "Like this," he said, as though I might not have understood his simple instruction. "You can press down on me," he continued. "Use me to keep yourself steady and just relax your body and float."

I tried, but I couldn't.

"Just relax," Ben repeated. "Let your lower half go floppy."

I pretended he didn't just say that and tried again, which just resulted in a hell of a lot of leg splashing.

Ben laughed.

"I'm trying," I protested.

"I know you are."

"I think I'm doomed to never swim."

"No, you're not," he smiled.

"I'm an idiot."

"No. *You're not.*"

Our eyes locked together at that point.

And I felt it again.

The same feeling as outside the pizza place that time.

His hands found my hips, and he stepped towards me, slightly weightless in the water.

I moved my hands down to his waist too, and he caught his breath and tensed. "Sorry," I muttered.

He didn't reply, just rested his forehead against mine again. "Hi," he muttered.

"Um . . . hi. Hello," I said.

His breath was heavy as he pulled me closer to him, our stomachs brushing under the water, legs intertwined, as he pressed himself into me and then his lips were on mine or mine were on his, I'm not quite sure who initiated it, and. . . It. Was. Epic. I mean, I really don't mean to brag, but my first kiss was happening with a really hot boy, in a *lake,* at *sunset,* no one was drunk, you know, I think that's definitely a *win.*

He kissed gently. So tenderly. Like every single one had been thought about and meant something and whilst this wasn't the time to be thinking of middle-aged women,

I thought of Maggie, because she was right. When the moment comes, you *do* know what to do.

We came to a slow, gradual stop, and he rested his head on my shoulder, nestled into my neck, and sighed.

"Great swimming lesson," I muttered.

He laughed.

"Can't wait for the next one."

He kissed me again, just once this time, and then sighed. I saw the look in his eyes – the same conflict I'd seen outside the pizza place. Not that again. "OK, Ben," I said. "I surrender. This is the moment I surrender."

He just stared at me, mouth slightly open.

I was going against every word of advice, but to hell with the advice. If this was going to be "too keen" then so be it, I was going to be that person. I was not going to be a game player any longer. "Ben, I *totally love you.*"

His eyes widened.

I nevertheless pressed on.

"You are so perfect. You're so nice. I know I'm doing this all wrong. I know I should be playing it cool and hard to get, but I want you to absolutely know – I am not cool about this. I am . . . the opposite of cool, I am . . . *really hot* about this. About you."

"Alex. . ."

"'Love' just felt like the best word, Ben. That's all. It's more than 'like' and it's not just 'lust' so what else is there? *Really* like? I *enormously* like you?"

"Alex—"

"OK, I do now regret saying it all like that."

He blew out a breath. "Let's get out of the water."

He reached for my hand and helped me out of the water, before we sat down by the lake's edge, legs drawn up, with our towels draped over our shoulders. "I'm sorry," I said. "Everything I said just then was all wrong."

"Don't be sorry."

"I don't even. . . Ben, I'm confused because I thought you were with Bella, in fact *you said* you were, and now. . . I mean, it's cool, whatever you are, even if you don't know, it's cool. I just . . . I guess I wanted *you* to know where *I* was at, anyway."

He hung his head between his knees and sighed. "But for ages, I thought you liked Caleb."

"No, I liked you!"

"But you said you liked him!"

"No, *you* said I did, and I went along with it because I thought if you were saying that, it meant you didn't like me!"

He blew out a breath. "OK, so we got quite a bit wrong then."

"*What about Bella?!*"

"OK, so, me and Bella have been best mates since Year Nine, and we went to prom together and we sort of kissed, and we kind of became a bit of a thing, except not really much of one. I dunno, it felt like everyone else was pairing off, and so we did too, except it never really felt quite right, if I'm honest. And I'm sure Bella would say the same. We both agreed the whole debacle was over whilst she was away traveling."

I wasn't sure I dared ask, but I wanted to know. "How did you know it was over?"

Ben looked up at me. "Bella knew before I did."

"How?"

He cracked a smile. "Because one day she said to me, 'You know all you talk about is this Alex guy?' And I was like, 'No!' and she said, 'Er, *yes*!' And she told me, 'You like him, don't you?' and as soon as she said it, it just slotted into place and, you know, I had to admit, yeah, I did. *I do*."

He was telling me he liked me, and my heart was pounding. "And Bella is . . . she was fine with this?"

Ben nodded. "Bella is such a cool girl. Nothing fazes her. And she knows me better than I know myself, pretty much. I mean, obviously, I think this proves it. She's been trying to get us together since she got back. That whole thing in the pizza place, when you were with Caleb? She was all, 'Let's feed each other dough balls, it might make him jealous!'"

"Oh . . . how . . . manipulative," I said.

Ben glanced across at me. "Caleb was doing the same with you, *blatantly*."

I stifled a grin.

Ben sighed. "But Alex ... you're going to have to be

patient with me. It's taken me a while to realize I like boys, so this is all new. It's why I got a bit funny with you in the cleaning cupboard that time – my head was all over the place, and I thought maybe you would want to talk about the fact I'd tried to kiss you the night before—"

"So you did try to kiss me!"

"Oh my god, yes! I mean, I'd kind of hoped you might kiss me first, you know, since you've clearly known you're gay for a while and I'm a total newbie, but you didn't look like you were going to, so I thought I might try, but I bottled it, so."

"I would have! Ben, I so would have, but Bella!"

"Yeah, I know," Ben said. "But then in work the next day, you seemed super weird, and I just assumed I'd overstepped the mark, like, you fancied Caleb, and I was just being all obsessed with you, like some lovesick puppy. And then you suggested bringing Bella to dinner, and that was seriously friend-zoning me. That's why I backed off."

I blinked at him. "Oh, wow. We're ridiculous. That's what I was thinking! That's why I backed off!"

"OK, wow. Yeah, we are ridiculous." He laughed. "Can we just … pretend that conversation never happened?"

"What conversation?" I waited to see if he got my little joke. "Hey? What conversation?!"

He laughed again, shaking his head at my appalling comedic efforts. Then his face softened. "I like you, Alex."

"Really like? Enormously like?"

"Yeah," Ben said. "And then some." Hearing that, it was like New Year's Eve and all the fireworks exploding at once.

He put his arm across my shoulders and pulled me into him, and we rested our heads against each other.

"It's been a tough year though," he muttered.

"I know it has."

"What with Mum, and then Dad sinking into this pit of despair . . . like, I was seriously wondering if anything good would ever happen again."

I put my arm around his waist. "It's not remotely the same, but at the start of this summer, I wasn't in the best place either. Everyone seemed to have moved on, except me. And I didn't think anything would change . . . and then I met you. And everything did."

"Snap," Ben said, giving me a little smile.

He shuffled round towards me a bit, rested his forehead on my shoulder and traced his finger along the path of a little droplet of water, running down from my shoulder. I gasped as his finger drifted over my chest, nearly exploding into a million pieces as he brushed past my nipple, then held my breath as he wandered down over my stomach, coming to a rest at the waistband of my swim shorts.

I was an absolute quivering mess.

"Can I kiss you again?" I asked.

"I was hoping you might," he said.

So we did.

CHAPTER TWENTY-NINE

It was Saturday, and I wasn't on the rota until midday, which meant I could have a lie-in, basking in the awesomeness of everything that had happened the night before with Ben, and enjoying the fact that tonight I would be going to the pool party with an actual boy, like some sort of regular person for whom things actually work out. A stupid grin spread across my face as I relived the previous night for about the ten millionth time – Ben's hand, gently tracing down my chest, towards my stomach, and the waistband of my swimming shorts. Our kisses, more breathless and urgent. I can't get enough of him. He's lying on top of me, and we're seconds away from tipping over into something neither of us would be able to stop – I can feel the blood coursing through me, adrenaline, excitement, but also *fear,* because I really don't know what I'm doing, and nor does he, and we both want to, but we also both *don't* want to, not yet, not quite yet. It doesn't matter. This is enough. He's trembling and so am I. It's because I want him so much. I hope it's the same for him. He whispers in my ear and I totally melt.

"Rise and shine, it's poached egg and avocado time!"

I crash about and whip my duvet practically up to my ears just as Kendra flings my bedroom door open, like she's never heard of the wisdom of knocking before you enter a boy's bedroom because obviously we wouldn't be doing anything other than a spot of cross-stitching, or crocheting some booties for the next-door neighbour's new baby.

"Hi, morning!" I gasp.

"Poached egg – protein. Avocado – one of your five a day. It's ready, so can you come downstairs now, please?" She crossed her arms and raised her eyebrows.

"OK," I said. "I'm coming."

She nodded. "I'll wait."

"No," I said. I definitely did not want her to do that.

"If I go, you'll just go back to sleep."

I shook my head. "I promise I won't."

"Get up, Alex. It's ten o'clock. You can't just fester here all—"

"I'm not festering!" I protested. "I'm . . . relaxing."

"The poached eggs will go hard," she told me, advancing into the room.

I mean, I literally couldn't have cared less about the eggs, but she was acting like the situation would start World War Three. I gripped on to the duvet, because I was pretty sure what was going to happen next.

"Up!" she demanded, tugging at the bottom of my duvet.

"No! Kendra! I am doing!"

"Up!"

"Please!"

She reached down with her other hand. She had both hands on my duvet. I also had both of mine on my end, but she was a woman with rock-hard abs who did kick-boxing, and I was a teenage boy with disappointing muscle development and no strength. The odds were stacked against me, so I went into damage limitation mode, gripping on to the duvet with every part of my body possible, while Kendra attempted to whip the whole thing away. I scrunched myself in a ball, and with part of the duvet wedged between my thighs, and another bit wrapped around my arms, I rolled off the bed, using the momentum as I dropped on to my bedroom floor to take the rest of the duvet with me. I ended up face down, my boxers still halfway down my legs because I hadn't had chance to pull them back up, with my bare arse in the air. But it was still better than the alternative.

"For the love of god, at least wear some boxers in bed," Kendra said.

I groaned into the duvet.

"One egg or two?"

Why was this still happening?

"I don't know – two?" I said.

"Do you want a side of spinach?"

"No! Thank you. No spinach."

I buried my face back in the duvet. I heard her move, and then felt a ripple of cold air across my bottom as she pulled the door shut after her. I waited until I heard her descend the stairs, then rolled out of my duvet nest and quickly pulled my boxers back up and then some joggers and a white T-shirt.

"Nice time with Ben?" Dad grinned as I walked through to the kitchen.

"Yup."

I poured myself a glass of orange juice, while Kendra silently mashed an avocado with simmering aggression.

"So, is Ben going to be your date for the pool party?" Dad asked.

I perched on one of the breakfast bar stools. "I guess." I tried to play it cool, but the smile I was suppressing spread across my face anyway.

Dad laughed. "Nice one, Alex. He seems like a nice lad."

"You've barely met him."

"I'm a good judge of character!" Dad said.

I came *this close* to raising my eyebrow and glancing

in Kendra's direction. Instead, I just smiled, and Dad squeezed my shoulder as he went to help Kendra plate up.

He glanced back at me after exchanging a few words with Kendra. "Alex?"

"Oh, sorry, what do you need me to do?" I said.

"Nothing. I was just going to say, I'm glad you're happy."

"Thanks, Dad," I smiled. "Me too."

I bounced along the pavement of the promenade, weaving between the lunchtime crowds of holidaymakers, most of whom were wanting to grab fish and chips or ice cream before returning to the beach to catch the afternoon sun. I had started this summer so down and out, but now, just a few weeks later, everything had changed. For the first time in my life, I felt excited about the future, and I was ready. I was ready to jump in and see where the rapids of life took me.

First stop, the bakery, to get some fresh blueberry muffins for the squad. I bought six, and just as I pulled out a fiver to pay for them, a little card fluttered out and on to the floor. And that's when I saw it:

Tyler Phillips

Managing Director, Develop Newsands Ltd.

I just stared at it. I hadn't made the connection before; why would I? Tyler told me he was on some sort of committee to help local traders, but his business card made it clear he ran the company who had recently bought the Bellevue Café.

Oh my god.

I ran out of the bakery, then ran back again and gave them back the muffins I hadn't paid for, and then ran all the way to where Efia and Ben were waiting on our usual bench.

"Guys!" I said. "Develop Newsands is run by Tyler Phillips, the same guy that offered to help with the PR for the relaunch, if he's behind this, if he wants Wonderland as well as the Bellevue, maybe he got all the press to come to the relaunch knowing it would go wrong, for maximum bad publicity!" I could barely breathe, but I had to get this all out. "He seemed like such a nice guy, but what if it's all an act? What if it's him?"

"We know," Efia said.

My eyes widened. "You do? So it's true?"

"Alex. . ." She looked away. "God, Alex."

I stared at them both, neither of them looking back at me. "I didn't know," I said. "He came up to me at the lemon, I mean you saw, but ask Caleb! He seemed genuine, I didn't even properly look at his business card, I—"

"Alex, we know it's not Tyler," Efia said, standing up to face me.

OK, now I was confused. "What?"

"It's not Tyler, is it?" Efia said.

I shook my head in bewilderment. "Then . . . who?"

She stared at me for about five silent seconds. "We know what you did, *what you've been doing*. Why don't you just come clean, Alex? Please? Just admit it, 'cause we know now."

I stared back at her, stomach tingling.

"At least do the brave thing and own it," she continued.

I swallowed. "What. . ." I looked between her (glaring at me) and Ben (still not even looking up). "I don't understand. . . *Tyler*—"

"Not Tyler, *you*!"

"What . . . what have I done?"

Efia gave a contemptuous laugh and shook her head. "You're playing innocent? Of course you are. You had us all fooled, so good job there."

I looked, desperately, at Ben. "Ben? I—" I reached out to touch his arm, but he shrugged me off.

"Stop it," he muttered, standing up next to Efia. "Just . . . stop it." He still wouldn't look at me.

"OK," I said. "I have literally no idea what any of this is about. I haven't done anything. Not that I know of. So, please, just tell me!" I blew out a breath and flopped down on the bench. "I mean, what the hell is this?"

"No, Alex," Efia said, handing me a sheet of A4. "What the hell *is this*?"

I looked over the typed letter, on headed paper from

"Foresight Properties Ltd" and addressed to Maggie at Wonderland. It was an expression of interest in the property, asking whether Maggie had considered selling, or whether she might consider it "for the right price". It was signed by someone called "Georgie Graham".

I frowned. "So, it's not Tyler's company, but property developers *were* after Wonderland?"

"Oh yes, but you already know that. You've known it all along."

"Efia, how would I know that?"

"Who's the registered director of 'Foresight Properties Ltd', Alex? Who is it?"

I held my hands out. "Literally, I've no idea!"

Efia nodded, then bent down to my level, so we were eye to eye. "Kendra King."

My mouth went completely dry.

"So, three months ago, Maggie gets this letter asking to sell," Efia said, while I sat staring at the letter. "She obviously refused, because Wonderland is still here and it's not up for sale. You then suddenly show up, get *injured*, start working here, and what happens? Threatening letters start to appear, most of which you just so happen to find. And then the ante is upped, isn't it? Kendra's little mole is planted right in the heart of Wonderland, and like a virus, you worm your way in, fooling everyone into thinking you're a harmless, sweet little boy, who wouldn't say boo to a goose. And all that time, you're plotting to bring the place down for your rich stepmother."

"She's not my step—"

"Who had the opportunity to plant the bad egg? *You.* Who knew which doors to tamper with in the Mirror Maze? Get the bad publicity, make the locals think we're trouble, turn everyone against us, so the takings drop, and Maggie is forced to sell to whoever will take it. And who'll be there when she does? Your stepmum and her property company, ready to regenerate the town – or rather, get rid of everyone who lives here and fill it full of people with money."

I shook my head. "No..."

"We liked you, Alex," Efia said. "We thought you were our friend. We thought we could trust you. And all this time..."

"Ben!" I said, hoping he would see sense. "Please!"

But his eyes were full of hurt, like I'd stabbed him.

"I swear to you," I said, trembling as my world collapsed around me, "I didn't know about any of this. I believe you, of course I do, but I didn't know! I barely even speak to Kendra, I didn't even know what she really does for a living, I—" My heart was hammering, my head was light, everything was swimming. "I didn't," I muttered. "I wouldn't..."

"But you did, didn't you, Alex?" Efia said. "Was it fun, Alex? For you? Was it all some undercover bit of excitement?

See if you can get away with it, yeah? Thing is, it's not a game for us. Me and Ben aren't working at Wonderland just to earn a bit of extra pocket money on top of our allowance from our rich parents who own companies. We need these jobs. But you wouldn't understand that. You wouldn't know what it's like to really struggle for money, as long as you and your family get richer, who cares, right?"

That wasn't true. I wanted to say that my dad wasn't rich, that after the divorce with Mum he'd probably have to sell the house, that Kendra wasn't family anyway, that—

"Anything to say, Alex?" Efia said.

I looked up at her, so angry, her eyes full of hatred. "Um." I swallowed.

"Um," she said, in a mocking voice. *"Um, I'm Alex, um. . . I put on this act so you'll feel sorry for me and think I'm harmless, um. . ."*

Ben tugged at Efia's arm. "Come on, that's enough, let's go."

My mouth was open. I just stared. I couldn't. . . I didn't know how to. . .

"Just don't show your face at Wonderland again," Efia said.

"Ben. . ." My voice was hoarse; I barely rasped his name. "Ben, please, I . . . please, Ben, please. . ."

He shook his head, his eyes cold. He walked off with Efia, leaving me on the bench.

CHAPTER THIRTY

There was no sign of Kendra or Dad when I got back home. I slammed the front door behind me, then barrelled up the stairs, kicking the door of Kendra's office in the back bedroom open. I needed verification. I needed to see this for myself. Trembling, I reached for the box files on the shelf to the side of her desk, ripped them open and riffled through the papers inside. I dropped the first box and started on the second, and halfway down I found what I was looking for: financials, charts, and letters to potential investors about the area on the promenade "currently occupied by Wonderland". "Currently occupied", like it didn't actually belong to Wonderland, it was just a guest, ready to be moved on whenever someone else felt like it. Money. Property. Profit.

The pounding in my ears exploded out of me. I swept everything off her stupid desk, papers, cups, pens, the pot plant all crashing to the floor, then I pulled the rest of the files off the shelf, letting them smash open on their way down, while I kicked everything now on the floor against the wall, smashing, destroying—

And the next thing I knew, I was sitting in the middle of all the wreckage, sobbing. I'd come so close. So close to everything being different and finally changing. It wasn't just about Ben, although, of course, he was a huge part of this. It was that place. It was all those people who had become friends. This summer, for the first time in my life, I was starting to become happy to be me. I'd started to believe that life might work out OK.

I laughed at my own stupidity, because I should have known better.

This whole summer at Wonderland had been little more than a dream – a really nice dream where I was different and happy and felt good about myself. But now it was time to wake up and realize none of those things were true.

Nothing had really changed at all.

Dad found me.

"What the hell, Alex?" he said.

He must have seen something in my eyes, pain or hurt or I don't know, but it was enough that he didn't go ballistic. Instead, he sat down in the middle of the wreckage of Kendra's office, put his arm around me and pulled me towards him. "What's happened?"

So I told him everything and when I got to the end, he was just silent.

"Did you know?" I asked.

He sighed. "Kendra runs a property development company, Alex. She's involved with deals all over the town; that's what she does. But everything you're saying, underhanded tactics, *threats*?" He screwed his face up. "That doesn't sound likely."

I gave a little snort and looked down at the floor. Dad had no idea what Kendra was really like. He had no idea how she made me feel. I knew damn well how evil that woman could be, but what was the point in telling him? He must have seen that for himself loads, but it hadn't stopped him being with her.

"Kendra plays by the rules," Dad continued. "She plays fair."

"*Fair?!*" I said. "What's 'fair' about trying to buy Wonderland? Booting us all out – lots of us love that place, Dad. It's where we go. You can't hang out at a luxury apartment block with a stupid bar on the ground floor." I sighed. "Well, not if you're sixteen, anyway."

"The town's changing, Alex. And honestly, I think for the better."

"Yeah? Better for who?"

He didn't answer.

I stood up and walked to the door. "Ground me, take my allowance to pay for the damage, I don't care."

I sat on the edge of my bed, staring at the pool party outfit that I'd got ready this morning, folded neatly on my chair.

They would all be finishing getting ready about now, maybe meeting up for a pre-party get together, before heading over to Splash Down! Everyone would know by now. Everyone would be disgusted at the snake who they thought had been living in their very midst. I opened Spotify and selected "Pity Party Playlist 1" because, yeah, I did have enough Pity Party playlists to warrant numbering, and just so you know, number one is the gloomiest, most pitiful, of them all, that starts with Green Day, ends with the Smiths, and has a whole heap of Manic Street Preachers in between. Oh, and some Coldplay, because "Fix You" always makes me want to weep uncontrollably.

I wondered who Kendra got to do her dirty work. Did she bung Drake a few hundred quid to put the bad egg in the goose and tamper with the Mirror Maze? Did she get him to press the fire alarm? Using her money to oil the wheels of injustice so she could get what she wanted? And maybe she still will. Maybe everything that's happened will still tip the place over the edge. When the holidaymakers leave, takings will drop massively. Maybe that's when the bank will close in, and with all the bad publicity, Maggie will just decide to sell after all. You can only fight for so long. Eventually, if the punches keep coming, you just get tired and give up.

I didn't know where to go from here.

I didn't even have any tears left.

There was just this huge, gaping emptiness inside me.

You can only fight for so long. . .

There was a knock at my bedroom door.

I swallowed and stared down at the floor, my leg bouncing, pulse quickening. I knew it was *her.*

The door pushed open.

I didn't look up. I just waited for whatever the next punch was going to be. It didn't even matter now.

Her footsteps.

She came to a stop just by me. I could feel her eyes on the back of my neck.

And then a sheet of paper in my field of vision. "Take it," Kendra said.

I still didn't look at her, but I took the paper, blinking at it through my stinging eyes, trying to focus on the words, but failing. It was all just swimming around. Letters, numbers, dates. . . I had no idea. I shook my head. "What even is this?" I muttered.

"It's why I didn't go through with my offer on Wonderland," she said.

I let her words sink in, staring at the paper.

"It's true I was interested in it, Alex. And it's true I made some initial enquiries about whether Maggie might look to sell. It's a prime location, and it's a good size."

I was still looking at the paper, and I still couldn't make sense of it.

"But there's one huge problem with Wonderland," Kendra continued. "So huge, it's a deal-breaker, so I had to withdraw my interest." She perched down on the bed next to me. "It's a listed building."

I swallowed. "I don't . . . what does that mean?"

"It basically has protected status, on account of the architectural style and when it was built. The upshot is, you can't ever demolish it. And you can't significantly change it, either. It makes it entirely unsuitable for my purposes. There was nothing I could do with it. There's nothing any developer could do with it. I don't want to buy Wonderland, Alex."

I shot her the briefest of sideways glances.

She released a long breath. "And for the record, however low an opinion you have of me, I'm not the sort who puts pressure on vendors to sell through dirty tricks, so whatever's been happening at that place, I can promise you, it has nothing to do with me. Although I hope that much is obvious, since I have no interest in buying it anyway."

"But you do hate the place," I said. "And maybe you'd rather it wasn't there? Maybe it'll put people off buying the new apartments you're building up the road?"

"It crossed my mind, Alex, yes," Kendra said. "But in the end, I don't think it'll make much difference. My clients are mostly Londoners who are selling up and getting out of town. Trust me, when you've seen the 'delights' living in London has to offer, an amusement arcade isn't really going to worry you."

"Huh."

"I think you should take that document and show your friends. Show them it's not me, and that you had nothing to do with this." She got up and walked to the door. "In any case," she said, turning back, "do they really think I'd use you to carry out a dirty tricks campaign?"

I looked at her. *Why not me?*

"Oh, come on, Alex. You're not exactly cut out for industrial espionage type stuff, are you?"

I sat up a bit straighter and pushed my shoulders back.

"Your talents lie elsewhere. If I was looking for . . . someone to be an assistant supervisor at a soft play centre, for example, I'd consider you."

Oh my god, not even supervisor, but *assistant*! Also, "consider" not "hire".

"Anyway," she said. "Go and put your friends straight."

"Kendra? I'll clear up your office."

"It's already done, Alex."

I looked at her. "I'm sorry."

She nodded and closed my door behind her. I knew it wouldn't be that easy. I would not be allowed to forget all this, and I *would* pay – terribly. But I'd have to brace myself for her emotional blackmail and passive aggressiveness masterclass another time. Right then, I needed to put something right. Because all this, *this sadness*, that was *old Alex*. And I wasn't that person any more.

I couldn't be.

I didn't *want* to be.

I paused Spotify.

And then I deleted the Pity Party playlists.

All frickin' twelve of them.

And I put on some better clothes, did my hair, and for the first time in my life, got ready to put up a fight.

You probably think I mean Ben.

I don't.

I was fighting for *me*.

CHAPTER THIRTY-ONE

The end-of-season pool party was pretty much how you might imagine spring break from American movies, only British, so a bit more crap. The palm trees were fake, the inflatables in the main pool were already looking limp, and, rather than stopping off on his tour of Ibiza, Ayia Napa and Cancún, the DJ had definitely more likely stopped off after a ten-year-old's birthday party, a garden fetê and the year seven disco.

It didn't matter though. The place was insane. Everyone was here and everyone was partying hard. Stalls placed around the main pool area were serving everything from cocktails and shots to burgers and tacos, whilst couples made out, groups danced, boys gave girls piggybacks, and girls gave boys shoulder rubs. In the distance, all the main rides were open, and the sounds of laughter and screams drifted across the pool, from the kids enjoying the rapids, log flume and the brand-new Mystery of Atlantis ride – opened just this year. Girls in bikinis, boys in swim shorts, and me . . . in chinos, because this, *this* was a "chinos situation" as my dad would have it, and I wasn't planning on staying long.

I may as well have been invisible as I worked my way through the debauched mob, being bashed every which way I turned, as though someone as dorky as me couldn't possibly exist in such a fun and cool place. I didn't care. This wasn't about anyone else, and I was done worrying about what other people thought. I knew I wasn't a bad person, and I knew I deserved better than anyone who thought I was a loser . . . or a liar.

I must have been standing watching them from about ten metres away for a full minute before they saw me. Efia, Bella, Caleb, Kem and Ben – they'd colonized a couple of sun loungers, and were sitting sipping drinks out of neon-coloured plastic cups, topped off with giant twisty straws and cocktail umbrellas. Ben was eating tacos. Efia had a cardboard tray filled with stir fry. They were all laughing. That hurt a bit, to be honest. They were all having such a great time. Without me. Like my absence didn't matter one bit; didn't even register.

"Can't believe you'd show your face," Efia said as I approached them.

"I'm not staying. I wanted to give you this." I pulled the paper out of my pocket and handed it to her. "Kendra *was* interested in Wonderland, you're right. But she pulled out." My voice was trembling. I swallowed. "Turns out it's a listed building, so it's useless for a property developer. She doesn't want to buy it. I don't think anyone wants to buy it. Anyway." I thrust my shaking hands in the pockets of my chinos. "I don't know who's been responsible for everything's that's happened. Maybe it was just a prank. Maybe it was Drake or Billy or Carl Hudson or whoever. I have no idea. I just know it wasn't Kendra who was behind it, and it wasn't me either. I didn't even know she was ever interested in buying it, but even if she had been, and even if she'd asked me, just so you know, I would have refused to have been a part of it. I love that place. And I've loved hanging out with all of you this summer. It's been my best summer. Best one, ever. No question. I wouldn't hurt Wonderland and I wouldn't hurt any of you." I looked at Ben. "I wouldn't hurt you. I wish you knew I'd never do something like this. I wish you thought as much of me as I do of you." I looked between each of their stunned faces. "I hope I haven't ruined your night," I muttered, turning and walking away.

I pushed my way back through the throng, forcing my way past people who didn't want to move, tutting at me for getting in their way. Tears welled in my eyes now, a mixture of relief that I'd told them, combined with injustice and disbelief and the deep-down pain that any of them could actually think that about me. I'd stood up for myself. But it turned out that felt like a small victory, compared to what I'd lost.

There was a hand on my shoulder. I tried to keep walking forward, but it was strong, pulling me back. I turned. *Ben.*

I blinked at him through wet eyes and swallowed hard.

He opened his mouth to speak, but his pained face already said it all. "I'm so sorry," he said, in a small voice.

"Don't worry about it," I muttered.

Ben shook his head. "No, Alex. We don't get off the hook that easily. You deserve better than that." He looked down at the ground. "Better than me." He glanced up at me again. "There's a chill-out area round the corner—"

I nodded and let him lead the way. I wasn't holding out much hope – it felt like things between us had been irreparably damaged. Maybe this would just be goodbye. At best, I thought it was probably going to be "well, we'll try to be civil to each other and I promise not to drag you on social media".

The chill-out area was festooned with huge beanbags and cushions, and surrounded by billowing drapes that sectioned it off from the rest of the party, and did make it feel like a sort of haven. The music here was some Ibiza sunset type stuff, all gentle and relaxed – would have been better if it was some heavy, dark break-up music. A couple of girls were lying across a mound of cushions and whispering to each other, but other than them, we had the place to ourselves.

We didn't sit.

"You said you wished I thought as much of you as you did of me. . ."

My eyes met his.

"I *do,* Alex," Ben said, taking my hands. "I think so much of you it hurts, sometimes. I think so much of you I often don't think of anything else. I think so much of you that if I really told you how much you'd probably think I was weird and obsessed and I'd be doing that 'too keen' thing you're always worried about."

"So why didn't you trust me? How could you think I'd be involved in any of this?"

Ben swallowed, loosening his grip on my hands. "Because I'm a screw-up. Because I didn't believe, and I don't believe, something as good as you could happen . . . to me. And I think. . ." He swallowed and tried to steady his breathing. "I think I was expecting it to go wrong, to be taken away from me, so I was looking for it. Waiting for the inevitable."

"You can't spend your life waiting for the crash, Ben! Waiting for disaster to strike! You miss all the good. And I know the world can be a shitty place, and I know it can feel like it's full of bad people, and bad, horrible, unfair things happen to the good guys, and they've happened to you, but in amongst all that, there is still good."

"I know. You're right. "

"Took me a while to find it too," I said. "But you came along in the end."

His lip was wobbling. "Same."

"Now you're crying," I said.

"It's just one tear." He quickly wiped it away. "That's not crying." He wiped away another one. "OK, I'm crying."

"Ben. . ."

"I'm just so sorry," Ben said. "*I'm sorry.* And Alex, I wasn't sure what to think when Efia found that document, but I didn't—"

"But you *did,*" I said. "And I . . . I really, I *liiiiiike* you *so much*, I honestly can't even."

He looked like a chastised little boy, full of remorse, desperate to make it better. He gave me a tiny, hopeful, smile. "I *liiiiike* you too, Alex."

I sighed and went in for a hug, because . . . well, because I liked him, and he was sorry, and everyone messes up sometimes. And everyone deserves another chance. If I'd screwed up, I'd want them to forgive me. Of course I would. These people were my friends. I loved them. And like Maggie told me once, no one behaves perfectly. I'm not sure perfect even exists, outside of movies and possibly a Starbucks gingerbread latte. And that's the truth of it. None of us are ever going to measure up to an over-sugared hot beverage you can only buy for three months of the year. No one is exactly how you'd like them to be, all of the time. Of course they aren't. Being human means being flawed, imperfect, messy. But you can't beat yourself up for that. And I don't think you can beat other people up for it either.

My attention was drawn by the curtains moving at the entrance. Efia appeared. "I'm sorry, I got it all wrong, I'm an idiot, I made assumptions, I would be a crap police detective, I should never have thought that of you, Alex, you're one of the sweetest, nicest guys I know, I mean, I'm getting down on my knees here—"

"Efia, no, please don't—"

"I'm down, I'm . . . ow! Netball injury from year eight, but look, I'm—"

I darted over to her and pulled her back up to her feet. "It's OK."

"It's so *not* OK. I really am sorry."

"I know. And I . . . accept that." I extended my arms.

She looked at me like she didn't believe me, so I nodded, and she came in for a hug. It felt so good to have them back, I didn't have room to be angry.

Caleb and Kem pushed through the curtains, looking slightly sheepish and loaded up with a selection of treats.

"Tacos, hot dogs, there's a burger. . ." Efia said, following my gaze. "And there's churros, a crepe, and a bag of fudge, slightly randomly."

"The churros are excellent," Kem said.

I was, it has to be said, starving. And the food looked great.

"All for you," Caleb told me. "Although, can I just say, I literally had nothing to do with Efia and Ben going crazy on you. If I'd have been there, I would have been much more reasonable." He grinned.

"Same," chimed in Kem.

"Anyway, we're helping with the massive backtracking!"

I raised an eyebrow. "Is there dipping chocolate for the churros?"

"Ta-da!" said Kem, producing a small bowl of molten chocolate.

"It's good chocolate, man!" Caleb said, dipping his little finger in the bowl, then licking it off.

I caught Efia smiling at him, *fondly*, when Efia's style would normally be to tell him off for being gross. And then Caleb put his arm around her.

"Ohhh," I said. "Are you two . . . you're not . . . are you?"

For the first time ever, Efia actually dropped her eyes and looked a bit shy.

Caleb gave me a sparkling grin and a thumbs up.

"Well, that's a nice surprise," I said.

"Not as surprising as. . ." Efia glanced at Kem.

Kem shifted about on the spot, scratching the back of his neck. "Yeah, so," he said. "I mean, I thought I'd made this clear, but apparently I hadn't, and who knew that after a couple of drinks these things could just be like 'BOOM! HERE WE ARE! BIG REVEAL TIME!' Ha! Ha!" He looked at me. "Right?"

"Kem, I literally have no idea."

"The girl I like? The one I've been trying to impress all the time you've known me?"

I nodded.

"It's Eve," he said.

My eyed widened and nearly popped out.

Kem shook his head. "Ever since I first saw her in Wonderland, man. She has this *allure*. Maybe it's the astral plane she's on, but there is something about her. Something ... *cosmic*..." He trailed off, seemingly lost amidst her mystical beauty.

"Turns out Kem doesn't have a big gambling addiction after all," Ben said. "Just an *Eve* addiction. "And maybe a small gambling addiction."

I nodded. "Wasn't Eve meant to be here tonight?"

"Yes," Efia said. "She was, until Kem, fuelled by a vodka and Coke—"

"*Two* vodka and Cokes," Kem corrected her. "I'm not that much of lightweight."

"Until Kem told her all this, in a ... brave and misguided attempt at honesty," Efia said. "Apparently the tarot did not foretell Kem's arrival, and as such Eve is now having some sort of existential crisis."

"My bad," Kem said. He looked at Efia. "Should I

send flowers?"

Efia shook her head.

"Well," I said. "Seems I've missed all the drama."

I gave Ben a little smile, and had just started tucking into the tacos when Bella appeared with a tray of drinks for us all. And after two cocktails, plus some shots that Kem procured from a guy at the main bar who wanted some tips on beating the odds at a Las Vegas casino he was going on honeymoon to, I was feeling a bit more perky.

Who am I kidding? I was halfway wrecked.

"I think we should rejoin the main party," I declared.

"Um – you don't have swim shorts," Efia said.

"I am hooched up and ready to go!"

Efia looked to the boys. "Don't let him swim in his pants."

"I am going to SWIM IN MY PANTS!" I said. "Swimming shorts are for *losers*."

I started pulling my clothes off.

"Is anyone going to stop him, or not?" Efia said.

"Don't need no special kit to swim in," I was saying. "Swim in normal things." I stood before them, in just my boxers, and held my hands out, like I'd just completed a magic trick, the big reveal of which was making a teenage boy in his pants appear. "Ta-da! Let's *swim*, baby!"

"Future note to everyone," Efia said. "Alex gets drunk incredibly easily and quickly. We already knew this. Why have we failed yet again?"

Caleb pulled his T-shirt off. "Let's do this!"

"Hell *yeah*!" I said.

"Alex, are you sure you're OK to swim?" Efia said.

"Buzzing!" I replied.

"That's what I feared." Efia shook her head. "Ben? Kem? Get in too. After everything, we cannot let him drown."

"Sexy swim time with my boys!" I sort of sang. Let me be clear – I'm fully embarrassed about all this, I'm just telling it like it was. Or like I remember it, anyway, which in the circumstances may not be entirely accurate. I glanced at Ben, and saw he still had his T-shirt on. "You!" I pointed at him. "I am not seeing your abs!"

I'm pretty sure he blushed a bit, then he smiled and pulled his T-shirt off.

"I have abs," Caleb said, patting them.

"I have abs *coming*," Kem added.

"All the boys want some attention, Alex. Don't leave them out now, they'll get jealous and start fighting," Efia said, rolling her eyes.

"You are all beautiful," I told them. Then I turned to Efia and Bella. "You both are too."

"You're an idiot," Efia said. "But a lovely idiot. And a very generous one. Come here." And she kissed me on the cheek. "Now go and swim."

So that's how I ended up in the main pool at the pool party, in just my boxers. I am well aware that is not advisable to swim whilst intoxicated, by the way, but as it turned out, there wasn't much swimming. The water was shallow, and we splashed about, gave each other piggybacks, laughed and, when no one was looking, I squeezed Ben's hand under the water. I didn't mean to start anything by it, it was just a way of saying maybe not everything's ruined. I could see he was still beating himself up about everything – I knew that feeling well, I could easily recognize it in others. I wanted to give him some hope. Because maybe, once the dust had settled a bit, maybe there was some hope.

It was a little after midnight, although I can't be sure how long. I know because the DJ told everyone, and then changed the music to "something a little more mellow". Without such a heavy thud of bass, it was easier to hear – a single siren at first, and then, not long after, several more. Lots of sirens, blaring through the night. That's an unusual thing in Newsands, because it's quite a small town, so you don't often hear police or ambulances, or whatever. Something was going down, although at that point, I don't think anyone was too bothered. The drinks were still flowing and the mood was gently simmering down from electric to something a bit more warm and chilled, and everyone was in a good place.

And then I noticed people whispering.

People pulling other people aside. Hushed conversations. Gossip spreading.

And there was a palpable shift in the mood.

People were getting out of the pool.

Others were grabbing phones and checking social media.

There was a mean-spirited cheer, like something bad was happening, but they were enjoying it.

Groups pulled on clothes and rushed towards the exit.

And then the word got to us too.

Wonderland was on fire.

CHAPTER THIRTY-TWO

We didn't bother to dry off. I tugged my chinos on over my wet legs and boxers, threw on my T-shirt and ran with the others out of Splash Down! and along the promenade towards Wonderland. Blue flashing lights flickered across our faces, the air thick with the stench of burning. A crowd had gathered at the police tape that was cordoning off the entire width of the road and pavement, but we pushed our way through to the front.

I don't know what I was expecting, but I wasn't expecting what I saw.

I didn't expect it to be . . . so *bad.*

All the windows on the ground floor were glowing a fierce orange. On the first floor, flames licked out of every single one of the six windows, and despite the fire crew currently doing their best to douse it with water from the top of their crane, half the roof was completely ablaze. Billy stood by himself on the edge of the crowd, the cocky swagger all gone, now just vulnerable, defeated somehow. Drake was over the other side, mouth open, restless. I spotted Eve, just staring into the flames, and then towards the back, Carl Hudson. I caught his eye, and he gave me a sympathetic nod.

But one person was missing.

I grabbed hold of Ben's arm. "Maggie wouldn't be inside?"

"It closes at eight, why would she?"

My mouth was dry. "Yeah, but, I dunno, what if she was doing paperwork late or—"

I felt cold to my core. Frozen.

BOOM! We were jolted back to reality by one of the ground floor windows blowing out. There was a smash of shattering glass, someone screamed, the firemen backed away, which was fair enough, but I still wanted to scream PLEASE JUST DO SOMETHING GET IN THERE – MAGGIE MIGHT BE INSIDE! The panic was rising from my stomach, because I could see which way this was heading. It was out of control. For whatever reason, they'd got there too late, the fire had taken hold, and now it was unstoppable. And if anyone was inside . . . no way were they getting out easily. I couldn't breathe. My chest, so tight, my throat, so tight, my heart fluttering and racing, and I wanted to cry and scream because THIS WAS HOME! THIS WAS MAGGIE! This was everything.

Ben's hand found mine. He squeezed. He muttered, "It'll be OK."

But I knew it wouldn't be.

And then my heart relaxed just a little bit, because she was suddenly standing beside me. *Maggie*. She stared towards Wonderland, letting out a strange, strangled gasp as her hands flew to her mouth. She had tears in her eyes. I reached for her hand, and Efia and Kem put their arms around her as Eve, Drake and Billy all found their way to stand with us, all helpless, all united in horror and shock and grief. To the other bystanders, this was exciting. An event. A piece of morbid theatre they couldn't tear themselves away from. For all of *us*, it wasn't just Wonderland that was burning down. It was our little corner of the world. The place where we all felt safe. The place where we'd found one another. The place we loved. And for Maggie, her life's work, the place she'd built from nothing, in memory of her only son.

A deep, painful creaking noise.

Something splintered.

I started shaking as I saw the firemen start to urgently pull the platform crane away from the building, and just as they did—

The whole roof collapsed.

Crash!

Imploding in on itself.

A shower of sparks, flames leaping up, feeding on the new fuel.

And the only thing I remember next was something Billy muttered:

"I haven't got anywhere else to go."

CHAPTER THIRTY-THREE

"Alex? Are you OK?"

I focus back on DI Griffin, clear my throat and rub my eyes. "Sorry," I mutter. It was only a few days ago; reliving it all so soon, it's too much. Too raw. It still frightens me. "Anyway," I say. "That's basically everything. Just like you asked." I sit back in my chair a little and have a sip of my Lucozade. Dad pats me on the leg, which I assume means "good job", but knowing Dad could also mean "OK, so there's some stuff we need to talk about later, mister." I'm not surprised. I knew there would be.

"Thank you, Alex," DI Griffin says.

I have a little more Lucozade. "Was it helpful?"

DI Griffin has a little smile playing on his lips. "Well,

I certainly know more than I anticipated about the love lives of the town's teenagers."

"Oh. I didn't know if—"

"No, no," DI Griffin says. "I asked you for everything, and you certainly gave me that." He sighs and leans towards me. "Everything you've said tallies with everything we already know, and everything your friends and your— Is he your boyfriend, I'm not clear?"

I shrug and look wistfully into the middle distance. "Nor am I." Things were left hanging that night, and we haven't spoken about it since. We'd arranged to go to Comic Con, of course, except we never did. It's not that I forgot, I just didn't mention it to him, and he didn't to me. Maybe the ball's in my court – he's giving me some space, which is exactly what I needed.

DI Griffin nods. "Well, anyway, everything about the threatening notes, the 'accidents' that may not have been accidents, Ben told us about that too. As did Efia."

I nod. I suppose that's good. Stories that match up are always a good thing in police dramas on TV. And I'm glad, because I know damn well what the rumours circulating say. I know they haven't yet established the cause of the fire, and I know there's speculation about whether we fireproofed the drapes in the fortune telling booth, or if the lights in the Roswell Experience were PAT tested properly – and I'm pretty sure the answer to both of those questions is a resounding no. There's a chance, a high chance, that we got carried away with all our ideas for the relaunch, and something we did caused all this. That *we're* the guilty ones. I can't even bring myself to think about it too much. How would Maggie ever forgive us?

"The problem we've got, Alex," DI Griffin says, "is whether this was a genuine accident, or whether this fire was deliberate. All the mysterious things you've described might point to it being deliberate. But then we have the thorny question of the identity of that person or persons. And their motive. Drake, for example, has an alibi for the night of the fire."

"What about whatever trouble he was in?" I ask.

DI Griffin rolls his eyes. "Drake borrowed money from a loan shark to buy his car. And yes, he's been cautioned about possessing cannabis, but we can't find anything else to implicate him. You were right about Tyler Phillips though."

I sit up. "I was?"

"In that your original assessment of him as a 'good guy' is absolutely correct."

I sit back again. "Oh."

"His name came up in our interviews with Ben and Efia, so we asked him to come in. He was sorry that you didn't realize he also ran a property development company, along with his work on the local traders' committee – he said it was on his card."

"It was." I shrug.

"And yes, he's bought the Bellevue and it's going to be demolished."

I sigh. "More fancy bars and shops then."

DI Griffin shakes his head. "Indie cinema in the basement, with an exhibition and performance space on the ground floor, along with a café bar. It's designed for the whole community and there's going to be a youth theatre based there."

"Oh."

And now I'd basically accused Tyler of torching Wonderland, guess who wouldn't be welcome at the brand-new place?

DI Griffin must read my mind, because he says, "Tyler did mention he'd be calling you. . ."

"Oh no."

"He said he wants some local teenagers to be involved in the new building, so I think he's hoping you might be part of that."

Dad ruffles my hair. "Quite the mover and shaker, aren't you?"

"Stop it!" I shrug him off and scowl at him, although I am quite pleased about being part of Tyler's thing, and hope there's a way I can get the others on board.

"Anyway, that's where we are, Alex. There's no one obvious suspect, is there? Just a lot of possible ones and some vague motives."

I shake my head. "We tried," I say. "As I told you, we tried to find out."

"I know, and yet, it seems all roads point everywhere and nowhere, all at the same time."

I crack a small smile. "Like the Mirror Maze," I say.

DI Griffin nods and closes his notebook. "Yes, I suppose so," he sighs. "Like the Mirror Maze."

Me and Dad sit in our Ford Mondeo in the police station car park for a good minute before either of us says anything. "Kendra and I are thinking about taking a bit of a break," he tells me.

"Ah, Dad, *no,* that's—" I'm totally flooded with guilt. "You don't have to do that."

"I know I don't *have* to."

"Dad, look, *please,* in another two years I'll probably go to uni or something. It's true I'm not keen on Kendra, but that doesn't mean you two should end it. Not if you're happy."

"Huh. Well, maybe I'm not," he says. "*Happy.*"

I can't say that massively surprises me. I don't know how he ended up dating her in the first place, even less how she ended up moving in.

"Maybe we did the whole moving-in thing too quickly, maybe we just don't have that much in common, maybe it was a midlife crisis. . ."

He smiles at me and I grin.

"But I also don't like the way she talks to you," he says.

"Well, sure, nor do I, particularly."

"You're my son."

I'm not sure how to respond to that, because it's sort of just a statement of fact; it's hardly a revelation.

"You're supposed to be the most important thing in my life." He looks at me. "And you are, by the way. Just in case . . . in case that hasn't always been clear?"

I smile. "Thanks, Dad."

He puts an arm across my shoulders. "Hearing it all just then, it's the right decision. You don't need people making you feel bad about yourself, Alex. God knows, you do a good enough job of that yourself."

"Excuse me?"

"Always been an over-thinker," he says. "Always winding yourself up."

We sit in silence for another few moments until Dad claps his hands together. "Hungry?"

"Yup."

"Fish and chips?"

"Ohh! What are we celebrating?"

"You being awesome."

He starts the car.

"Dad, you're gonna make me sick if you talk like that."

He grins and takes the handbrake off. "You are though. You're on the up, Alex. It's only up from here."

And as we pull out of the car park, I smile, because deep down, in spite of everything, I think he might be right.

CHAPTER THIRTY-FOUR

Two weeks later, I'm back at school, and with all the excitement of starting year twelve (No uniform! Free periods! Will being really sheepish and suggesting cinema trips to try and salvage our friendship!), parts of the summer are already starting to fade. Other parts, though, are as vibrant and crystal clear as if they were happening right now. The fire is one of them.

The night at the lake with Ben is another.

It's a Saturday afternoon when Maggie sends a group text to me, Ben and Efia, and asks to meet us outside the ruins of Wonderland. The fire burned through everything, leaving only the shell of the structure, although most of that has now been deemed unsafe, and requires demolition. I've been past it a few times, and once I stood for a whole hour just staring at the ruins through the temporary metal fence they've erected around the site, but seeing Wonderland like this is still heartbreaking. Amongst the rubble, I can make out the odd machine – a claw grabber, smashed and on its side, the charred remains of a Penny Falls, and a huge teddy bear, its body burned and singed, covered in dust.

I jump when I hear his voice. "I still can't get my head around it."

Ben's standing a couple of metres away from me, and he's brought Artoo Dogtoo with him. The weather's more autumnal now, and he's wearing jeans with a blue hoodie, cheeks slightly pink with the colder air, looking as adorable as ever.

"Hey," he says.

"Hey." I glance down at Artoo Dogtoo, who's wagging his little tail at me. "Hey, buddy."

Ben smiles and comes to stand beside me, and we both stare at the ruins through the metal fence. "Sometimes bricks and mortar are just as important as people," I say. "You said that, didn't you?"

Ben nods.

"So where does that leave us?"

"Well, I guess that's just it," Ben says. "It leaves *us*."

He's right. Wonderland, the place, might be gone. But everyone who made it truly special was still here. And everything that had happened this summer, it was all still ours, and always would be. If we wanted it to be.

I turn to him. "I've missed you."

His eyes are hopeful; he opens his mouth a little, but no words come out.

Words don't feel like they're going to cut it anyway, and I want him close to me so badly that I just step towards him and throw my arms around him, burying my face in his shoulder. He responds by wrapping his arms around me, pulling me tight into him, so close, like we're never going to let go of one another again. And we stand like that, whilst Artoo Dogtoo sits watching (I swear he makes an "Aww" sound at one point), and I'm so happy that it's like this again, I could cry.

He's on the brink of tears too. He pulls back from me a bit, and his eyes are wet, and he's shaking. "Sorry," he mutters. "Thank you. Thank you for giving me another chance."

"Well, you're pretty, so." I smirk at him and he laughs.

Then he glances briefly over my shoulder, and I know what he's doing, so I glance over his, and then he meets my eyes, asking if the coast is clear of anyone who might cause us trouble, and I give him the smallest of nods, and he leans in to kiss me. And that kiss, it's so epic, so utterly spectacular, it's fireworks and confetti cannons, it's glittering, it's golden, a million dollars, and I don't mean to brag, but we are *so good* at it, and the world just stops, like everyone tells you it does, and it's just me and him—

"*Boys.*"

. . . and now Efia. Which means we must have been kissing for at least a minute because she was nowhere to be seen when I looked up the road.

We break apart. Efia grins. Ben pulls his hoodie down a bit, looking sheepish. "Hey," he says, cheeks seriously flushed.

"*Good,*" Efia says. "You two being back together is good news. I'm glad. That is what's going on here, right? That wasn't some weird break-up snog?"

"Is that a thing?" I ask.

"Everything," Efia says, "is a thing."

I reach out and take Ben's hand in mine. "This is Ben," I say, and I'm feeling like the world is mine at that moment, so I just say it. "He's my boyfriend."

I flick my eyes to check his reaction, and he's grinning, and then he leans over and pecks me on the cheek.

Artoo Dogtoo barks his approval and definitely looks like he's smiling.

"Cool, that's cute," Efia says. "Double date with me and Caleb soon, then, yeah?" She sighs, and then it's her turn to look through the fence at the remains of Wonderland. And we all just stand there, *looking*, remembering, still not quite believing.

"It's all gone." It's Maggie's voice, behind us. I turn, and there she is, wrapped up against the slightly chillier September air in a huge fur coat that I hope is fake, and smoking a real cigarette rather than an electric one. "Hello, my loves," she says.

"Do they know how it started yet?" I ask.

Maggie takes a drag of her cigarette. "Doesn't seem like it." She blows out smoke. "They think it started in the back office, and perhaps something was thrown through the window – but it's hard for them to be sure. Seems it spread quickly, though – apparently it ripped through the Roswell Experience like actual wildfire – they were asking if we flameproofed the drapes." She looks at our horrified faces. "I'll take that as a no."

"Maggie, were we meant to?" Ben says.

Maggie nods. "Yes, dear." She sighs. "But that's on me – I should have overseen it better."

Ben looks crushed, like all this is his fault.

"Seems the place *was* a dangerous fire trap," Maggie continues. "I know they've been looking for the person who wrote the notes and tampered with the maze and the eggs, but seems like they've drawn a blank. Seems like maybe it was just 'kids'. That's what they said to me. 'Kids playing pranks'." She shakes her head and laughs. "Some prank."

Something in the back of my mind nags at me, but I can't place it.

"What about the insurance, Mags?" Efia asks. "Are they gonna pay up? Maybe that'll mean you can rebuild, start again—"

Maggie holds her hand up to stop her. "I may have fallen behind on paying the premiums."

Efia's eyes go wide.

"That's right – technically speaking, I wasn't insured," Maggie says. She throws her cigarette on the floor and stamps it out. "So that's that."

I look between Efia and Ben, desperate for one of us to say the words of wisdom that will solve all the problems. A great idea, a solution, a way forward, anything. But I can tell from their faces they're as stumped as I am. This is insurmountable.

"I'm so sorry, Maggie," I mutter.

Maggie sniffs. "Well, then again, maybe this is possibly . . . good news."

"What? On what planet?" Ben splutters.

"Based on the fact my insurance won't pay out and the building is totally wrecked, the local planning authority have given permission for the whole thing to be demolished and the land to be sold. They've agreed I can sell to one of the property development companies – it's no one you guys know, before you all get your knickers in a twist – and they can build apartments with retail units on the ground floor. As a nod to the listed status of the original building, the developers have agreed to reclaim some the original bricks and recreate part of the original design. I think the council knew it was either that, or they'd have a plot of land that no one wanted anything to do with, so they let it go through."

Efia wrinkles her brow. "So, where does that leave you?"

"The company is buying the land from me. I'm using the money to pay off my debts, and the rest. . . Well, I'm finally doing what I always wanted to do. I'm getting out. Moving on."

"Where to?" I ask. "Like, Devon or something?"

Maggie screws her face up. "Why *the frig* would I move to Devon?"

"I dunno." I shrug. "It's pretty nice there. Good scenery. Scones."

"*Scones?!*" Maggie practically screams. "Alex, I don't want *scones*, I want excitement! I want many, many years of completely outrageous *living*. I want late nights drinking, great food, wild adventures with crazy friends, I want fabulous sex!"

I think we all groan in a grossed-out sort of way.

"I'm moving to Ibiza," she says.

"WHAT?!" we all squeal.

"Found a lovely little apartment near Santa Gertrudis. It's within easy reach of beaches, nightlife, good restaurants. . . Loves, I'm going to be doing yoga on the beach and finally finding my bleeding chakra. Hopefully with the help of some ludicrously hot Ibizan with a penchant for the older lady."

She gives me a wink and I nearly puke.

"But, Maggie, surely Wonderland is . . . I mean, what about the memory of your son?" I say.

Maggie blinks at me. "My what now?"

"Your *son*!" Ben says.

Maggie looks blank. "What son? Have I got a son?"

"The son who. . . He disappeared, didn't he?" I say. "You built Wonderland because—"

"I have no idea what you're talking about," Maggie says. "You think I'd ever want to be lumbered with some stinking kid? Changing nappies and mopping up puke?"

I'm totally stumped. The story was legend. Everyone knew it. What the hell?

She's still staring at me like, *have you gone entirely mad,* and I feel stupid now, so I push it to the back of my mind. "So, um, when are you. . ." And then I see the suitcase she's standing next to, and it hits me. This is goodbye. "Now?" I say.

Maggie nods. "My solicitors are sorting out the details this end and completing the sale. What's the use of hanging around? I've got a lot of living to do, and I don't intend to waste a moment. You know what my final little piece of life advice to you would be? *Don't cling on to the past.* Embrace change. Some things are worth saving, worth trying for, and some things aren't. Learn to work out the difference." She looks at me and Ben. "But I think you've probably worked that out for yourselves."

I glance at Ben, and we both share shy smiles. And then I look back at Maggie, who just nods, knowingly.

Drake screeches up to us in his souped-up Fiat Panda that definitely wasn't worth being beaten up for.

"Ah. My ride," Maggie smiles.

"One-way trip to Gatwick?" Drake says, leaning across the seat towards the open window.

I pull Maggie to one side. "Are you sure this is what you want?"

"I'm taking an opportunity," Maggie says. "I'm lucky, in many ways. I'm very lucky, Alex."

I nod. I can see she's set on this new path. I give her a sad smile, and she smiles back.

"Thank you for everything," I tell her. "Thank you for taking a chance on me. And for the advice. It helped. I'm going to miss you. We all are."

Her face softens. "You're a good kid, Alex. You deserve some luck too."

Drake's car revs behind us.

"Well, you know, you make your own luck," I say, repeating back the advice she gave me many times.

Maggie smiles and leans into me for a tight hug. "Oh, I did, Alex," she says in my ear, in a low tone. "I did make my own luck. . ."

I freeze as everything slots into place.

Oh, *shit*.

She breaks away from me and climbs into the passenger seat of Drake's car, smiling and waving to us all. "Adios!" she shouts cheerily. "And whatever happens, never let the bastards get you down! Remember, *the house always wins*!"

I turn to look at Ben, and he sees my open-mouthed expression.

His eyes widen in understanding.

Maggie.

And just like that, like some illusion, or trick, she's gone.

ACKNOWLEDGEMENTS

Linas Alsenas, whilst I'm not really a believer in fate and destiny, I thank my lucky stars that we ended up working together. Thank you for being the best cheerleader (sans pompoms – but I could get you some?), thank you for your insightful, brilliant notes, and most of all, thank you for making every part of this process fun and enjoyable.

Joanna Moult, at Skylark Literary – thank you for always having my back, for being the best sounding board, and for all your wisdom and support.

Sarah Counsell, you're simply the best! When I hit a roadblock in the manuscript, you always manage to calm me down with your unwavering support and belief in me, convince me I need to "step away from the screen" and that I shouldn't throw my laptop out of the window. Thank you. This book might have ended up in the pond if you hadn't been there to catch it.

Liam Drane, yet again you have designed a spectacular cover, and Debbie Powell, your cover illustrations are brilliant and perfect – thank you, both!

Huge thanks to the rest of the wonderful team at Scholastic, especially Harriet Dunlea and Kate Graham in the PR and marketing department for everything you've done to promote me and Alex.

Thank you to the school librarians who have championed my books in their schools, and arranged for me to come in and deliver talks and workshops to their students. I'm going to miss some off inevitably (apologies), but thanks to Debbie Haynes, Sally Baker, Laylah Moore, Amanda Phelan, Susan Mulkern, Jane Hill, Joanne Hunter, Rachel Eckford, Christine MacCourt, Kate Kenward, Lucy Georgeson and Julia Hale, and a special mention to Laura Ferguson at Wirral Grammar School for Girls for organizing my epic trip to schools around the Wirral, and the always cheerful Tony Higginson for driving me around everywhere and tirelessly promoting and selling lots of my books. Heroes, all of you.

On the subject of selling books – the team at Gay's The Word bookshop have been every shade of awesome, so the biggest hug to Jim, Uli and Erica. And to all the other wonderful booksellers – you know I love you, SO MUCH.

A shout out to some fellow authors for your friendship and support, especially Becky Albertalli (thank you for that quote!), Matt Cain, Perdita Cargill, Juno Dawson, Beth Garrod, Sara Grant, Alice Oseman, Lev Rosen, Chloe Seager and Julian Winters.

To all the bloggers who have been so kind and spend

so much time reviewing, promoting and generally shouting about books – the biggest thank you.

Thanks to all you readers who are so passionate and so supportive – it means a lot. I've been fortunate to meet a lot of school students at events in the last year and it warms my heart when you bound up to me after a talk and introduce yourselves as "The Gay Kids" or variations thereof. Keep being you. And know that whenever some people want to silence you, shame you, or pretend you don't exist, we've got your backs, we're here for you, and those people aren't ever going to win.

Mum, Jonathan, Liz, Alfie – now I've finished writing this one, I can come and visit! Sue and Peter Counsell – thank you again, for everything.

Whilst I was writing *Alex in Wonderland* my dog, Bella, passed away. Bella was a beautiful soul – loving, brave, kind – the best dog, such a good girl. I miss her terribly, but before she died I promised her I'd dedicate this book to her, so everyone would know what a special dog she was and she wouldn't ever be forgotten. So here it is, Bella. We love you so much, and always will.

Simon x

ALSO BY SIMON JAMES GREEN

"Side-splitting comedy... A riotous, real-feeling YA debut."
Guardian

"I loved Noah's voice: warm, lovable, awkward."
The Bookseller

"We're calling it. Simon James Green's *Noah Can't Even* is officially the funniest book of 2017."
Maximum Pop

"Funny and smart and warm hearted..."
Daisy Buchanan, The Pool

"Sure to leave you with a smile on your face. ★★★★★"
OK Magazine

"Young adult fiction just became seriously fun."
Attitude Magazine

"Simon James Green is one of the most hilarious, heart-flippingly romantic, charmingly observant writers in the game right now."
Becky Albertalli, author of Love, Simon